In Knots Over You

The Ladies Alpine Society
Book 1

Edie Cay

ARE YOU SIGNED UP FOR DRAGONBLADE'S BLOG?

You'll get the latest news and information on exclusive giveaways, exclusive excerpts, coming releases, sales, free books, cover reveals and more.

Check out our complete list of authors, too!

No spam, no junk. That's a promise!

Sign Up Here

www.dragonbladepublishing.com

Dearest Reader;

Thank you for your support of a small press. At Dragonblade Publishing, we strive to bring you the highest quality Historical Romance from some of the best authors in the business. Without your support, there is no 'us', so we sincerely hope you adore these stories and find some new favorite authors along the way.

Happy Reading!

CEO, Dragonblade Publishing

Chapter One

London, 1866

ELEANOR PIPER WISHED she had her practice string. It wasn't a string so much as a length of cotton rope, which sounded even worse for a young lady to be toting around a ballroom. Instead, she smoothed her wide, pale yellow skirts and looked into the sea of brightly colored finery. Very few faces looked familiar, but she likely knew their names from the society columns her mother had foisted upon her in the last few months. No one ever looked like their scandal column sketch.

"Don't fidget," her mother hissed. She smelled strongly of mint and rosewater, which shouldn't have been eyewatering, but somehow, on her mother, it was.

That's why I need my string, Eleanor sulked. Her father wanted Eleanor to make a Society match, given that the queen had passed him over for special recognition for service to the Empire. While the British had theoretically not taken sides in the American Civil War, some shipping companies had aided the Confederacy in hopes of maintaining good cotton prices. Piper Shipping & Co. did not. After the war, the Americans had forced the British government to pay reparations for the ships that aided the rebels. Mr. Piper thought he should have gotten a medal, if not a title, for that fact that his company had saved the Crown money that would now be handed over to the Americans for the other companies' tomfoolery.

"May I visit the retiring room, Mama?" Eleanor asked. The women in their bell-shaped gowns and the men resembling black ship masts felt overwhelming. The mingling of musky ambergris perfumes, lemon-and-beeswax polish, and wine suffocated her.

"Return soon. I don't want you hiding all night," her mother said, snapping her fan open. It was not yet warm in the crowded room, but her mother seemed to always be "glowing."

Eleanor escaped, unsure if she should meet the gaze of other women, or keep her eyes demurely cast down. She'd had a governess and finishing classes, but the best parts of her days had been spent down at the docks in her father's offices. Smythe, her father's business partner and former ship's captain (before he lost his eye), amused her with new and ever-increasingly difficult knot-tying challenges. It was he who gave her the practice rope, and it was he that understood her nervous energy. While her governesses and elocution instructors had threatened and cursed her constant movement, Smythe just gave her harder problems, capturing her attention.

A body appeared in her path, forcing her to look up. And up. And up. Distracted by his height, she ran straight into him. Her heavy crinoline cage, covered in petticoats, swung into his legs, and she almost fell over as the momentum pulled her first toward him and then away.

She emitted a very unladylike grunt. Her coiffure—the same silly braids as Queen Victoria favored, pinned and looped—fell out of place, and a curl tumbled over her eyes. She fumbled for words as she pushed the errant hair out of the way. "My sincere apologies, I—" but her mouth stopped working.

He was beautiful. Not the dangerous kind of beautiful a man could be, but the sighing angel kind of beautiful. He was golden-haired, golden-skinned—more sun-kissed than most of her countrymen. His blue eyes were the color of her father's paintings of the sea, the opposite of her brown hair and brown eyes. He was a study in contrasts, while she was a study in . . .

brown. Muddy, basic, forgettable brown.

"No, my fault entirely, my dear Miss . . . ?" He looked at her, apparently sincere, for she wanted to believe whatever came out of his golden god-like mouth.

But her voice had not yet resumed its duties. And they were jostled again, this time by two young misses.

"Tristan, must you always be in the way?" one of the girls, matching his golden hue, hissed.

He rolled his eyes at her, annoyance obvious. Their family resemblance was not subtle. Eleanor smiled, as she had no siblings, and had always wished for one. But alas, her mother's health was always on the brink of failing. She fired the visiting physicians, one after next, who declared her in perfect health.

"I am speaking with someone," the golden god, apparently named Tristan, said.

"Well, speak to her elsewhere; this is the entrance to the Ladies' Room. Haven't you some other way to meet women?"

Tristan seemed to ignore the jab, turning towards his sister, forgetting about his trespass against Eleanor completely. Which was understandable, since Eleanor was eminently forgettable. "What are you in such a hurry for? Will you force me to call for pistols at dawn again?"

"You are such a prig," declared the other girl, whose deep, glossy auburn hair was shining and perfect. Eleanor recognized her from the caricatures on the scandal sheets. That was Miss Justine Brewer, or *Bad News Brews*, as she was nicknamed. Beautiful, impetuous, and wealthy, she was the object of every man's dreams and nightmares both. "I can't believe you're still whinging about that. Now, out of the way, we have an emergency."

As the two young ladies swept into the retiring room, Eleanor crept in after, not bothering to excuse herself from the presence of the man called Tristan. He'd already forgotten her anyway.

"I can't believe we are an hour into a ball and my dress is

falling apart," wailed Tristan's sister. She pulled off her long white gloves and fussed with a tear in the ruffled gown. "How am I supposed to look like I can lead if my very *clothes* won't follow directions?"

Eleanor agreed the dress was not hanging correctly. The light blue ribbon trim was meant to encircle the gown and return to a pin at the waist. Two ends of the ribbon hung limply halfway down the belled skirt.

Miss Brewer stepped back and eyed the misbehaving ribbon, her mouth canted over to the side in a perfect pout. It should have wrinkled her face into a terrible scowl, but that was Justine Brewer—cute as a button, no matter her expression. Eleanor wished her face was half as pleasing in even one attitude.

"I could tie it into a bow," Miss Brewer suggested.

"That's too last season," Tristan's sister complained. "What am I going to do? I have to get back out there."

This was a problem she could fix! Eleanor took a step forward. "May I make a suggestion?" Her boldness surprised her, but after all, these were just other young ladies, and not ones that would judge her for forwardness.

"Please," the sister wailed. Even Miss Brewer looked relieved.

"Could I just show you?" Eleanor stepped closer.

The dress's owner huffed in frustration. Miss Brewer gave her a skeptical once-over. "Of course, Miss . . . ?"

"Piper. Eleanor Piper. How do you do?" She gave a slight, reflexive curtsy because she didn't know the rank of the other woman.

"Of Piper and Co. Shipping?" Miss Brewer asked, exchanging a look with her friend.

"Mr. Piper is my father, yes." Dismayed by the distraction, Eleanor looked to the golden-haired young miss. "May I?"

With a shrewd look in her eye, the young lady nodded. "Go ahead."

Eleanor knelt in front of her, smoothing out the ribbon, finding the edges of each side. There was a loose tie that had come unpinned from the waist. It wasn't secure without a proper knot. Stripping her gloves off, Eleanor quickly tied a double butterfly, careful to flare out each wing to make the knot's namesake clear. The width of the ribbon wasn't easy to work with, nor was the slippery satin easy to tie, but Eleanor was happy to finally be comfortable.

"There now." Eleanor backed away, pleased with her work. Instead of a plain hook of ribbon, there was now a jaunty butterfly pinned midway down the wide skirt of the young miss.

"Oh," Miss Brewer said in surprise.

"That was fast," the other said, looking down. "Oh. It's a butterfly." She sounded disappointed.

"Do you not like butterflies?" Eleanor asked, her stomach plummeted.

"Who doesn't like butterflies?" the miss replied, though her tone made it very clear: *she* did not like butterflies.

Eleanor squared her shoulders. "Not to worry." She knelt once again, untying her butterfly and looking up at the woman who was now peering down at her as she worked, judging her to be the type of person who preferred fewer feminine frills. She tied a double figure eight knot instead, fashioning the ribbon to make the geometrical pattern of the infinity sign pleasing to the eye.

"Ophelia," Miss Brewer said, her voice full of admiration. "Come look in the mirror."

The young lady—Ophelia—moved past Eleanor to the mirror hung on the wall. She moved this way and that. "Oh, that's good. That's very good. Miss Piper, you have my undying gratitude."

Eleanor smiled and got to her feet, careful not to step on petticoats and balance the hoop of her dress. "My pleasure."

"You seem to be quite the expert on ribbons," Miss Brewer said carefully.

"Not ribbons, really." Eleanor smiled. "It's one of those things anyone might learn if their father dealt with ships. Knot-tying is essential aboard any vessel."

Ophelia got a strange look on her face, an expression that

made Eleanor almost nervous. "Miss Piper, I would very much like you to call on me tomorrow, at my home."

Eleanor blinked rapidly. Had she made friends so easily? And did she want to be known as a friend to an associate of *Bad News Brews*? "I would be delighted. May I inquire as to your address?"

"Belgravia Square. Lord Rascomb's residence." Ophelia smiled.

Eleanor stood stunned. This was *The Honourable* Ophelia Bridewell. And her golden-god brother was *The Honourable* Tristan Bridewell. Her stomach sank. They were so far out of her social sphere, she might as well be on the bottom of the ocean. "Of course."

Miss Ophelia gave her an impish smile. "Did you not recognize me?"

Eleanor shook her head. Oh, her father would be pleased to call on Lord Rascomb, with his wealth, his title, and his two unmarried sons. "I apologize, I have not been keeping up on the social *on dits*."

Miss Brewer gave her a kind smile and folded Eleanor's hand in her arm. "Why don't you let us make introductions tonight? It's the very least we can do."

"That isn't necessary," Eleanor said weakly, wanting to pull her arm from her new friend's grasp.

"I'm afraid it is," Ophelia sighed. "After all, once Justine makes up her mind about a friend, you'll have a devil of a time changing it. Besides, tomorrow, you'll be a member of the club, so we might as well introduce you as one tonight."

"The club?" Eleanor asked, having a distinct feeling that things were about to happen *to* her, whether she wanted it or not.

Both young women smiled. "The Ladies' Alpine Society."

Eleanor echoed the name back. "I'm afraid I've never heard of it. What does it do?"

"It raises money," Justine said.

"For what?" Eleanor asked, her whole body tingling.

"For the first women to climb the Matterhorn." Ophelia took

Eleanor's other arm.

"And who would those women be?" Eleanor sagged against them.

"Us, of course," Miss Brewer answered. "Come, let's go raise some money."

"WOULD YOU INTRODUCE me to Miss Brewer?" Blakely asked Tristan. He'd been in America too long and didn't know what he was asking. The other men in the group chuckled.

"Not if you value your time," Jacobs chirped.

"Or your immortal soul," said DeWitt.

"Wasting your breath, but I will if you'd like me to," Tristan said to him. He liked the man, mostly because he generally liked everyone. Blakely lost too frequently at cards, but that was another reason that Justine would eat the man alive. Justine didn't like losers. Or really, winners, for that matter. Justine Brewer disliked about every man she encountered, which was fine by Tristan.

He'd given her a wide berth since childhood, when she'd climbed up to the slate roof of their townhome and performed a jig because he'd dared her to. He didn't expect her to do it, which was the entire reason he'd said it; any reasonable person would have seen the risk of breaking one's neck. The girl was patently insane, and he wanted no part of her antics.

"Oh, hello there, who's that other one on Miss Brewer's arm? Haven't seen her before," Jacobs said, peering over Tristan's shoulder.

Tristan glanced, expecting to see another one of Ophelia's constantly changing chums. But no, it was that young miss he'd bumped into earlier. It was entirely his fault. He'd been charging towards the card tables, hoping to catch Francis, Justine's older brother, who was just back from the Continent, when he'd stepped right into the woman's path. He was such an oaf at times—of which Ophelia had no compunction reminding him. His height and width had sprung out of nowhere at the ripe age of eighteen, and in the years since, he'd spent most of his time outside. He still had trouble remembering just how far his stride carried him when inside a building.

"I don't know her name," Tristan confessed. There was a softness about her that he liked. Where his sister's friends were typically impetuous and bold, this woman didn't seem like she would run him over.

He glanced at his mates, all standing around gawping at the trio of women making their way through the ballroom. He wasn't about to let any of those idiots get the upper hand on a pretty girl. "Excuse me, gentlemen."

They booed as he walked away, a grin on his face. Blakely caught up. "Introduce me?"

"It's not worth it, mate," Tristan said, a grin on his face.

"What do you care? Aren't you seeing Mrs. Fitzroy?"

Tristan's step faltered. "We've parted company." Mrs. Vera Fitzroy was an actress whose greatest joy seemed to be torturing him. She'd been nothing but sweetness when he first courted her, but she'd grown more acerbic as they spent time together. Finally, he realized that he'd not known her at all. He gave her an emerald brooch to commemorate their time together, and she'd been seen in the company of an older man the very next night. Tristan had felt insulted, though he knew he had no right to begrudge Vera her happiness—or her livelihood.

Finally they reached the trio: his sister, Justine, and the mysterious young miss.

"How is your evening thus far?" Tristan asked Justine.

"I haven't yet gotten a sponsor for the Scotland expedition, if that's what you're asking," Justine said curtly. She was all business with him, which suited him fine.

"Quite," he said. "May I introduce my friend Mr. Terrance Blakely? Blakely, this is my sister's bosom companion, Miss

Justine Brewer." He didn't add her nickname, *Bad News*, which admittedly, he'd given her. It wasn't his fault he knew the editor of a few papers.

Justine gave Blakely a tepid smile, but Blakely was all aflutter. Maybe she could wheedle more money out of him for the expedition, just as the rest of his money had been relieved from his pockets at the card tables.

"Since we are introducing everyone," Ophelia announced, "may I present Miss Eleanor Piper, the newest member of the Ladies' Alpine Society."

Tristan's brows shot up. He had not pegged this young lady as an adventurer. Miss Eleanor Piper blushed furiously, which he enjoyed watching. So she was as timid as she seemed. He hoped she could keep up, otherwise Ophelia and Bad News would chew her up and spit her out. Not to mention what the mountain would do to her.

"And this is my brother," Ophelia continued. "Mr. Tristan Bridewell."

"I'm not truly a member," Miss Piper stammered. "In fact, I've only just heard of it."

"Nonsense." Justine said. "She's coming. And that's final."

Tristan caught Miss Piper's gaze. Her brown eyes were deep and velvety, carrying a softness that melted him. "You must have shown some kind of acumen that makes Miss Brewer so adamant."

"She's an absolute genius with knots," Ophelia said. "You should have seen how quick she was, too. Look at my dress. Look at this!" His sister turned to show off the side of her dress, where a perfectly tidy double figure eight knot was dressed out to perfection. Their father could not have done half so well with a ribbon that thick.

"That's impressive," Tristan admitted.

"See? We must have her," Justine said.

Blakely turned red at the phrase, no doubt hearing a double entendre.

"Your skills would be quite the asset," Tristan said, making that delicious eye contact with her. She blushed again; this time, the heat spread delightfully across her chest. The off-the-shoulder fashion displayed so much, and for that Tristan was eternally grateful. "How did you come to know such a thing?"

"My father is in shipping," Miss Piper said, her voice small.

"Ah, this must be him now," Ophelia observed as an older couple approached.

Miss Piper did the introductions, and Tristan noted Mr. Piper's disapproval when she named him. Tristan's reputation was perhaps not the most ideal. He played cards—gambling was an easy way to raise the money for their expedition, after all. But he did use some of his winnings on keeping women like Vera Fitzroy happy, it was true.

Yet Tristan was convinced he could win over a man like Mr. Piper. Not that he had any designs on Miss Piper, of course. Any friend of Ophelia's was immediately off limits, and doubly so if she were someone who might accompany them on their expedition. One oughtn't dip one's pen in the company ink, so to speak.

The goal was the Matterhorn. It had been successfully ascended not even a year earlier, by a British team. Unfortunately, Lord Francis Douglas and three other members of the expedition had lost their lives in the descent. Queen Victoria was not pleased that aristocratic blood had spilled on mountain, but it spurred Tristan's father on. Somehow, that burning desire to conquer was made all the more palpable by the fatal mishap that had befallen Lord Francis Douglas's team.

Ophelia shared that desire with their father. Tristan wanted to be a part of the ascent, not out of a desire to conquer, but for the view. He was always a boy climbing a tree, looking for a lofty perch. What could be loftier than the distinctive perch atop the Matterhorn? How far would they see? The challenge of climbing a mountain that proved not only impossible but lethal to so many was intoxicating.

Tristan gripped Mr. Piper's hand—he tried to greet all industrialists with a hearty American-style handshake, as they seemed to respect him more for it. Given that he wouldn't inherit his father's title, he needed to prove himself in some other way. "Mr. Piper, a pleasure."

Mr. Piper's grip was firmer than he expected, his hands solid and square. Clearly the man had worked shipboard before he became a businessman. "Mr. Bridewell," he grunted, a voice like gravel. "I've heard you and your father are in search of adventure."

Tristan gave his best rakish grin. "I daresay it isn't a search, as we've found our target."

"And what would that be?" Mr. Piper was fishing, and Tristan would be happy to reel him in.

"The Matterhorn," Ophelia announced, giving Mr. Piper a pristine smile of her own. "You see, we're hoping to make me the first woman to the top."

"I beg your pardon!" Mrs. Piper exclaimed, swaying as if she might topple at any moment.

"Mr. Whymper has proved the ascent possible. I've met him, and while he is perfectly decent, he is no god among men. I believe I can also accomplish the task just as well," Ophelia answered serenely.

Justine, miraculously, kept her mouth shut about joining the expedition.

"Is this true?" Mr. Piper asked Tristan.

"Of course," Tristan replied. "But my sister will not be alone. My father and I will also be on the expedition. Surely you know that my father, Lord Rascomb, is an accomplished mountaineer."

Mr. Piper frowned but nodded. "I'm not sure I can condone such an exercise for a woman. Their natural frailty seems a deterrent."

Tristan didn't bother looking to his sister, who had heard the sentiment time and again. But he would pitch Ophelia against any man when it came to endurance. Their father had taken them on mountaineering projects many times, from Mount Snowdon in Wales to Mont Blanc in France. They were slogs, each one of them, and while his older brother Arthur complained, Ophelia kept her head down and her feet moving.

"I harbor no qualms about my sister's abilities."

"Mrs. Piper," Ophelia said, bypassing Mr. Piper's authority. "I've asked Miss Piper to call on me tomorrow. She has some skill that I had hoped she would impart upon me."

Mrs. Piper straightened, her previous frailty forgotten. "Oh? And what is that?"

"Her skill in knot-tying is quite extraordinary. It would be most advantageous to have such abilities on a treacherous climb such as the Matterhorn."

Tristan smiled at Ophelia's cunning. She didn't say she wanted Miss Piper on the expedition, nor did she ask for lessons. That was Ophelia for you; dance around the issue so that by the time the trespass has been committed, the persecuted doesn't realize they've been manipulated.

"We would be happy to call on you tomorrow," Mrs. Piper answered, clearly dazzled by the idea.

Even Mr. Piper finally looked pleased. Tristan wanted to sigh. The obviousness of their social climbing was depressing. His father's title baited more than one family. Technically, his brother Arthur, the heir, was unmarried. No doubt they wished to shove Miss Eleanor into the wandering, aloof gaze of Herringbone.

It wasn't Arthur's fault that his courtesy title was Lord Berringbone, nor was it his fault that he was born with eyes so wide and so very far apart, like a trout. It was only a matter of time until someone came up with his nickname. That it was Tristan was . . . not unexpected. But Tristan had not sold this nickname to the papers. It was just what he called his brother from childhood, and then when they ended up at the same school, since Arthur wasn't that much older, well, the other boys definitely picked up on the fish-related ideas.

Tristan didn't begrudge Herringbone inheriting all the money. Or the title. Or a guaranteed purpose in life. But looking at the shy Miss Eleanor, he did begrudge Herringbone the chance to court her, sight unseen. Tristan was here, and an excellent conversationalist and dancer. Why should his brother get all the respectable women?

The musicians returned from their break, striking up another Viennese waltz. He might as well do his part to raise Miss Piper's esteem in the eyes of Society. "Miss Piper, may I have this dance?"

She looked astonished to be asked, and he couldn't help but wonder who had ignored her so often as to make her believe herself invisible. She was a stunning girl, her hair and eyes a study in warm luscious brown, like the dark Swiss chocolate he'd come to enjoy.

"Go on, go on," Mr. Piper muttered, shooing her off with his hands.

There was Tristan's answer. Those people—her parents—were the ones who had ignored her. If nothing else, between him and Ophelia, they could make Miss Piper feel important. He held out his hand, waiting for her, hoping she could at least take this dance. It was her due as a young lady at a party.

She composed herself and slid her gloved fingers into his. "Thank you," she whispered as he led her to the parquet, already swirling with couples. Belled skirts swirled in yellows, lavenders, azures, and emeralds.

He gave her his best rakish smile, as he'd done to win over her father. "I have a feeling that by the end of the night, I'll be thanking you."

THE DANCE FLOOR was distracting. How did one remember steps amidst all these swaying multi-colored dresses? But then, how did one remember one was on the dance floor at all, when Tristan Bridewell's hand was settled heavy on her waist? He was beautiful. And not a gentleman she would ever consider, either.

Not that a gentleman like him would be interested in her. She needed to reject that idea immediately. This was clearly a bid for her father's money for whatever their Society was about. Even in the retiring room, Ophelia had asked if she was related to Piper Shipping. That was fine. Understandable. They needed to raise money, and Eleanor was the lock holding back her sizeable dowry. This Society needed the correct key. Whether that was friendship or something more, so be it.

But surrounded by Tristan's very firm arms, the scent of him different than the salty ocean smell of Mr. Smythe, her father's captain, best friend, and the teacher of all her wonderful knots, Eleanor was hard pressed to remember this was not about her. That Tristan's clear, exceptionally beautiful blue eyes staring at her as if she were something extraordinary was because of her father's money.

"Have you been to many balls?" Tristan asked, pulling Eleanor out of her own spiraling thoughts.

She looked up at him, momentarily lost in the absolute charming beauty of his symmetrical face. "No, not many, I'm afraid."

"Oh, were you in the country? Or traveling?" Tristan asked. A small frown line appeared between his brows, and somehow he became more attractive. How was a man with a lined face *more* attractive? But he was.

"No," Eleanor said. "I was . . ." What was she doing? Reading books, tying knots, drawing pictures of dogs and cats that she wished were her pets if her mother wasn't *deathly* allergic. Emphasis her mother's, of course.

Tristan's hand adjusted at her waist, causing the sensation to renew. That was very distracting. "And you?" she asked. "Have you been to many balls?"

His eyes flashed wide open in acknowledgment. "I fear that being the son of a viscount obligated me to attend every ball in a forty-mile radius of London since my fifteenth birthday."

"What happened on your fifteenth birthday?" Eleanor asked automatically, not thinking that it might be an impertinent probing.

Tristan barked out a laugh. "I grew into my feet." He leaned down to whisper in her ear, "I was clumsy as a boy."

Eleanor had to concentrate very hard on listening because his mouth so near her ear was making her feel faint. Maybe she had inherited her mother's sickly constitution, because dancing with Tristan was inducing all sorts of concerning symptoms. "And now?" She hoped she didn't sound breathless.

He grinned, which really ought to be a crime, because the pleasure on his face was so handsome, Eleanor was surprised she wasn't felled right there on the dance floor.

"You tell me," he said. "Have I stepped on your feet at all?" He spun her around, which did nothing for her dizziness. He let go of her hand and bowed. It was only then that Eleanor realized the music had stopped and the dance was over.

Oh dear, he was a dangerous man. And Eleanor knew from the scandal sheets that he found company amongst the opera singers and the demimonde. He was not a man in search of a wife. If she weren't careful, he would seduce her out of her petticoats with one alluring smile. No, not her. He was looking for her father's money. This was about the money, and not about her. She had to remember that in order to keep her head on straight, as her father would say.

They returned to their circle of people, her parents, Miss Ophelia, and Miss Brewer. Then quite unexpectedly, Tristan announced, "It's settled. Miss Piper has agreed to teach us her knowledge."

Eleanor shot him a look that could only be construed as surprise, couldn't it? Not gratitude for including her, not delight that it would compel her to spend more time in his company. But maybe those things too. Her heart fluttered in her chest, and she looked to her parents, who both eyed her skeptically.

"Well then," her mother sniffed. "We shall begin tomorrow, I suppose."

❦

Chapter Two

MARY ELIZABETH PIPER, Eleanor's mother, was what people called a handsome woman. Never beautiful or dainty, as she had the wide, capable hands of a stablemaster, and the shoulders of a coalminer. According to Mr. Smythe, the ship's captain, who knew her parents when they were courting back in what must have been the Dark Ages, Mary Elizabeth had the mouth of a sailor. But as she became Eleanor's mother, all that capability and brashness shrunk into propriety.

Mr. Smythe would lean back in his chair, hands folded over his growing belly and *tsk*. "She were a right powerful woman, your mama. Too bad she changed for the docile."

It was in the set of her mother's mouth that Eleanor could see that boldness as they handed off bonnets and gloves and pelisses at the Rascomb townhouse. Mary Elizabeth Piper had set about getting her daughter a fine match, and it dawned on Eleanor then and there that the docility Mr. Smythe complained of was all for Eleanor's sake. That her mother had given herself over to propriety for twenty-five years for exactly this moment—calling upon the house of a viscount.

Eleanor was determined to be the most gracious, most helpful, most demure daughter that there ever was. If her mother could do this for twenty-five years, Eleanor could manage for a fifteen-minute visit.

They were shown to the drawing room, and Eleanor had not

expected the scene before them. Neither the twenty-five years of propriety nor her mother's childhood in Kent would have prepared either of them for what they encountered. Eleanor decided that there was absolutely nothing proper or predictable about the Bridewells.

Miss Ophelia was climbing a rope that was secured to the ceiling of the drawing room in some manner. A blonde woman, presumably Lady Rascomb, was standing with her hands on her hips, evaluating Ophelia's ability. The blonde woman leaned against the wall, next to a cane. Tristan was sprawled on the settee, covering a smile with his hand. And then she spotted Lord Rascomb in the corner sorting through a pile of items that looked to be samples of ropes of different calibers and colors and lengths.

"Even without the damned hoop, how am I supposed to climb with all the fabric of petticoats and skirts? This is ridiculous!" Ophelia said, catching sight of guests as she threw herself off the rope. "Oh! People."

The butler announced Eleanor and her mother, only to have the other family all snap to proper positions. Tristan bolted to his feet, Lady Rascomb's hands floated down in front of her, Ophelia smoothed her skirts, and Lord Rascomb dropped the ropes and stood.

Eleanor glanced to her mother, wondering what she made of the chaotic scene. Her mother's face was implacable, and Eleanor was suddenly jealous of her ability to be so even tempered.

"Mrs. Piper, Miss Eleanor, welcome. I'm so glad you took the time to visit," Lady Rascomb said, her tone even and gracious and not at all embarrassed. She bid them sit with a wave of her hand, and shooed Tristan and Lord Rascomb out of the room.

"Miss Eleanor," Tristan murmured in a low voice as he walked past.

"Mist—mist—mist—" Eleanor couldn't even manage his name as that fresh air scent that heralded his person wafted close as he passed her on his way out the door. Oh, dear.

Her mother covered for her and properly acknowledged Lord

Rascomb and Tristan Bridewell, while Eleanor bobbed her curtsy before settling her gaze on Miss Ophelia and Lady Rascomb.

"Refreshments will be up shortly," Lady Rascomb said, ushering them in. "But in the meantime, please sit, tell us how you found last night's ball."

"Very lovely," Mrs. Piper said with a bland smile. "We met a great many wonderful people, such as yourselves."

"Yes," Miss Ophelia piped up, settling next to her mother on the opposite settee. "I feel as if it were the hand of Providence that guided Miss Eleanor to me."

"Don't blaspheme," Lady Rascomb whispered to Ophelia. Ophelia returned her mother's comment with wide eyes as if she couldn't believe the scold.

Considering the cursing Eleanor had witnessed while Ophelia was up on the rope, she was surprised too.

"Please excuse my daughter, Mrs. Piper. I let her spend a great deal of time with her father. They both believe in the unconquerable adventure, and I fear that has influenced her speech." Lady Rascomb batted her eyelashes.

No wonder Miss Ophelia was not married nor connected to anyone. They had a hard time behaving decently. Eleanor quashed her own glee. Ophelia's glow of enthusiasm was refreshing, and Eleanor wished she had it as well. Maybe they could be friends, regardless of whatever the mess of this adventure Society was.

"Quite all right," Mrs. Piper said, looking about the room. It was a beautiful room, with exceptional curtains, portraits in gilded frames, and the exact pristine wainscotting that Mrs. Piper wanted for her own drawing room. "My Eleanor also spent a great deal of time at my husband's office, and no doubt has some choice phrases that she won't utter in my presence."

A partially true statement, that. Eleanor had spent a great deal of time at her father's office, Piper Shipping & Co., but Mr. Smythe's presence and knot lessons kept her from wandering amongst the former sailors on the bottom floor who had the truly colorful language. Had she heard snippets? Yes. Did she know curses in some interesting languages other than English? A few.

But she mostly kept herself upstairs, busying herself with intricate knots and creating lever pulls similar to the ones that loaded the heavy crates onto her father's boats. It was obvious why she did it—it was the play that garnered praise from her busy father.

"Is that where she learned her extraordinary skills?" Lady Rascomb asked.

"I believe so. Eleanor?" Her mother prompted.

"Yes, Lady Rascomb." Eleanor wasn't sure what she should say. In fact, she was surprised they were talking about this at all.

Fortunately, a servant walked in with a tray, and suddenly, it was all business of tea and scones and cream.

Miss Ophelia poured, no doubt to showcase her skill, lest Mrs. Piper doubt Ophelia's feminine training. After handing Eleanor the final cup and saucer, Ophelia glanced at her mother and then back to Eleanor.

"We have a salon later this afternoon, if you would like to join us. I do hope you will."

"A salon? For your Society?" Eleanor asked.

"The Ladies' Alpine Society," Ophelia corrected. "Yes. It is open to the public, but our members will be there. We discuss our upcoming project and teach basic skills that might prove interesting to other attendees."

"Do you get a great many of the public?" Mrs. Piper asked.

Miss Ophelia actually looked abashed. "Not many. Mostly those who just want to see the inside of the house."

Mrs. Piper frowned.

"They are mostly ladies, these attendees from the public," Lady Rascomb added. "Often in hopes of finding my eldest son, Lord Berringbone."

Polite understanding flitted across Mrs. Piper's face. Eleanor understood as well. They were mamas and young ladies hoping to nab a viscountcy. Not unlike them. Mrs. Piper sipped her tea.

"Then it shouldn't be scandalous for my Eleanor to attend."

The trap had been so expertly baited by Lady Rascomb, dangling her son for Eleanor's mother. Eleanor couldn't help but admire the subtlety of the woman.

"Thank you, Miss Ophelia," Eleanor said. "I should be glad to attend."

And it wasn't so much Lord Berringbone who she hoped would be in attendance, but the younger brother that she already called Tristan in her mind. It was far too familiar, and far too presumptuous, and possibly even dangerous. She might slip and call him by his first name in company, which would be far too embarrassing. No, she should endeavor to refer to him as Mr. Bridewell. But he looked like a Tristan, with his beautiful golden hair and blue eyes—

"Eleanor, pay attention, girl!" her mother whispered at her.

Eleanor snapped back to the conversation at hand. "I do apologize. Woolgathering."

Ophelia gave her a sly look. What was that for? She couldn't possibly know that Eleanor was daydreaming about her brother. "I was saying that I have some journals and pamphlets you might like to borrow, all written by woman who climb mountains."

"Oh no," Eleanor said. "I'm not really the type—"

"That's fine," Ophelia interrupted smoothly. "Would you mind doing a short presentation of some knots for us? It would be quite educational."

"I can do that," Eleanor said. "But the best way to learn a knot is to tie it at least one hundred times. Everyone ought to have a practice string of their own."

"Do you have one?" Ophelia asked. Lady Rascomb looked at her with interest.

"Yes, it's a length of cotton rope about two feet in length. Small diameter, easy to tie and untie."

Lady Rascomb and her daughter exchanged looks. Eleanor panicked.

"I used to use hemp, as that is the type used on the docks to load crates. It does well when wet," she explained. "But it is harder on one's hands."

"I believe I can procure cotton or hemp for our attendees this evening," Lady Rascomb said. "Mrs. Piper, do come. Your husband as well. It's quite the evening, and we do serve refreshments."

"I shall, and I will send to Mr. Piper about it as well. I don't know how busy he is today, but I'm sure he'll be interested."

Eleanor was already thinking of the different knots she might show them. Tying the same knots in the different fibers would be an excellent showcase to help them with their decision-making. While she had no intention of climbing any mountain, she would hope they might include a thank you to her at the end of whatever paper they published at the end of their adventure. To think, her name in print!

OVERALL, TRISTAN USED the Ladies' Alpine Society salons to covertly drink. He kept a hipflask on his person, filled with the best Irish whisky he could get his hands on. Sometimes even his father would take a nip or two. One could only hear Ophelia and Bad News extol womanly optimism for so long before boredom set in.

But tonight, he had a feeling the hipflask would stay full, because in walked the Pipers. Mr. Piper, of Piper Shipping & Co., which of course Tristan had looked into, narrowed his eyes the moment he walked into the drawing room, as if this might be an ambush—which indeed, given the expedition's need for funding, it might be. Following the man of industry was Miss Eleanor Piper. Her brown eyes were warm and darted around the room, and when they caught his gaze, her cheeks turned a lovely pink.

That was a shame. Tristan nodded his acknowledgment, he wasn't a complete cad, after all. But still, Ophelia's friends were off limits to him. Bad News Brewer was just the obvious example as to why. Still, a social climbing shipping heiress was not appealing to him nor anyone he knew.

Mrs. Piper rounded out the set of figures entering the room, and when she saw Tristan, her dislike was palpable. Ah, so she'd read about him on the scandal sheets, then. All the more reason for them not to throw Miss Eleanor at him—oh. They weren't here for him, that's right. He remembered now. They were going to throw her at Herringbone. What a waste. Maybe his flask would be emptied tonight.

But Herringbone wasn't coming tonight. He rarely did. Tristan didn't know if he felt excluded since he was forbidden to go with his father on these adventures. Tristan was the spare, so it didn't matter if he risked his neck. It offered a sense of freedom, but also a reminder that he was expendable.

The hipflask grew heavier in his pocket as Mr. Piper approached. "Mr. Bridewell."

"Mr. Piper. So good of you to make it to one of our events." Tristan gave a practiced smile and moved his body to make a pathway to his father. If anyone could gain the shipping magnate's confidence, it was him. "Let me take you over to my father, Lord Rascomb. You met him last night, did you not?"

"I did, yes, thank you," Mr. Piper said, his gruff voice smoothing out into the higher pitch of the more polished class.

It rankled Tristan, this pretense. Not that Mr. Piper conducted business in a different accent or even a different register of his voice, but all of the class wars. It seemed like a lot of silly bother. But, as Vera had once pointed out, it was easy to see it as silly bother when one was on top of the pile.

Tristan passed the man off to his father and wandered over to Ophelia and Bad News. "We have an audience tonight," he stage-whispered to his sister.

She popped her hands to her hips. "Maybe you won't be so focused on your pockets tonight, since we've got actual company."

"What are talking about?" Tristan asked, annoyed by the sheer idea that someone was critiquing his behavior.

Bad News rested her hand on his arm, batted her long, dark eyelashes as she stared up into his eyes, and whispered, "Is that drink in your pocket, or are you happy to see me?"

Tristan yanked his arm away. "That's disgusting! Whoever have you heard say something like that?"

Bad News snorted, tossing her auburn ringlets. Other men found her captivating. Tristan found her to be nothing but a swarm of fire ants in petticoats. "If I had a shilling for how many times men have asked me what I thought was in their pockets, I'd—"

"Have a shilling?" Tristan asked politely.

Bad News narrowed her blue eyes. "I wouldn't need a dowry."

Tristan threw his hands in the air, very uncomfortable with the entire scene. "I don't know what we're even talking about anymore."

"I do," Ophelia said, seeming to relish his discomfort. "We are discussing men's pockets."

Miss Eleanor Piper chose that moment to join their trio. "Oh, are there new fashion plates out?"

Bad News laughed, but at least had the decorum to cover her mouth. Tristan shot daggers at her. Her reputation was notorious, and she didn't need to tarnish Miss Eleanor by association. Or by the ghastly things that came out of her mouth.

"I'm afraid not," Ophelia answered her. "But we are so happy you could make it, Miss Eleanor. I do hope you are ready to share some of your skill set with us."

At the mention of her skills, Eleanor's face lit up. She was an attractive enough girl when expressionless, but when speaking of her passions, she was positively radiant. As she spoke, her hands moved artfully, weaving in the air, and Tristan realized she was tying knots. He also realized he was staring at her. He shuffled his feet, leaning in that rakish way that women seemed to appreciate.

He honestly could not be bothered by Ophelia's friends.

"I brought fifteen lengths," Miss Eleanor said.

Tristan was absolutely lost by her words. He hadn't been able to listen and watch at the same time. *Lengths?*

"Ah yes," Ophelia said, gesturing to a carpetbag on the chair in the corner by the door. "That must be the satchel that Ferris brought up."

Eleanor turned and spied it, scurrying over. She opened it, counted out four and returned, handing it to each of them. "This is a practice string."

"String?" Bad News asked, eyebrows raised.

Eleanor gave her a stunning smile, and Tristan was envious that Bad News elicited such an expression on her lovely face. Then he kicked himself mentally and focused on the practice string that looked rather like a hearty rope.

"I call it a string, but yes, it is a length of manila rope. It's a bit rough on the hands at first. Eventually the natural oils on your hands will transfer, and it will soften up. I recommend using a quality hand cream nightly. It isn't nearly as bad as handling hemp rope, which is definitely less flexible and harder to work with."

"I should say," Bad News said.

"Should we wear gloves?" Ophelia asked.

Eleanor shook her head. "Not at first. At the beginning, we must get each knot so thoroughly in your hands that you could tie it while being highly distracted."

Oh, Tristan could think of something that would be highly distracting. Namely, watching proper Miss Eleanor standing closer to him. He ran his hand along the length of the rope, and it felt oddly similar to another activity he had been engaged in more frequently since his parting with Vera.

"Like reciting a poem?" Ophelia suggested.

No, Tristan thought. Absolutely nothing like reciting a poem.

"Exactly!" Eleanor said, again bestowing a gorgeous, full-toothed smile. One of her incisors was tilted in a most endearing way. Oh, stop. He wanted desperately to like her, as he liked most everyone. But if he allowed himself to like her, then he'd be at risk of *liking* her.

"What is our first assignment?" Bad News asked. "I like to be the best, you know. Give me a head start."

Eleanor let out a light, tinkling laugh. Tristan almost growled at Bad News. "Shouldn't we wait until the entire salon may be addressed?"

Ophelia looked up, scanning the room, and Tristan did the same. They had Tristan's father, himself, Ophelia, Bad News, her brother Francis who was over talking with Mr. Piper, and then the Piper family. It was not a good turnout. But it rarely was. Ophelia winced as Tristan caught her eye.

"I may have forgot to put a notice in the paper." Ophelia twisted the rope in her hands.

"It does make it difficult to attend a party one doesn't know is happening," Tristan scolded. "If you're going to be the leader of this expedition—"

"I've been focusing on other aspects, Tristan," Ophelia hissed back.

"If you cannot delegate, then you have no business—"

"You don't know what I have been doing because you're either not here or—"

"Bridewells! Bridewells!" Bad News stepped between them. "It doesn't matter at this moment. We have all the attendees we'll receive this evening. Let's get started. And don't bicker in front of the teacher." Bad News winked at Miss Eleanor, and it made Tristan furious.

Bad News flirted with everyone and everything. The silly chit would flirt with a gas lamp if she were bored enough. Meanwhile, Tristan was doing his absolute best to be a gentleman. It was enough to drive him to the back of the room and indulge in his hip flask.

Eleanor flushed—perhaps with pride, if Tristan had to guess. He would wager that she'd never before been praised for her unique talent. If that wasn't just like Ophelia to find someone's weakness and draw it out for her own purposes. She was cunning, his sister. Pushing aside his resentment of Bad News, he let pride in his sister flush through his veins.

"And Eleanor." Ophelia grabbed the girl by her wrist, making Tristan wonder what it might feel like, how small her wrist might feel beneath his own hand. "Please return those pamphlets and journals I let you borrow. We have a new member of the Society, and I want to make sure I reel her in."

Tristan tried to keep himself from grumbling and flung himself into one of the seats. Ophelia clapped her hands to get everyone's attention.

The rest of them stopped talking and took seats obediently. These salons were meant to educate the public about their hope to climb the Matterhorn in a few years, to educate them on the perils and trials they would face and how they would overcome them. It was also a way to make them pay for a subscription to the writings they would publish during the adventure, and hopefully open their pockets even further to help pay for all the preparations still needed.

Three men had lived after conquering the Matterhorn, requiring something like fifteen attempts: Edward Whymper, an illustrator, and the two German guides. How many attempts would it take them? And how could they even get this motley group of woolen skirts to Switzerland to try?

Tristan had no doubts about Ophelia. His sister was remarkably stubborn, and she had proven herself when the family went scrambling up mountains in France over the last few years. People applied the word *stubborn* to all manner of beasts and people, but the definition didn't come to its pinnacle until Ophelia. She would die with snow in her boots rather than walk down a mountain without reaching the top. And Bad News? Best to not underestimate that one. Tristan didn't know the true extent of the girl's powers, nor did he want to. She was Bad News for a reason.

But Miss Eleanor Piper. If they took this soft beauty up a mountain, they might kill her. Half of Edward Whymper's team died, and those were seasoned climbers. And men, of course. Could Miss Eleanor overcome her staid, proper upbringing to become a physical creature that could conquer a mountain? Not many Englishmen could—could many Englishwomen? Any risk they took gambled their lives—individually and as a group.

But his father had several exercises for them to engage in over the next few months: the intensive at Berringbone Hold, and then the trial expedition in Scotland. Climbing Ben Nevis wouldn't be easy in the least. It would be cold and wet and foggy, all conditions they might find on the Matterhorn. It was the closest they could get to a test before leaving for the Continent.

"This is Miss Eleanor Piper, everyone," Ophelia announced, straightening her shoulders as Tristan had told her repeatedly that she must do if she expected to get anywhere as a public speaker. "As you know, safety on a mountain relies on the strength of your ropes. Your ropes are only as strong as your knots. So let us welcome Miss Eleanor, who will no doubt keep us safe."

Tristan raised his hands for a lazy clap, feeling awkward about applauding someone in a crowd of less than ten people. He hoped he could focus well enough to learn what she had to teach—if anything. He was already strong in his basic knots. He'd been up several mountains, and been in peril many times. Including the times when Vera took to her dramatic opera roots and threw a vase at his head.

"EVERYONE SHOULD HAVE a length of rope to practice along with Miss Piper," Miss Ophelia said, scurrying around, handing out the lengths to those who hadn't gotten them yet. Once the task was done, Ophelia sat down in the settee next to Miss Justine.

There were so many eyes looking at Eleanor. Honestly, must

everyone have two of them? Heat crept up her cheeks, and she began to *glow,* as her mother would say, under her arms. She swallowed and gripped the length of rope. This was her comfort, more than any doll or blanket or book.

"Hello everyone, I am Miss Eleanor Piper." She gave a short curtsy bob before realizing she had already been introduced. "I'm the daughter of Mr. Bruce Piper, owner of Piper Shipping & Co. I learned all of my knot-tying skills from one of his esteemed captains, Captain Smythe. While knots are employed in various professions, the ones I know pertain to sailing and the hauling of cargo."

Eleanor glanced across the room. Tristan Bridewell was giving her the most bored expression, even if his eyes were pretty and blue. She probably wouldn't say anything new to him, and he was likely finding her gauche and beneath him. But her father was here, so that must have more than made up for her presence. That was what they wanted, and he'd been very clear about it in the ballroom—they needed funding.

"You likely already know some basics, like a square knot," she folded the length of the manila rope over itself and through. "This is a basic knot that is very intuitive for almost everyone. But it can showcase for us why it's important to dress out your knot."

She caught confusion in Justine Brewer's eyes.

"What I mean by dressing out your knot," Eleanor explained, "is to carefully keep each line of the rope in clear view. No twists or sloppiness. The twisting of the rope can degrade the strength itself."

There was a masculine grunt from the back. Was that Lord Rascomb? Or her father? She glanced over to her father. His burgeoning belly was relaxed against his thighs, but he had a dreamy look on his face, his rope held loosely in one hand. Eleanor straightened. He seemed *proud* of her.

"Ow!" Miss Justine shrieked, sticking a finger in her mouth. "I think I have a splinter."

"Why are we not using cotton ropes, Miss Piper?" Lord

Rascomb asked.

Eleanor felt her cheeks heat. Cotton was probably better for practice knots, and indeed, what she used at home. But she hadn't had enough available at such short notice. Manila was the next best thing, and indeed, what she believed they should use on a snowy expedition. "My apologies. Perhaps this was a poor idea."

Ophelia shot to her feet. "No, this is a wonderful idea. And we likely won't be using cotton rope on expedition, will we, Papa?"

Rascomb shook his head. "We have some hemp, but I'm worried about rot."

"Manila is a good flexible fiber," Eleanor said. "Next time, I can bring cotton rope." It came out of her mouth before she had time to think. Was she really proposing to teach them on another night? This couldn't be interesting or even lucrative for them. This felt like utter failure and she dared not meet her father's eyes. "Perhaps if you tell me what scenarios you think to encounter, and I can figure out the best types of knots to show you."

"I can show you our packing lists," Rascomb said. "Ophelia can make you a copy to take with you. You'll see what we need to bring. Then of course, we rope ourselves together in storms, or places that it is treacherous."

Eleanor nodded, pleased to be considered by the viscount. He wasn't dismissing her because she was a young lady, and that was a very pleasant feeling. She liked him, and she liked Ophelia, even if she felt an utter fool standing in front of them, pretending to know something.

"Perhaps you could show us another knot to practice?" Ophelia prompted.

Eleanor nodded, grateful for the direction. She certainly didn't want any of them getting splinters from the manila rope, but if she convinced them of its qualities, then they would need to grow accustomed to it.

"To determine what you need, I'll clarify some terms. A hitch is when the rope will hold fast to another object."

"Like hitching a pony to a cart?" Justine asked.

"Yes, very good." Eleanor relaxed her shoulders. "A bend unites two rope ends, and a knob is well, a knob in the rope, to help provide a handhold. What type would be best for you to learn?" Eleanor expected some discussion, but instead, the room looked to Ophelia. And it was then that Eleanor realized that this expedition was not Lord Rascomb's project, it was his daughter's. She would lead. The very idea of it was unexpected, and frankly, revolutionary.

"What would be the best knot for us to use when tying into a safety rope?" Ophelia asked.

Eleanor frowned. She didn't know that term. "A single rope that goes around each climber's waist?"

Ophelia nodded.

Eleanor bit her lip. "I'll think about it more, but right now, that would be classified as a hitch."

"A hitch, then, please." Ophelia smiled, clearly encouraging Eleanor.

"Right. Well, I think since the purpose of a safety rope is to prevent one member from falling, then we should learn a noose."

"Sounds terrible," quipped Tristan from the back.

"Someone ought to put a noose on you," Justine shot back.

Eleanor didn't know how to respond to their comments, so she plowed on. "A noose is a sliding knot, so when walking, it shouldn't be too constrictive, but it will draw tight when the standing part—that would be the long portion of the rope between people—is pulled."

They all looked at her expectantly. She didn't know how to use words to describe what she was doing, so she held up her rope instead. There were several nooses that would be appropriate, but she wondered what her pupils would be able to learn well. A familiar shape ought to work. "Today we will learn the figure-eight noose, as it draws up quite smoothly."

Everyone in the room, including her father, followed along. It was one of the simpler knots, and made a clear figure eight, the infinity sign.

"Just like on my dress!" Ophelia cried when she made fast her noose.

Eleanor nodded, pleased that Ophelia remembered. She bid them practice, and they set about, working their manila practice ropes. All except her father, who showed off to her mother by tying intricate designs instead. Her mother giggled, their hold over each other firmer than any knot.

At that moment, Lady Rascomb came in, her cane striking the floor ahead of her steps. Eleanor was suddenly very curious about this woman, as she was the exact opposite of Eleanor's mama, who was currently looking extremely impatient, with her lips pressed together in a thin line.

As all the faces swiveled to the door, instead of still facing Eleanor, she sighed in relief. Lady Rascomb caught her posture and smiled. "A rather small gathering tonight. Are you finished for the evening?" Lady Rascomb asked Ophelia.

Ophelia looked at Eleanor, noting no doubt the sag of her shoulders. "I think so. We will practice these two knots until Miss Piper meets us again."

"Perhaps the Pipers should like to join us for some tea?" Lady Rascomb addressed her question to Eleanor's mother, who jumped to her feet.

"Oh, we would hate to impose." Which wasn't true at all. Her mother would use the viscountess's name to impress her friends and acquaintances for months.

Tristan stood. "I have to meet a friend. My sincere apologies. Excuse me."

The other man in the back, whom Eleanor had not met, stood as well. "If you have a friend to meet, then I do as well." His button nose was an echo of Miss Brewer's, so Eleanor assumed he was her relation.

But the excuse was clearly a flimsy one. Eleanor tried to not feel slighted, but she did. Was she so boring? Was she so inconsequential that he couldn't manage an entire evening in her company?

"Port for the gentlemen who remain, of course," Lady Rascomb smiled. Her blonde hair was clearly where Tristan and Ophelia had gotten theirs. "Darling, will you escort Mr. Piper to your study, since the boys won't be staying, while I have the footmen tidy things up in here?"

❖

Chapter Three

Tristan stood idly in the ballroom, trying to look as if he enjoyed himself. The dancing had just begun, and given that he was the spare—even if he were objectively the more attractive brother—he was ignored. It was not unpleasant.

Herringbone was here tonight, already dancing with the carousel of respectable ladies with adequate dowries and determined mamas. His brother caught his eye, not betraying anything to the wider public, but Tristan could see his exasperation. Tristan raised his cup of overly sour lemonade to his brother as if to toast his dedication. That's what a title got you. Well, tedious time in a ballroom, some dilapidated country houses, and frustrated tenant farmers. Tristan was happy to think about mountains instead.

If Tristan were honest with himself, he was waiting for the Pipers to arrive. He looked forward to seeing what Miss Eleanor was wearing, yes, of course—he was still a hot-blooded male of his species—but also to furthering a discussion with Mr. Piper about sponsorship. It would be expected for him to dance with Miss Eleanor as Tristan's father talked with Mr. Piper. And there was a certain delight in dancing with her, not just because she acquitted herself well.

She was clearly knowledgeable about rope quality, and yes, knots. There was information to be gained there, and he was not such a blowhard as to refuse to learn from a woman. Besides, he did like her. She was pleasant, and she thought him handsome. It was obvious, after all, that she did. And who would blame her? He'd heard it all his life, that he was the handsome one in the family, and it would be terribly false to say he wasn't.

All in all, it was that reason that Tristan was watching the entrance to the ballroom, not for any other. Because he was not the sort who watched for young ladies. Or a young lady in particular. Tristan simply wasn't the sort. However, he was the sort who enjoyed lying to himself.

"Looking for someone?" Francis Brewer asked, coming up for air from the card tables.

"Have you finally lost enough money for the evening?" Tristan responded, sipping his sour drink and struggling not to make a face.

"Just getting started." Francis was Bad News's brother, and a classmate of Tristan's from boyhood. It was, in fact, how the girls met each other and then became inseparable. For a time, the families had hoped that Tristan and Bad News might wed, but their rapport was not suitable to matrimony. Bad News was likely to push him down the stairs, and Tristan would be apt to go join a war just to get away from her. "You seem to be unusually focused on the majordomo."

"I have to look somewhere, don't I? This way no young lady can later claim that I was gazing at her across the ballroom."

Francis clapped him on the shoulder. "Or you could tell me who you are waiting for."

"Don't you have a boat to lose to someone, somewhere?" Tristan asked.

Francis leaned against the wall and folded his arms. "Why? You want a boat?"

"Not particularly."

"Do tell me who she is."

"Who?"

"This lady you await, your Isolde," Francis teased him, using the familiar names from chivalric tales. It had been one of the first ways Francis, bookish as he was, chose to mock him. It had never caught on, because none of the other schoolboys were that smart.

"For your information, it's Mr. Piper, who, as a businessman of some experience and acumen, might object to being referred to as Isolde."

Francis groaned. "Still with the Matterhorn?"

"Always with the Matterhorn. You know how we Bridewells are. Like mastiffs, unable to let go once we've sunk our teeth in."

"After that little display at the salon last week, I'm shocked you still think Piper will give you any money. Justine says you plan on taking the girl with you? No possible way."

Tristan felt the same way, frankly. Miss Eleanor should not accompany them to the Alps. If the Matterhorn killed avid male adventurers, that girl had no business in Switzerland. But he disliked Francis telling him what to do. "We aren't going this year. Hell, we aren't even going next year. She has plenty of time to acclimate to the physical demands the mountain requires. We would never put a member of the expedition in danger."

Francis smirked. "You like her."

Tristan rolled his eyes. "You think that about every woman I look at."

"You like beautiful women, and Miss Eleanor Piper is objecively a beautiful woman. How she's managed to remain unmarried, I haven't the foggiest. Perhaps just being the daughter of a tradesman has kept her from making a decent match."

"I'm not terribly interested in why Miss Eleanor Piper has not been brought to the vicar." Tristan shifted his weight, and then straightened as he saw Mr. and Mrs. Piper appear on the threshold. Miss Eleanor stood right behind them. He couldn't hear the announcement of their names from across the ballroom, it was far too crowded, but at last.

She wore a dark wine-colored dress, her dark brown hair shining and lustrous in the light. Before he even could check his own behavior, he was cutting across the ballroom, barely able to give his excuses as he worked his way to Miss Eleanor.

Fortunately, he came to his senses before he reached them. What on earth was he doing? He'd been obvious that he wouldn't be dancing the first set. He'd been clear he would not be courting anyone, let alone a friend of Ophelia's. Had he lost all of his faculties?

"You look lost."

Tristan whirled as a woman's gloved hand snaked onto his forearm. But it was only his sister—the other one, the married one, the only reasonable Bridewell among them—Portia Preston, neé Bridewell.

"My goodness. What has you at a hair-trigger?" she asked. Her husband, Garrett, a barrister and a fellow second son of the nobility, stood by.

With a quick glance at Eleanor, Tristan turned back to Mr. and Mrs. Preston. "Nothing, I'm quite well."

Garrett's dark eyebrows raised in skepticism. "You looked like a tomcat on the hunt."

Damn the man's perceptiveness. Tristan made a strange sound, one he'd never made in his life. "Not at all. I was only . . ." he trailed off, not able to even come up with an excuse.

Portia didn't look impressed. In fact, she looked rather like their mother at the moment, her forehead wrinkled and lips twisted. Tristan felt like he'd been caught lying about having worms in his pockets. Again.

"Anyway, you're here now. And that is lovely. I wasn't sure you'd be attending." Tristan gave them both a brilliant smile. Which didn't work in the least.

Portia flipped her fan out with a harsh thwack and cooled herself furiously. "I sent a note to the house yesterday reminding everyone of our attendance."

"Yes, well." Tristan dared a glance over at Eleanor. Brian Fulk, that nitwit, was bothering her. Perhaps he should rescue her. Brian had been at school with him and had the absolute worst halitosis. The man's breath was notorious; all through school, it smelled as if something had crawled into his mouth and died. Tristan shrugged. "Correspondence."

"I beg your pardon?" Portia fanned even faster.

"I don't believe he's paying attention to anything you say, darling." Garrett moved and stood in front of Tristan's gaze, blocking his view of Miss Eleanor Piper.

"I am paying attention," Tristan insisted. "But that's ol' Fulker, over there."

"Who?" Portia asked, standing on tiptoes. She was the only one who hadn't inherited the Bridewell height, and was indeed the shortest of them all.

"Where?" Garrett asked.

"Bothering the Pipers. Portia, he has the worst halitosis of anyone you've ever met. If we want Mr. Piper's sponsorship, we must save them."

"I daresay," Garrett observed with a faint grimace. Garrett was a few years older than Tristan and Francis and ol' Fulker, but the reputation was widespread.

"Is it really that bad?" Portia asked.

"Worse," Garrett said. "By all means, off with you."

Tristan grinned and cantered over to the Pipers and ol' Fulker, who was now joined by Jacobs, the swine. He did another survey of the ballroom as he advanced, clocking Ophelia and Bad News in one corner with his mother and Blakely, the poor idiot.

"Ah, Mr. Bridewell," Mr. Piper said, stepping infinitesimally across their circle to welcome him in. "Good to see you here."

Tristan performed a formal bow, one that he knew was appreciated. "Mr. Piper, good of you to grace us with your presence, along with your lovely wife and daughter. Mrs. Piper, Miss Eleanor." He moved to join their group and acknowledged ol' Fulker with a nod. It wasn't just the halitosis, or the unfortunate name. It was that even at the age of ten, the boy looked and acted fifty. He was roughly thirty now, which meant he would act the age of what, seventy, eighty?

"Bridewell," he said.

"Fulk," Tristan said in return, catching himself before uttering the man's nickname. "Jacobs."

Jacobs performed a brief head nod in lieu of speaking, eyeing Fulk harshly.

"I trust you're doing well." Fulk always did have fine manners; he'd give him that.

"Yes," Tristan took a big breath of air. "Picture of health."

"Always were, always were. Gallivanting up some mountain, I hear? I'm surprised to even find you in London."

Tristan resisted the urge to narrow his eyes. Fulk had never been friendly with him, and this felt very much like a trap. What was the trap? Damn and hellfire, he'd never been good at figuring out these sorts of interpersonal manipulations. "We are preparing for an early autumn ascent of Ben Nevis as a preparatory excursion to a larger expedition."

Fulk chuckled and shook his head as if he were a child. It rankled him. Fulk gripped him on the shoulder, as if it were a friendly gesture, but it wasn't at all. "Some men are all adventure. And that's wonderful! The world needs men like you, Bridewell. But me? I've spent my career carving out a position at Drummonds. It's an excellent institution, and we do well. I'm the youngest vice president in its history, you know."

Oh. Tristan looked at Miss Eleanor, who was theoretically the intended recipient of all the bragging. Yet, it was Mr. Piper who would be the most impressed, if Tristan had any judge of the family. But Miss Eleanor looked mildly pleased by ol' Fulker, and that further irritated him.

"Miss Piper, would you be so good as to honor me with the first available dance on your card?"

Well, if that didn't take the cake. Tristan controlled himself, willing himself to not ball his fists. 'Ol Fulker was earning his nickname right along. He'd been a snitch that time with the toads, and now he was worse.

"Me as well," Jacobs said, speaking finally. As if he couldn't have defended Tristan earlier.

"If you'll excuse me," Tristan said, doing his best to not grit his teeth. "I need to speak with a friend, but before I go, Miss Eleanor, please find a place on your dance card for me as well." Tristan gave a perfectly placid smile to everyone, but he could see 'ol Fulker sulking.

ELEANOR WAS NOT stupid. The two men clearly had an old rivalry, and Mr. Jacobs was there to show obeisance to her father. Manners bid her to accept a dance with Mr. Fulk, who seemed perfectly polite, but could wilt a bouquet of flowers at twelve paces. She knew she was blinking rapidly in the onslaught of aroma, and she hoped it was not being interpreted as coquettish flirting. In fact, her eyes might begin watering at any moment.

She allowed her dance card to be filled by Mr. Fulk, Mr. Jacobs, and Tristan respectively. No, she really must address him as Mr. Bridewell even in her mind. Oh, but he was so handsome tonight. His formal dress was almost identical to that of every man there, but he sported a blue lapel pin that was a perfect match to his sparkling eyes, and it was most fetching.

Not that she enjoyed looking at his lapel, as it accented his broad shoulders, his coat stretching to accommodate them. Or how his flaxen hair caught the gas lamp flame in such a way that it seemed like liquid gold. He gave another exquisite bow and left their company, followed by a bow from Mr. Jacobs, and left only themselves and Mr. Fulk.

Mr. Fulk, stout in his brocade waistcoat and formal black evening kit, suddenly seemed put out that he had no one to mock in conversation. "Er . . ."

"Thank you, Mr. Fulk, for your attentiveness. Eleanor will be at the ready for you when the next set begins." Mrs. Piper, accustomed to an entire life before Eleanor had been born, one that Eleanor was not privy to, shooed the gentleman away. Mr. Fulk slunk off, but as he did so, Ophelia and Justine were making their way through the crowd towards her. "Not too long with those girls. But they are quite a breath of fresh after that gentleman."

Eleanor smiled at her mother. Having a strong sense of smell was not an asset at the docks, and apparently, it wasn't in a ballroom either. She smoothed her skirts once again, her hands raw inside her gloves from tying new knots in preparation for the next salon. She'd practiced late into the night, not needing nor wanting illumination. She wanted to be able to tie the knots in the dark, and behind her back. She'd even lain upside down, hanging off her bed, tying them. She had to be the expert, and she wouldn't let the Ladies' Alpine Society down.

"There you are," Ophelia said. She should have been breathless, any other corseted girl would be after that march through such a throng. But then, Ophelia seemed to be made of sterner stuff than anyone Eleanor had ever known. Maybe even Captain Smythe.

"We arrived not long ago," Eleanor said.

Ophelia nodded tersely, as if she were a military commander and this was a battlefield.

"Mr. Piper, Mrs. Piper." Justine curtsied and smiled. She elbowed Ophelia.

"Miss Bridewell, Miss Brewer," her father said.

Apparently Ophelia was not keen on observing social niceties? Or couldn't be bothered with them at the moment, at any rate. Ophelia performed an obligatory nod to them and turned back to Eleanor.

"I hadn't believed it, but I think we have a fourth member of the Ladies' Alpine Society." Ophelia looked as if she might hyperventilate.

"I thought your brothers were also members?" Eleanor asked. "They were at the salon."

Ophelia gave a look that was not complimentary for either of them. "They aren't *ladies*. So they cannot be members of the *Ladies'* Alpine Society."

Eleanor looked to Justine, who lifted a pretty, bare shoulder as a shrug.

"Her name is Mrs. Cabot. She's an American." Ophelia twisted this way and that, trying to see through the crowd of people. "I think she's an excellent candidate."

"Why?" Eleanor couldn't help but ask, even though she had absolutely no right to do so. It wasn't her club, and she wouldn't be climbing any mountains. "Is it because she's an American?"

"Not just an American," Justine whispered. "She's from *Minnesota.*"

Eleanor shook her head. "I haven't the faintest clue where that is."

"Neither do I," Justine said.

"That's the point!" snapped Ophelia. "She's perfect. And look at her shoulders. That is a woman who has done some work!"

Eleanor frowned, scanning the crowd for someone who might look like she was from Minnesota. She still wasn't sure who they were speaking of.

Her mother leaned over. "Please do not make comments on the bodies of other women. It isn't seemly."

"Yes, Mama," Eleanor said, knowing she was right. It was a sore spot for her mother, she knew.

The set finished, and all three young ladies looked up. There was the shuffle of people and instruments in the suddenly music-less hall.

"I shall have to find Blakely," Justine said, her mouth finishing into a pursed moue that would have seemed an unbecoming pout on any other person, but on her looked adorable enough to cuddle.

"Oh dear," Eleanor said, looking down after seeing Mr. Fulk clearing a path back to her.

"Ugh," Ophelia said, noticing Mr. Fulk. "He's such a braggart."

"I thought you might have noticed his halitosis," Eleanor said. "It was quite overpowering."

Ophelia waved her hand. "I've partially lost my sense of smell. Frostbite! The wonders of an adventuring life."

"Maybe you ought to dance with him, then," Eleanor said.

Ophelia shook her head. "Mr. Fulk hates Tristan, and by extension, the rest of us. He blocked anyone at his bank from supporting our expedition as a result. It's been a bit of a trial." Ophelia's shoulders sank, but then she brightened. "But maybe you can convince him otherwise? Oh Eleanor, you're a genius! I'll slip off then."

"But—" Before Eleanor could protest that she had no intention of going on the expedition whatsoever, Ophelia threaded behind their group into the wallflowers and matrons, disappearing into the crowd.

"Well then, Miss Piper?" Mr. Fulk said, offering his arm.

Eleanor glanced at her mother, who gave her a polite smile. "Thank you, Mr. Fulk."

Meanwhile, Justine was whirled away by a dashing young man. Her light-hearted laugh rang out, her mouth open, and carefree. Oh, to be as unencumbered as Justine was. Justine didn't participate in Ophelia's plotting, she didn't fuss about being a scandal, she merely existed the way she liked. If only that were available to someone like Eleanor. She glanced back at her parents, older than most of the other chaperones. They were staid and staunch, unflagging and thoroughly gray in their quiet love of her. She knew that. It was security and expectation, all rolled into one.

Mr. Fulk placed them in relation to the other dancers, and they stood quietly waiting for the music to begin. Eleanor hadn't the experience in dancing with actual men to know the best way to converse, so she waited, hoping he might fill in the gaps.

But he didn't. He looked over her head, also waiting. Finally the music began, and they swayed to the rhythm. Eleanor had dance instruction, but Mrs. Bernard had always been her partner. While Mr. Fulk acquitted himself well, Eleanor hoped she did likewise. But he didn't speak. So neither did she.

As the long minutes ticked by, Eleanor let her mind drift. She caught sight of Tristan watching her from the sidelines, an amused smirk on his face, she determined she would speak to Mr. Fulk. Tristan was not the entirety of her suitors. Best to make a go of it.

"Are you having a pleasant evening?" Eleanor asked, wincing as it came out. How very unoriginal.

"Thus far." Mr. Fulk glanced down at her with a tight smile. "And you?"

"Thus far," she echoed. Well, that was stunning. Both her ingenious conversation and his breath.

After some minutes, Mr. Fulk cleared his throat. "The Bridewells, are you well acquainted with them?"

Eleanor considered how to answer it, but not knowing any of the politics, went with the truth. "I've known them scarcely a week. I like Miss Ophelia Bridewell very much. She's so . . ."

Mr. Fulk gave a snort that couldn't be construed as anything but dismissive. "Don't be taken in by her sort, Miss Piper. They may have a title, but they aren't Quality."

"Oh." Eleanor caught sight of Tristan once again. Was he not Quality? By many people's standards, she herself wasn't Quality. They had no title, no illustrious lineage. Her father was a ship's captain who happened to be an excellent businessman with a head for political winds.

"Perhaps Miss Bridewell could be, if she were given a firm, guiding hand," Mr. Fulk continued, as if he were considering buying her like one might buy a racehorse.

"I beg your pardon?" Eleanor couldn't believe what she was hearing, or perhaps it was the tone in which he said it.

"A firm, guiding hand," Mr. Fulk repeated. "By a husband, since her father nor her brother seem to be reining her in. Traipsing off to climb mountains indeed! A waste of time, and a waste of her health, when she ought to be settling down, raising a family."

"What is wrong with climbing mountains?" Eleanor asked.

He swung her around, her wine-red skirts billowing.

"If men kill themselves doing it, then certainly a woman would topple in the face of it. Men are inherently heartier than women. That's just a fact."

"Have you heard about childbirth, Mr. Fulk?" Eleanor asked pleasantly. "They say it's quite painful. Given how many women die from it, one does think women have quite a solid constitution."

"See? That's my point exactly. Women are made to have children; therefore, it shouldn't be difficult in the least. But so many women die from it, which only shows how weak they truly are." Mr. Fulk gripped her closer, as if this entire conversation was building his passion. "You confuse facts with biology. Women are meant to breed. And like a prize mare, a man must be there to guide the process, making sure every line is its strongest."

Eleanor didn't know if she should step on his foot or slap his face. "I'm surprised you are willing to say such things with a woman on the throne."

"Ah! Another great fallacy of our time! Queen Victoria is ordained by God himself. She isn't merely a woman, though she is doing a fine job of keeping up with her lineage, as required by her biology, but able to govern, as appointed by God."

They passed several moments in silence, spinning and swaying, and Eleanor could not wait to be free of him. "Would you have spoken to me at all during this dance if I had not spoken first?"

"No," Mr. Fulk admitted. "For what is the point? I intend to court you, pay suit, woo you as it were, but the conversations must be held with your father, not you. Conversing with you is . . ."

Eleanor's eyebrows were so high up her forehead, it felt like they might lift off like birds. She could not believe the gall of this man.

". . . extraneous, at best. But like petting a dog, or brushing down a horse after a long canter—"

Eleanor could take it no longer. The dance was still going, the music still playing, but she thrust herself away from him, shaking loose from his hands. "I am no dog, sir. Good evening." She spun on her heel and marched over to where Ophelia was standing with Justine and the woman who must be the American Mrs. Cabot.

"I'll climb your bloody mountain if I die doing it." Eleanor stomped off to get some air.

~◆~

Chapter Four

"**T**HANK YOU ALL for coming," Ophelia announced, looking around at their small assembly. His sister looked through him, as if he were any other member of the team. He stifled a smile, in case she thought it was to mock her, when he was just so proud of his baby sister. She was doing it. She was leading her people.

It was the first real expedition meeting they'd held. This wasn't a salon, nor was it a tea. This was for budgeting, scheduling, working out the nuts and bolts of their plan. The Ladies' Alpine Society was assembled, Ophelia, Bad News, Miss Piper and the new one, Mrs. Cabot. But there was more to the team than just the lady mountaineers: there was his father, Tristan himself, and the expedition financier, Mr. Leopold Moon. He handled the books for all aspects of the expedition, and there wasn't a single shoelace he hadn't accounted for. Tristan had suggested he come, not trusting they would remember every detail of what would be required of them, even for their trial climb of Ben Nevis.

He hadn't been properly introduced to the new woman in the crowd, but Tristan had a hard time thinking of manners when he was doing his best to stay on the opposite side of the room as Eleanor Piper. All the ladies were dressed in their most serviceable gowns, hair tied back in severe chignons, and he did not know why, because it made no sense, but it made Eleanor Piper look even more regal.

They sat in the Rascomb drawing room. But this time, they were all business. Spring was nearly over, and that meant they needed to train if they would be climbing Ben Nevis in May.

Even with this temporal urgency, he could not stop thinking of Eleanor. His forearms prickled with awareness. He'd held her in his arms while they danced last night, his gloved hand resting on her small, pinched waist. The only thing she spoke of was Ol' Fulker, and she was spitting mad. It was glorious. Her anger had her heaving, and he almost tripped over his own feet not looking at how her chest moved in response. That lovely expanse of skin was tantalizing. Smooth as cream, and he wanted to be the cat to lick up cream such as this. A rough tongue that would make her eyes widen in pleasure and—he cleared his throat, flexing his thighs to clear the blood that was beginning to build in his trousers. Enough. Time to pay attention.

"This, if you have not yet been introduced, is Mrs. Cabot. She is from Minnesota, and she is a widow, and she is joining our expedition."

"That's one more mouth to feed," murmured Mr. Moon to himself, flipping open his ledger and notating it. Ophelia shot him a quelling look that he did not notice.

"Tristan, would you like to come up and tell everyone about what to expect on Ben Nevis?" Ophelia prompted him.

Tristan took his weight from the curve of the pianoforte and sauntered to the front of the small assembly. "Greetings to you all, thank you for being here. Our goal is to climb the Matterhorn, and make my sister Ophelia the first woman to summit the mountain. I would be happy to add your names to the list of ladies to summit its height as well. As you may know, Mr. Edward Whymper was the first to do so last year. However, you may also know that this is a treacherous, difficult climb, both up and down, and it killed four of his expedition, including Lord Francis Douglas, Mr. Charles Hudson, Mr. Douglas Hadow, and Michel Croz."

Tristan surveyed the ladies to see if any of them blanched at such a prospect, but they all remained stoic. They must know of the danger in this attempt.

"Some believe," Tristan continued, doing his best to not look at Eleanor, "that Mr. Hadow was at fault for being inexperienced. I knew Hadow from finding him in those places of mountaineering, and indeed, from his spectacularly swift climb of Mont Blanc. He was young, and in excellent shape. But I believe he did not understand snow, and that, my friends, is what we are going to prevent in our excursion."

Eleanor lips pushed off to the side in an off-center purse, as if she were chewing the inside of her cheek. Her lips were a distraction. He had to stay focused! He was the safety expert, after all.

"This summer, we will be climbing Ben Nevis in Scotland as a practice expedition. Before then, we will be training with ropes, terrain, and yes, even vocabulary. Hearing each other on a mountain can be very challenging, especially if we hit bad weather, so we will be going over the words we use to describe specific emergencies."

Bad News seemed to actually pay attention, which was shocking in and of itself. This was the first time their proposed expedition felt real. They might actually go to Switzerland. This could be an actual ascent. He was happy to share the accomplishment with his sister, and did not care a whit if she gained notoriety for it. This was the challenge of a lifetime.

"We will be hearing from Mr. Moon regarding our expenses, and then, as no doubt you all saw from the rigging on the staircase, we will be practicing a climb."

"A climb from the entryway to the drawing room?" Bad News asked.

He hadn't heard any of her usual disdain dripping from her words, which was a welcome change. "Yes. We are going to practice tying into a rope, set the order of our climb, and get familiar with our equipment. Any questions?"

Eleanor continued to chew on her cheek, but raised a finger.

Tristan nodded at her, because he couldn't chance saying her name aloud. He wasn't sure he could address her formally as was her due and the correct thing. He'd been thinking of her first name because it was so soft and musical. And then it became habit, and now he had to concentrate to address her properly.

"I was under the impression that in the case of the Matterhorn expedition the rope snapped, and that was the cause of the fall?" Eleanor said the statement as a question.

"The rope did indeed snap, yes," Tristan affirmed. "However, it was likely secondary to the fall. If you've spent time in the mountains, you'll realize that the give-and-take of the rope between climbers does not often grow taut. So if it snapped, perhaps because of an inherent weakness, or a sharp rock, it was because there was some undue strain, like a fall."

Eleanor nodded. "What kind of rope was used?"

Tristan grimaced. "That news has not yet been provided."

"So we'll need something that is both flexible and strong. That will not rot or degrade in wet conditions, is that correct?"

"Yes, though we do have some ropes already—"

"Equipment discussions can happen at a later time between you and Miss Piper, son." Rascomb stood as he said it, perhaps not only to forcibly take control of the conversation, but also to remind everyone that it was at his grace that everyone was going. Despite giving Ophelia the lead, he was *allowing* his daughter to go, he was funding the bulk of the mission, and it was his time they were wasting. "Let's get to the finances, so that we can get to the training."

"Of course. Mr. Moon?" Tristan gestured to the tall man as he unfolded himself from his chair. "The floor is yours."

ELEANOR LOOKED UP to the fourth step of the Rascombs' front staircase where Tristan stood with his father. They were demonstrating how to tie into a rope, using the figure eight noose Eleanor had taught them, and it was very hard to pay attention as Tristan stood in only his shirtsleeves, so that the view of his waist wouldn't be obscured. Her cheeks colored, and she looked down.

This was why women didn't climb. Who would allow their daughters to gaze so unashamedly on the male form? Eleanor tried to think of Tristan as a classical statue instead. Many of those stood around London and in museums. If she was allowed to appreciate that beauty, then learning about the safety provisions that might prevent her death was entirely appropriate..

"As you walk up the mountain, you will have your hands free to use your walking poles, or what have you. And on descent, you will be able to use your hands to steady yourself. Please try to stay upright at all times. The lives of your fellow mountaineers depend on you." Ophelia stood on the bottom step of the staircase, addressing them all. Her brother and father descended and moved to their places in the order of climbing.

Oh, she liked that, being called a *mountaineer*. She could just picture Mr. Fulk sneering the word at her. The mountaineers stood in a line, spaced out by a few feet, wrapping through the black-and-white checked foyer with the heavy hemp rope snaking alongside them. Ophelia was first, naturally, and behind her was Justine. Tristan tied into the rope as the third member of the team, then Eleanor fourth, Mrs. Cabot came fifth, and Lord Rascomb was sixth. Two men, four women. Mr. Moon was up in the drawing room, likely enjoying tea and cakes and thinking about how absolutely mad they all were.

She watched as one by one, the party tied into the solid hemp rope with the figure eight noose she'd taught them. Then it was her turn, noting to speak to Tristan about changing out the hemp rope for a sturdy manila rope. Hemp was excellent for many things, but it had a tendency to rot in wet conditions. While it was commonly used aboard ships, it was also regularly painted with tar to protect it from the saltwater spray.

Their first goal was an ascent of the volcano Ben Nevis, in

Scotland. She'd never been there, and certainly not to Switzerland, but she doubted either place would be exceptionally dry. She wouldn't want to risk rope rot, not when she knew better. And it turned out, Tristan was the one to speak to about equipment. So she must speak to him. For purely safety reasons.

"We are going to practice going up as a team first, then we will get into harsher scenarios. Everyone ready?" Lord Rascomb boomed.

Ophelia's face was shining with anticipation. Clearly this was her passion, her one true love. Eleanor envied that certainty. Ophelia knew that there was no other place she'd rather be. But Eleanor? What did she want? A tepid marriage? The agony of childbirth? But why would she think it was so awful, when the rest of the world seemed to celebrate those very things? Because it didn't seem like enough to her. But what enough meant, she had no clue.

"Am I to just go?" Ophelia turned and asked her father.

"Is that a bit of vocabulary we should discuss?" Justine asked, turning as well.

There was enough slack in the rope that their movements didn't impact her or Tristan. Still, Eleanor felt the itch to move. She closed her eyes and whispered, "Just go, for heaven's sake."

Tristan snorted and glanced back at her.

Oh. She hadn't said that as quietly as she thought she had.

"What about a one-word description of what you are about to attempt?" Rascomb suggested gently.

Ophelia thought for a moment, turned back around and announced, "Climbing!" And began a slow ascent of the staircase.

It was a bit silly, to stand in a fine entryway in Belgravia Square with marble accents, roped up as if they were defying God's wrath, but if such rehearsal would help them in the end, Eleanor would do it.

They practiced ascents and descents, falls and group rescues. All seemed so theatrical, not at all what such peril would be like in the real world. But then, not a bit of it felt real. And that seemed ominous to her. The danger proposed was quite true. So why did it feel like a game?

"Refreshments will be served in the drawing room," Ophelia said, unknotting herself from the heavy rope, once Lord Rascomb pronounced them finished for the afternoon. "Tristan, Eleanor, perhaps this is a good time to discuss whatever concern you had regarding our equipage?"

Eleanor nodded, picking at the knot around her waist, fumbling with the heavy fibers. Ahead, Justine huffed and puffed, unable to undo her figure eight. Frustrated, she sucked in her gut and slid the rope down her body, wriggling free of it as if it were a petticoat. Eleanor was shocked on a number of levels—what did Justine think she was doing leaving a rope knotted like this? And why did the rope not cinch as it was supposed to? Tristan eyed the knotted rope lying on the stairway, shaking his head at Justine as she abandoned her place and went to the drawing room.

Mrs. Cabot moved silently behind Eleanor, giving her an encouraging smile as she ascended the staircase. Eleanor pondered her as she went. She seemed of the same age as Eleanor, even if she were already a widow. But at her stagnant age of twenty-five, it was not all that surprising. She'd heard shocking tales of the American frontier. And unlike the Americans gossiped about in Society, Mrs. Cabot had not spoken to Eleanor other than to say, "How do you do."

Her beautiful honey-blonde hair, darker and redder than the flaxen Bridewell trait, was something that Eleanor would have given her dowry for. She watched Tristan's gaze as Mrs. Cabot passed him, wondering if he would notice her.

A silly part of Eleanor was relieved when Tristan didn't bother to look up at the trim figure of the newcomer. Given that Ophelia and Justine were bosom friends, it made sense that she and Mrs. Cabot would pair off as well. But what did she have in common with an American widow? But then, they hadn't had time to have a proper chat. Perhaps in the months to come.

Tristan wasn't yet untied, but he went over to Justine's mess and began the task of unpicking the knot. "Your concerns, Miss Piper?"

Eleanor's eyes snapped to his form. Yes, she had concerns. Standing next to him for seven hours as they ascended a mountain might be one of them. No, no it would not, because he was unattainable—any man who looked like that would be. "Ropes."

He looked up at her, snaring her with his cornflower blue eyes. "Ropes? Yes. We have many." Once he looked back down at the knot, she could think once again.

The heavy rope around her waist helped ground her, and now that she had slack from behind, she was able to work on untying herself as well.

"I mean that the hemp rope as the actual climbing rope is a poor choice."

Tristan picked at the knot, until he snatched away his finger. "Bloody hell!"

"Did you bend back your fingernail?" Eleanor asked, stepping closer.

Tristan popped the offended digit in his mouth, biting down on his nail. "Felt like the whole bloody thing would pop off."

Eleanor clucked in sympathy, ignoring his curses. Nothing she hadn't heard from Mr. Smythe or her father. She knew the feeling. "May I? I have a pricker."

His eyes looked like they might pop out of his head. "A what?"

Eleanor tried not to blush as she produced the small metal spike with a beautiful wooden handle. "It's a sailor's tool to help untie difficult knots."

Tristan handed over the rope, the size of a crabapple. Because the heavy rope stretched end to end on the staircase, she couldn't move far from where he stood. Besides, he was still tied in, and she worked the knot in the rope in the place in front of him. He loomed over her as she picked at Justine's sloppy, mess of a figure eight. She worked gently, giving slack at one end.

"You have a great deal to teach us, don't you?" He seated himself on the step, so that their heads were almost at a level, as she stood on the step below.

She shrugged. "Only what is useful. And I'm still learning what that is in these situations." Glancing up from the knot, she realized she had licked her lips. She hadn't meant to; it just happened. He seemed to be looking right at them. "This doesn't feel real."

His eyes seemed transfixed. "No," he said softly.

She swallowed and went back to the knot. "I know knots that are strong, knots that are flexible, knots that can haul a great deal of weight—oh!" Suddenly the knot popped free. She slid the rope out of its hold and pocketed her pricker. "There it is."

He stood quickly, the rope slithering down the polished wood stair with a distinctive hiss. "Watch out," he warned, grabbing at the top end.

The movement sent her backwards, off-balance. Instinctively, she pulled at the rope in her hand, which was still wrapped around Tristan.

Afraid she would tumble backwards and hit her head, she pitched forwards, falling onto him, as the rope cinched behind his ankles. With a shout, he fell on his bottom, pulling her down with him.

They slid down the stairs, Eleanor scrambled for purchase, but couldn't stop the fall. They landed on the floor with a thud.

"Oof." Tristan moaned.

Eleanor blinked, trying to get her bearings. Her ankles were tangled in rope. She was gripping the deep V of Tristan's waistcoat. Her teeth felt like they might rattle out of her head. Wincing, she lifted her head to look at Tristan. He was so very close to her. His chest was very firm under her, and she realized his arm now snaked around her waist, his hand resting on her hip.

"How are you faring?" Tristan asked, letting his head rest on the stair behind him.

"I—" How was she supposed to speak when she could smell

him? A tinge of horse, a bit of pine, definitely the earthy hemp—

"That good, eh?"

She ran her tongue over her teeth to make sure they were all still firmly in her mouth. The action drew his attention, and she felt a new heaviness. She did not want to stand. "You're quite the ride."

Tristan's mouth opened and closed.

Then she realized what she'd said, and blushed furiously. "I mean because of how that happened, and the falling, and . . ." His hand bunched the skirt fabric at her hip, catching some of her skin. It was so absurd. All of this was absurd. She burst out laughing. She covered her mouth, leaning more of her weight on him.

A moment later he joined her. He moved his hand off her hip, which left that area feeling surprisingly cold. "I'm so glad you are on my safety team," he said between chuckles.

"We are the experts," she said, her smile so wide it hurt her cheeks.

If she hadn't been half in love with him before, how was she supposed to not be now?

"What is taking so long?" called Ophelia from the drawing room. She let out a frustrated huff. "Get in here, Tristan! Stop flirting with Eleanor. We have plans to make!"

THE DAYS SPED by in a flurry of mundane activities. Or at least, it seemed that way to Tristan. Ophelia bemoaned the slowness of the days until they reached Berringbone Hold, their family's ancestral seat, which was nothing more elaborate than a pile of stones. It was once the site of a town and a Roman fortress that became a Norman fortress, but ever since that fateful plague centuries ago, no one had bothered to return to it. Not even an abbey or a hut had graced Berringbone Hold in the intervening centuries. But it belonged to the family, and more importantly, to Herringbone's honorary title, and it was an ideal place for the Ladies' Alpine Society and friends to hone their outdoor skills even further.

Tristan was in a daze, and he knew it, as his sloppy grin had been ridiculed at the card tables around town. Blakely had openly mocked him, but he didn't care. He was going to climb a mountain! They would change the face of climbing! And all with Miss Eleanor Piper gazing up at him with those liquid brown eyes that made him go soft in the head and hard everywhere else.

He enjoyed this feeling of infatuation, because he knew that was all it was. She was a friend of his sister's, and she was a member of the expedition. Nothing *should* happen, so nothing *would* happen. It wasn't responsible, it wasn't safe, and it wasn't a good match anyhow. They'd never suit: him an outgoing son of a viscount, her a quiet, tame daughter of a merchant. He'd find a daughter of the nobility at some point, and their bloodlines would continue on as safety measures to their families.

Yet how was it that thinking of her made him feel both weak and invincible all at once? He didn't even care that Jacobs took all his money at the last game they'd held. He'd invited them all to the next salon, where Eleanor would teach them more knots. She'd said she had a better idea of what kinds were required, and that she would make sure they would be well prepared for any eventuality that involved rope.

Did his mind wander a bit at the idea of what situations could involve rope? Yes. Of course. However, he was a gentleman, and she was a lady, even if she wasn't born to it, and he did his best to not think of those images . . . until nightfall when he took himself in hand. At which point he was like a whiskerless boy, frigging himself mad at every opportunity. It was only so that he wouldn't have an unfortunate tent in his pants at the worst moment, or find himself saying inappropriate things to her if he happened to find her in his mother's drawing room with Ophelia and Justine. And that new woman. The American widow.

"Oi! Hullo! Tristan!" Blakely appeared, jumping up next to him on the street.

Tristan was heading home to attend another salon, yet another chance to see Miss Eleanor Piper. "What's all the ruckus for?" He twisted round but didn't see anything worth a hullaballoo.

"You, you daft fool! I've been calling after you for ages, and you've been ignoring me. Are you trying to snub me?"

Tristan was mortally offended. "I'd never snub you, chum."

"Of course you wouldn't," Blakely agreed. "Which is why I've been running after you like some kind of Bedlam escapee. Are you deaf, or are you merely lovestruck?"

Tristan gave a winning smile. "Can't be lovestruck, you know that. Far too practical of a bloke for that."

Blakely gave a disbelieving snort. "Right."

"Are you attending the salon? Is that what you are doing following me?" Tristan asked.

"Will Miss Brewer be there?" Blakely asked.

"You know she will." Bad News didn't miss a single mountain-related, climbing-related, alpine-related moment in London. Even when women weren't welcome, she attended anyway and challenged those old farts to throw her out. Typically, they didn't have the gumption to do so. Probably because she promised them a healthy sponsorship from her father if she was allowed to stay. Money did make the world go 'round, after all.

When they turned the corner and arrived at the Rascomb townhouse, there was a crowd outside. They were not entirely orderly either. "What the devil?" Tristan said.

"Ah, yes. Not only did a notice appear in the paper regarding the salon, a rather ambiguous headline was attached: 'Tie a Woman in Knots' was advertised, I believe."

Tristan's stomach plummeted. This was not the sort of advertisement they wanted. The Ladies' Alpine Society needed to be above reproach, scandal-free. How else could Ophelia achieve her dream and not be marked for life because of her ambition? As her older brother, he had a duty to keep her away from gossips and fortune hunters who would hobble her, which was difficult enough when she was bosom friends with Bad News.

He and Blakely pushed through the crowd. Ferris, the Rascomb's butler, stood at the steps, interrogating the guests one by one. "I say," Tristan began, but Ferris beat him to the outrage.

"I do not know how many people can be properly admitted to the drawing room, sir, but we are already quite full."

Tristan glanced at the crowd. "And the drawing room is already full?"

"Her ladyship and your sister are dealing with that crowd, which is hopefully more docile than this one."

While an entrepreneurial spirit was often lost on an aristocrat, Tristan suddenly felt it spark to life, in the style of Victor Frankenstein. "Give me one moment, Ferris. I shall return shortly with a solution."

Tristan sprinted through the doorway and up the stairs to the drawing room, Blakely on his heels, and shouting from the outside trailing after. Ferris had told the truth about the drawing room. It was already stifling and standing room only. Ophelia looked at wit's end, while their mother barely had room to move with her cane. He waved them over.

"This is insanity," he said, marveling.

"I put it in the papers," Ophelia said. "I didn't realize it would be such a draw."

"We're going to have to serve punch or lemonade. I'm afraid the heat will only worsen in here and someone will pass out." His mother gazed about the room, looking as perturbed as she ever looked. Which was to say, placid to anyone who did not know her.

"Fortunately for you both, I am brilliant, and I can solve this." Tristan was grinning, he knew that looked a fool, but he didn't care.

"Oh?" Ophelia said, folding her arms.

"We shall move this to the ballroom and charge a shilling

apiece for entry. That should thin some out."

Ophelia scoffed, "We'll be left with no one, then."

Tristan grinned. "You haven't seen the crowd outside hollering to be let in."

Blakely found his way to their huddle. "I say—"

Ophelia waved away his commentary. She turned to her brother. "You announce the price to this crowd and the ones downstairs. I'll organize the maids to open the ballroom and the footmen to carry chairs and stand guard for any house wanderings."

Their mother smiled broadly at their cooperation. "I shall go speak with Cook about refreshments for such a crowd."

It felt good for them to work in concert. This was how it was when they were on the mountains; why it fell apart in town, he didn't understand. But they were back to it. Tristan clapped his hands to get the attention of the crowd as his mother and sister slipped out of the room.

Not long afterwards, the ballroom was full of patrons, a soup bowl was full of shillings, and Miss Eleanor Piper stood in front of a crowd of strangers with surprising aplomb. The ballroom had gas lighting—an extravagance that their father insisted upon after he'd had the experience of gas lights in Parliament. Indeed, it was convenient this afternoon to turn keys on the gas-lit chandeliers as opposed to lighting hundreds of candles, which would be far more time consuming.

Tristan sat in the front row with the other members of the expedition, including his father. The second row sported Mr. and Mrs. Piper, Mr. and Mrs. Brewer, Francis, Blakley, Jacobs, and a few others. The clamoring strangers sat in the rows behind them.

Ophelia spoke to the crowd about the Ladies' Alpine Society, Ben Nevis, the Matterhorn, and the efforts they would go to in order to prepare for each project. Beside her stood Bad News, Eleanor, and Mrs. Cabot.

"Now for why you came this afternoon. Miss Eleanor Piper will instruct us all in the art of knot tying, and specifics to what an expedition team such as ours will require. Miss Piper." Ophelia ushered the other women to sit down in the front row, while Eleanor stepped forward.

She swallowed pointedly, but then collected herself. Unlike what most pictured when thinking of an adventurer, Eleanor looked sweet, almost delicate, with her hair piled on top of her head, dressed in a fashionable green and white day gown. She pulled her gloves off and laid them on a small table next to her. Lengths of various types of rope were carefully stretched out on the table as well. She cleared her throat, picking up one of the ropes. She talked of snowy conditions and dunked three of the lengths into different buckets of water, which a footman hauled away.

"One of the issues that came to mind after hearing details of Mr. Whymper's ascent of the Matterhorn was the idea of splices." Miss Eleanor Piper took two steps forward, taking two different lengths of rope from her display table. "A splice, as some of you may already know, is tying two lengths of rope together in a way that strengthens the line instead of weakening it. One might need to do this in the case of a break."

Murmurs went through the crowd, no doubt familiar with the tragedy of a broken rope that killed the four men. Like the rest of the exhibition, Tristan had his own selection of ropes so that he might rehearse along with her. He hadn't thought about a splice before, which was ridiculous. Nor had he believed that knotting two separate ropes together would ever equal or outweigh the strength of a single line.

"Not one in twenty sailors can do a decent splice," a man from the back protested.

"Everyone knows once a line is cut, it's done," yelled another man.

Tristan turned to look at a young man who had scoffed, but who now got to his feet several rows back. He was well dressed, but not someone Tristan knew. Either new to London, or a scion of the merchant class, straining to climb into the aristocracy. He had light brown hair worn in a sloppy longer style. Tristan disliked him immediately and immensely.

"I'm not sure how I can possibly prove it to you," Miss Piper said. "Unless you have a suggestion."

The young man glanced around as if garnering support. "Why should anyone take your word for this? How many alpine ascents have you made?"

Eleanor put the ropes down on her table and folded her hands together neatly. "None."

The young man scoffed, again looking 'round. "Then how would you know?"

"I've learned all of this at the hands of one of London's best captains. My knowledge is from the sea trade, not mountaineering."

"And you've been aboard ships, is that what we are to believe? You, miss, are a fraud!" He pointed his finger at her.

Tristan wanted to snap it off his hand. He moved to get to his feet, but a single look from Eleanor quelled him.

"Would you be a better tutor? If so, I invite you up to share your knowledge." Eleanor gestured to her demonstration table.

"I would. I, too, grew up with the shipping trade. And I'd wager I had far more training as the eldest son than you ever had." The man edged his way past the other seated guests, shuffling to the aisle.

"Your name, sir?" Eleanor still maintained a very calm, decorous manner.

Tristan had found, in his short life, that it was the inexperienced or incompetent who would screech and protest their proficiencies. The capable and qualified knew where their strengths lay and where they needed knowledge. Eleanor's calm seemed very much like those old men they'd met in mountain huts—ancient, quiet, shockingly strong, and reliably competent.

"I am John Martell," the young man said with a bearing that seemed to indicate all should know who he was.

Indeed, recognition flared in Eleanor's eyes, and a snort came from Mr. Piper behind him. Must be a rival of sorts.

"Ah yes, Mr. Martell. I'm sure you know exactly who I am, then." Eleanor gave him a very polite smile as she made way for him up front. The subtle bend in her tone seemed very much like she was laying a trap. "What sort of knot would you believe would work best for this expedition? Our very safety relies upon it."

"First of all, I would recommend cotton rope, as it is far more comfortable on the skin, and much lighter weight." He looked across the crowd with a smile, as if he were discussing how very silly Eleanor's suggestions had been.

Tristan found himself balling his hands into fists with such ferocity that his knuckles ached. That smug bastard. He had no idea. But Eleanor politely stood by as he spewed his idiocy.

"Of course, a simple square knot does the bulk of the work." He picked up one of Eleanor's ropes and tied a quick and clumsy square knot.

Even to Tristan's barely trained eye, it looked sloppy. Eleanor signaled a footman, whom she whispered to discreetly before sending him on his way.

"Any others?" Eleanor prompted this rude interloper.

Mr. Martell stared at the knot, thinking. "Perhaps a slip knot?"

Eleanor said nothing, but gestured for him to continue. Mr. Martell fumbled with the rope, the point of his tongue darting out to the side. Tristan was unimpressed.

The footman returned, hauling a bucket full of water. While Mr. Martell struggled, more footmen hauled in two more buckets, and then handed Eleanor a twig. She thanked them and turned her attention back to Mr. Martell who had finally executed a simple slip knot.

"Thank you, Mr. Martell. Very informative." Eleanor gave him an encouraging smile, which seemed to confuse him. She should be red-faced and indignant in his estimation, no doubt.

"Of course, this is simple common sense. Any right-thinking person would know this. Frankly, it's clear that giving this kind of education to females only muddles their brains." The man didn't know how to exit the stage.

Eleanor didn't crack, even though Tristan heard Bad News shifting in her chair. Ophelia was pale with anger. Indeed, Tristan wouldn't mind taking this man to task for his arrogance.

"Indeed. Perhaps I can show you why I didn't consider your suggestions in the first place. Now, Mr. Martell, you were late to the demonstration, so you weren't here for the section where I dunked a length of hemp, manila, and cotton ropes into these buckets of water."

Martell shook his head, folding his arms. "And?"

"So, while cotton is a tempting option because of how much smoother it is on human skin, I'd like to demonstrate what happens to cotton fibers when they get wet. And, when climbing in snow, the rope will likely get wet." Eleanor used metal tongs and pulled the length of cotton out of the bucket. It dripped, but she took it in hand, putting the tongs down. She pulled it apart, and it stretched further and further. "Now, with the fibers stretched so thin, we can infer that the strength of these fibers has been compromised. As the son of a prominent shipping merchant, I'm surprised this was not one of the first lessons you were taught. Myself, I spent time down at my father's office and watched how impossibly heavy crates were taken off ships. These jobs were typically done with manila fiber ropes because they fare so much better in wet weather."

Martell had the sense to duck his head.

"Indeed, hemp, which is typically used on board ships, is very strong, however—" she pulled the hemp length from the bucket, "while it doesn't have the stretch the cotton fiber does, you'll see that it is very absorbent." She wrung out the rope, producing a stream of water so prodigious that the audience squirmed and chuckled at the prolonged cascade. "If you spent time aboard your father's ships, you would have seen them applying tar to the hemp ropes to prevent the rot that can occur in the saltwater. While we won't be in seawater, given the location of the

Matterhorn in landlocked Switzerland, rot could still occur should we be trapped on the mountain for any length of time, which would lead to breakage."

Martell huffed and reddened. Tristan smiled as Eleanor calmly picked him apart in front of the crowd.

"As for a square knot," Eleanor made an apologetic grimace to the audience, swiftly tying a knot and producing the twig the footman had given her. She shoved it right through the middle of it. "A knot that is so easily compromised isn't strong. It can collect debris, and is easily broken when pulled taut across boulders, as could have been the case in Mr. Whymper's expedition. Any sailor will tell you that a square knot is responsible for more deaths than any other knot." Eleanor smiled sweetly, as if she was thanking Martell for a dance. "So you see, Mr. Martell, anyone with the knowledge and experience with these materials understands that there is a deeper level of thought required when entering these life-or-death situations."

Ophelia applauded, as did Bad News. Tristan dropped the practice rope he'd been death-gripping to applaud as well. Soon the entire crowd did so, and Martell slunk out the door. Eleanor finally blushed, the color high on her cheeks in a way that charmed him even further. While Tristan wanted to protect her from a blow-hard idiot who hated women on principle, Eleanor proved she didn't need it. She was quite capable of holding her own against a man like that.

Ophelia urged Eleanor to curtsy, as if she were an actress on the stage. She did, humbly, and Tristan's heart surged. He got to his feet to control the crowd. It gave him the opportunity to whisper *excellent job* in her ear and touch her back to usher her to a seat.

He thanked Eleanor for her expertise and patience, made a plea for money, announced refreshments, and then dismissed the crowd.

Bad News was up like a shot, pulling Eleanor to her feet again. Tristan wanted to take her hands. He wanted to beam at her. But no, as a gentleman, he couldn't be seen engaging in that sort of behavior in public. But by God, that was impressive. The woman should run for Parliament, if they'd only have her.

Chapter Five

"THIS IS ABSURD!" her mother said, pushing the fish around in the sauce on her plate. "Whoever heard of anyone doing this?"

"Indeed, whoever heard of a woman climbing a mountain?" murmured Eleanor. She didn't like fish, and she didn't like the sauce, but she didn't want to offend Mrs. Branson, who had been their cook for as long as she could remember. Mrs. Branson, for a short time, watched after her on the days when her mother would take ill. Those days had been filled with baking, sneaking juice-soaked currants, and learning how to lay a precise fire.

Her father leaned back in his chair and slapped the side of his belly. "I'm all for it. You can find no better chaperone than Lady Rascomb."

"You're only saying that because Eleanor gave that Martell boy such a put-down at their salon." Eleanor's mama huffed and took a bite.

A footman stepped forward and cleared Papa's plate. Eleanor wished she could signal that she was done as well, but she'd wait until her mother had finished pushing things about.

Papa leaned forward. "I couldn't have engineered such a delight. Well done, Eleanor! Well done. I've been wanting to put those upstarts in their place ever since they jumped into bed with the American rebels. Fools! All that man's crowing for those years about his profits. Well now look at him, broke and near bankrupt for all his smug nonsense. Paying restitution for idiocy!"

Eleanor flushed with pride. Rarely had her father singled her out for praise, and it felt good to have his solid attention, rather than her mother's fluttering worry. Either way, it was nice to have both of them aware of her presence at the dinner table. They usually talked between themselves, not bothering to solicit or even allow her contribution to the conversation. Once, when she was much younger, her father had accidentally left her at the office after he'd gone home for the day. No one realized she was missing until well past the eleventh bell. Moments like that seemed to stick with her, despite the apologies and the blame that had circulated in the house for weeks on end. The blame was never addressed to Eleanor, nor was an apology. She was more like an expensive vase than a child to them, sometimes.

Her mother pushed the fish away as if it were the source of her frustration. "It was one thing when this, this, this training retreat as Miss Ophelia called it, was to be at their country home."

The footman stepped forward to clear her mama's plate, and Eleanor waved at him to take hers as well. "No one ever said that, Mama. You assumed that."

"Because it is only natural to assume that when someone invites you to the country it is to stay *inside* a house and not beside it!"

"But to be acclimated to such difficult physical work will require me to sleep outside, under the stars," Eleanor protested.

"We are not so beneath them that we must be kept outside like livestock!" Her mother sniffed, as if she were receiving a snub in public.

"We shall all be outside. If it is good enough for the viscountess, it is good enough for me." Eleanor tried to modulate her voice to sound respectful, but she wasn't sure if it had worked. Her mother had been saying the same thing for the past week, ever since she'd heard what would really be required of Eleanor. It wasn't like her mother would be going and sleeping in a blanket bag, either. She'd be snug and warm at home in her own feather bed.

Her father pointed at her and snapped his finger. "Exactly so. I've always said you had quite the head on your shoulders. Dear, if you want her to snag the heir, she has to prove she can fit into his family. What better way than let her tag along on this outing?"

Eleanor blinked. This was an adventure, not a marriage proposal. And Tristan wasn't even the heir.

"Haven't you been paying attention? The heir isn't on the trip! He stays home!"

The footman placed the pudding in front of Mama and backed away slowly.

"Eleanor, is that true?" Her father looked across the table at her, lines burrowing deep in his forehead.

"Yes. Lord Berringbone doesn't even attend the salons. He's busy with his own affairs."

"Then who is that chap with the shiny hair who moons after you?"

Eleanor blushed and looked at her hands. "I'm sure I don't know who you mean."

Papa scoffed. "Oh please, he mopes about like someone's taken away his puppy when you've turned your attention on another man—whether it is at a ball or at these salons. I know! I've watched him! He's Rascomb's son."

"The man you are referring to is Mr. Tristan Bridewell," Eleanor managed, still pleased and embarrassed all at once that Tristan might be paying extra attention to her.

"He's the second son," Mama explained, halfway through her pudding. "The spare."

Eleanor winced. She didn't know why, but she didn't like anyone calling Tristan the spare. He wasn't the spare to her. He was essential. And she knew that he was absolutely a necessary part of this expedition. Even if his knots were still too rushed and sloppy.

Papa grunted his thinking grunt. "A second son, eh? No title, but your children might be able to snag one, if you get enough of my money."

"What is so important about a title?" Eleanor asked, finally exasperated by her parents' machinations.

"It's automatic power. Respect. Authority." Her father stared her down, all humor drained from his face. "Those are things money cannot buy. No matter how hard I work, no matter how much we earn, the government can turn 'round and take it. Because we are no one. But to have a title! Then you are part of the land itself. You have become the conquerors, and all that is yours stays yours."

"Who would take things from you?" Eleanor cried, so frustrated. Why must her parents invent hardship?

"These are things you needn't worry about, girl," Mama soothed. But there was a glance between her parents that shared information that Eleanor wasn't privy to. "You shall go on this odd outing with our blessing."

TRISTAN HAD RIDDEN from the train station on his own horse. The idea of being stuck in a carriage with that number of skirts and petticoats for three hours was stifling. And sitting so near Eleanor yet having to share conversation with Bad News was too much for one man to bear. As it was, he'd sat in a different compartment with his father, leaving the ladies to chat amongst themselves, if they could, given the loud rattle of the train.

Part of the trade was that his horse was laden with a number of supplies, and a groom came along with him. They still had servants attending to them—but most of the servants would be staying at an inn at the nearest town and brought in by carriage every morning. While the company dealt with equipment and techniques and training, the servants would cook food, find water, and tidy the campsite.

Neither Ben Nevis nor the Matterhorn would require camping on the mountain itself. But they would need to have a camp set nearby. Ascension would require waking at likely three or four in the morning to assure they could be down again before nightfall. Therefore, they needn't practice upkeeping their own campsite.

Tristan got to the site of the ruins in the early afternoon, well before the carriage. It was a beautiful day, the air chilled, the nip of spring still biting, but with the promise of lovely days and sunshine to come. The rolling hills of the countryside were green, and the birds in the trees were active and loud, even in his presence. The sheep that sometimes grazed here were elsewhere at the moment, but they would surely appear at some point during their trip.

The ruins were unchanged. One full wall stood in half-repair, the wall opposite not as well-formed. The rooms where people had lived and eaten and danced were obvious from the large stone foundations. One arched doorway stood closest to the trees. Tristan's mother claimed it was once the gateway to the herb garden—the domain of the mistress of the house.

He loved the days and nights they'd spent here. When he was young, they would all come out, eat hamper picnic dinners and frolic in the trees and the stones. It was idyllic and wild, the fantasy of so many people, but for them, a reality. The only reason they had such freedom was his mother.

Lady Rascomb was a daughter of an eccentric earl who loved exploration, and it was that feeling of inherent freedom that attracted Tristan's father—at least, the way his father told the story. According to his mother, it was her ample dowry and her ample bosom that caught his eye. But she had been dragged along with her father to the ends of the earth, spending time aboard boats and skis, trekking in all climes. They'd lost her mother in childbirth, and the earl refused to part with her, regardless of her age or her gender.

Lady Rascomb was a unique spirit, and she seemed happy to

pass the torch on to her children. The avalanche a decade earlier had brought her outdoor life to a halt. Tristan still felt guilty for it. He'd wanted to stay longer on the mountain, push harder, explore more. While his father and siblings had gone down the mountain, his mother stayed up with him. Mont Blanc was impressive in its own right, but the French never wanted to climb it when snow was present. Which meant they only climbed it during a two-week window mid-summer. That wasn't convenient for the Rascomb schedule, and so they climbed earlier—in June. But it had gotten warmer earlier that year. And on the descent, his mother first down the mountain, Tristan trailing, he'd accidentally triggered an avalanche. One misstep, and the next thing he knew, his mother was swept away by a sheet of rotten snow.

He'd descended as fast as he could, scrambling and sliding, a frantic mess, pawing through the snow with wet gloves and frozen hands until he reached her. She was still breathing. Excavating her was agony. Fortunately, the avalanche had been loud enough that his father had sent the rest of them down, called for a stretcher, and headed back up. Between the two men, they got her out and carried her on their backs until they met the stretcher most of the way down the mountain.

Her leg was broken in a most obvious and horrific way. It was clear that despite the best efforts of a gentleman physician who happened to be staying at the same inn, she would never walk unassisted again.

It was deep guilt that Tristan carried with him—to be the person who took his mother's first love away from her. She would no longer watch a sunrise from a mountaintop. No longer could she see the world unfurl around her in every direction. The feeling of accomplishment that accompanied a summit. The sweat drying in the cold, unobstructed wind. It had been her girlhood, her connection to a doting father who had passed, a way she spent time with her husband and her family, and what did Tristan do? Snatched it out from under her with his carelessness.

Indeed, he was not so unaware of himself to not realize that he harbored some of the same fears about this expedition. That he'd have to be particularly vigilant to not damage the young ladies on this trip, either his sister or someone else.

He took in a deep breath and walked his horse over to a tree where he could have time to graze in the shade. Just as he'd done when he was a child, he climbed over the entryway stones and entered the fortress ruins. This place had once been a haven and a home. Moss covered some of the stones, others were covered in mud. It made him think of legacies, and how he was left out of his family's.

Primogeniture was a blasted rotten way to rule a country. Tristan folded his arms against a chill breeze. It deprived him, a second son, but it also deprived his sisters, Portia and Ophelia. Of the four of them, Portia was clearly the smartest. She had a better head for numbers than either Herringbone or himself. And as an adventurer? He loved it, but it wasn't as all-consuming as it was for Ophelia.

During the trip to Mont Blanc, as their mother recovered the following evening, Ophelia had told him in a fit of passion that she would happily die on a mountain rather than in a bed. There was nothing she wanted more in the world than to be at the top of these grand cathedrals of stone. It had discomfited him at the time. No one wanted to hear a young person speak of death, especially not after his harrowing venture on the mountain with his mother.

But Tristan knew she meant it. She wasn't the sort to die of old age. She'd rather fly into one of the Matterhorn's glacier fields like poor Lord Douglas. If she wasn't careful, she'd get her wish. All the more reason to emphasize safety and caution, since Ophelia didn't possess any. And who was Tristan? Not the heir, not the brains, not the adventurer . . . he was the other one. The boy with the charming smile. Fun to have a drink with. A good storyteller when enough port was available. Not particularly good at anything, nor particularly passionate.

He picked up a stone and threw it into the forest, over the arched doorway, startling his horse. In response, the beast eyed him, as if to scold him. What was he supposed to do with his life then? Support his family, yes, but what would he do? Help Herringbone with the estates? How? Get married and have babies? Who wanted a second son when estates were being parted out, no longer the generators of exorbitant wealth?

Picking up another stone, he looked at the horse, who stared him down with a steady glare. "Fine," he muttered, tossing it to the slick stone floor. He'd unpack and start setting up camp. The carriages would arrive in a few hours, and the ladies would like a place to have a decent cup of tea from the hamper after their journey.

GETTING TO KNOW Prudence Cabot was definitely the highlight of the carriage ride from the station to Berringbone Hold. The rail journey had been loud, mostly. Cold, as well. Eleanor had traveled via rail before, but it had been with her mother and attendants. They'd been well-stocked with hot water bottles, warmed bricks, and nibbles of scones and cakes to keep their stomachs settled amidst the jostling of the railcar. This journey had been much different. They were chaperoned by Lady Rascomb herself, while Tristan and Lord Rascomb went into a separate car.

The carriage ride, however, was cozy with the four young women together in one carriage and Lord and Lady Rascomb in another. Tristan, disappointingly, opted to ride his own horse, so there was no excuse to talk with him.

Yet Prudence Cabot was interesting. Eleanor had never spent so long talking with an American, and she found the flattened vowels and incessant smiling charming. They were all of an age,

Eleanor being the oldest by a few months. Prudence was next, then Justine and Ophelia were within weeks of each other. But it was odd to be the oldest and have the least amount of experience with the world.

It would be easy to feel shame about such an instance, whereas Prudence had not only been married, but widowed, and had the experience of running her husband's company. And now! She'd traveled across the Atlantic and was traipsing through foreign countries. The freedom seemed dizzying.

Yet Prudence was easy to be around—she exuded warmth without a need to impress. She was pretty in an unaffected way— no ringlets or braids decorated her coiffure, her gowns were simple, yet well tailored. She seemed to be exactly what she portrayed herself to be, which was refreshing. Her gray eyes were wide and watching, and she already had small lines around her mouth from smiling.

Eleanor found an urge to categorize Prudence. Was she descended from the English? Or perhaps the Scots? Even German could be found in her features. But she supposed that was part of the charm of the Americans. They escaped the categories.

"I'm not sure what to expect this week," Prudence said, voicing the fear Eleanor also had.

Justine and Ophelia looked at each other with delight sparking in their eyes. "No corsets."

Prudence seemed delighted, but it frankly frightened Eleanor. She *liked* her corset. It held her, kept her upright. She had come to depend on her corset like an invisible governess in the corner, whispering *stand up straight!*

"There must be more than that," Prudence said with yet another wide, disarming smile. Eleanor found herself smiling back. Oh, that habit would be difficult to break. By the time they finished this country excursion, Eleanor would be grinning at everyone like a deranged fiend.

"Oh, there will be," Ophelia assured her. "Papa has made a grueling schedule. As it needs to be, in order to get us all into shape."

Eleanor enjoyed watching Justine's very expressive face go from enjoyment to curiosity to disgust. "Grueling?" Justine asked.

Ophelia turned to face Justine, as they sat on the same side. "Utterly."

"I imagine it must be," Eleanor said. "It is, after all, the peak of human achievement."

Justine giggled. "Oh, did you not intend that pun? Peak?"

Eleanor did her best not to blush. The pun hadn't occurred to her, and Justine was so very quick.

"Eleanor is quite right," Prudence said, giving yet another smile. Really, did she never stop showing her teeth? "The Matterhorn has claimed the lives of many men. Let's be the group that proves the mountain only eats the males of our species."

"Hear, hear!" shouted Justine, making Eleanor wince. "Prudence, I knew I liked you."

It seemed strange to be on such intimate terms with these women so soon, but Ophelia had insisted they needed to be close in order to function as a team. So they dropped all courtesy and used first names to show familiarity. Eleanor hadn't minded, but it just felt odd. Like a new pair of leather shoes that needed to be stretched.

They arrived at the site of the ancestral hold. Prudence's gray eyes were wider than usual, taking in the land that had belonged to one family for centuries. Eleanor had heard Americans hadn't the concept of such a thing, or at least, the Americans born and raised far from New England. She'd been given to understand that the Native Americans didn't have as many permanent structures, preferring to roam about the land from season to season. Not terribly unlike British aristocrats, come to think of it. Eleanor began to suddenly wonder about Minnesota, Prudence's birthplace. How truly wild was it when a heap of English stones dotted with sheep droppings caused her awe?

The carriage door opened, and instead of descending, Lady Rascomb entered, squishing them very tightly. "Ladies," the viscountess announced. "Before you descend, I have a few things we must go over to appease my own mind."

Lady Rascomb surveyed them all with her crystal blue eyes—the same color as both Ophelia and Tristan's. "In order to succeed, we must maintain our decorum. We are in the wilds, yes. We are freer than when in London, yes. However, we still must behave within the bounds of humanity."

Eleanor wished she could glance around to see if the other girls understood what was being said, because Eleanor surely didn't.

"Begging your pardon, my lady, but you know I have not done anything to earn my reputation," Justine protested. It was the most polite sentence Eleanor had heard out of her mouth in three hours.

It also made Eleanor wonder why Justine was labelled Bad News if she hadn't done something to deserve it. She had the reputation of a wild girl, unpredictable and fun. The kind of girl a respectable man would never marry, and one the rake would entertain for perhaps a month.

"I know it isn't your fault, Justine. But I say this also to Mrs. Cabot and to Miss Piper. Forgive me, ladies, I know that it is uncouth to be so direct. But we cannot have any missteps."

"Perhaps this is one of those cultural barriers, Lady Rascomb," Prudence said, frown lines forming between her pretty brows. "But I'm not clear on what it is you are cautioning. As an American, I need more directness, not less."

"Of course, Mrs. Cabot. What I mean to say is, we must not fraternize with any men we meet. Not the porters, not the servants, not anyone. That is an easy warning here in the countryside, but it won't be that way in Scotland or in Switzerland. I know widows enjoy their freedoms, but you cannot engage in that sort of behavior around unmarried ladies like my daughter."

Prudence colored, and her mouth dropped open. "I would never—"

Lady Rascomb gave her a smooth look of appreciation. "I'm glad to hear it. Now. Let's descend and take off these blasted corsets."

Justine howled with laughter and the ladies climbed out of the carriage. Eleanor was last out, happy to sink into the corner and stave off her own embarrassment. The problem namely being that she *wanted* to fraternize with Tristan. Very much so. How was she to avoid him when he was literally tied to the rope eight feet in front of her?

Now that she left the carriage and could smell the sweetness of grass and fresh country air, she could see why Prudence was gaping. It was lovely, right out of a pastoral painting. The ruins were majestic in their own way, an arched doorway still hanging onto relevance, the rooms of the building outlined on the floor.

A thick copse of trees threatened to grow into the archway, creating shade and cool for the horses. They couldn't have asked for a better spring day. She got away from London often enough with her mother, yet never to a place like this. Their getaways were to seasides where her mother could take the waters. But this was proper inland English countryside. Off in the distant rolling hills she spied white dots. Sheep! Even with the appropriate livestock.

Curtains had been strung amongst the trees as the ladies' dressing area. It was secured by clothespins, so even the wind couldn't create a scandal.

"Here's a hint," Justine said, glancing sideways with a mischievous grin. "Take your stockings off and walk barefoot in the grass. It's the next best thing to Heaven."

Eleanor caught Prudence's expression of disbelief. "Have you . . . not done that before?"

Ophelia shrugged with a pert raise of a brow. But Eleanor shook her head. "Never. Where would I do such a thing?"

And honestly, where? London? They had gardens but not lawns. And they didn't own a country house because her father couldn't be persuaded to leave his business. Mother only went to the seaside, where grass was at a minimum.

"You must try it, Eleanor," Justine said.

Prudence nodded. "It is the most human thing one can do, I think. It's been far too long for me." The widow unbuttoned her traveling boots and shucked off her stockings, all while Eleanor stood gaping.

Laughing, Ophelia and Justine did the same.

"But—" Eleanor protested. Hadn't they just received a lecture on propriety from Lady Rascomb?

"We won't go near the men," Justine said with a wrinkle of her nose. "Who needs them, anyway?"

Eleanor unbuttoned her new traveling boots, the leather still stiff. The other women were all heading out the back of the curtained area, away from the ruins and the horses. "Oh, wait, please."

"Come on!" Ophelia laughed, gesturing broadly.

Eleanor shed her own stockings, as if she were a snake molting its skin, and skipped after them.

They emerged out of the copse of trees into a wide, sunny meadow. The grass was cold enough to feel wet, but the sun was warm on her hair and shoulders. Long strands of grass slid between her big toe and first toe, slipping almost as seamlessly as water. A breeze raced through, the grass whispering in response. It felt like magic. The four of them, standing in the sweet country air, as if they were collectively taking the hand of a loved one.

A great peace descended on Eleanor. Emotions that she'd never felt swept over her, confusing her, overwhelming her. The world was big and vast and she was so very small in comparison. And she loved it so much, and while she wasn't sure *where* she belonged exactly, she belonged somewhere. If she could take care of the world, the world would take care of her.

Her eyes welled with tears. Ophelia saw it and took her hand. "It happens that way the first time."

Eleanor sniffed. "What happens?"

"That feeling. The overwhelming love the first time you truly step into nature. Wait until you get on top of a mountain. You'll never want to stop climbing them."

Eleanor turned to Justine, attempting to wipe away her tears discreetly. "It happened to you too?"

Justine nodded. "Except I was a far bigger mess and not at all pretty about it."

Eleanor had a hard time believing that.

"I grew up in the farms and the lakes, so this isn't nature to me. This view still has too much of a human touch for me. But I am quite looking forward to losing my dignity once we crest our first mountain together." Prudence took Eleanor's other hand and squeezed.

The enormity of their endeavor hit Eleanor. "What we are doing is quite mad, isn't it?"

Justine laughed. "Extremely mad."

Eleanor felt the world tilt, and if it weren't for her bare feet touching the cool grass and damp earth, she would have fallen over, giving in to the dizziness. "Will we even be able to do such a thing as climb the Matterhorn?"

Ophelia's face settled, not as if she were angry to be questioned, but rather more determined. "The number one thing we need to succeed is the will to move forward. If we give up before we begin, then we haven't a chance."

"I'm not giving up," Justine said. "I'm going to the top of that mountain. And every single other one I can get myself to before someone convinces my parents I must have babies."

Prudence laughed.

"It isn't funny," Justine protested.

"Oh, it isn't funny in the least," Prudence agreed. "It's only—I came to London to take a lover. And instead I'm going to climb a mountain."

Eleanor couldn't help but gasp. "You *didn't*."

"I did," Prudence confirmed, her expression open and guileless. "I'm a widow at the age of twenty-five. My husband was old enough to be my grandfather. I wanted to see what it was like to have a young man adore me. That isn't wrong, is it?"

Eleanor looked to the other young women. Wasn't it wrong? She was beginning to wonder. Weren't they supposed to be scandalized by such talk?

Ophelia nodded just once at Prudence. "Seems very practical of you."

Prudence smiled, even though she clearly didn't need Ophelia's approval, nor Eleanor's for that matter. "Thank you."

"It's going to be an uncomfortable week, isn't it?" Eleanor asked, as it dawned upon her that walking up a mountain took a great deal of physical expertise.

Justine grinned. "You cannot begin to guess."

Chapter Six

T RISTAN LIKED RUNNING at sunrise. This early in the spring, he
still wore a woolen jumper, like a dock worker, as the frost
crunched beneath his feet. He loved the faint purpling of the sky
fading to whitish yellow, and then finally, the feeling of sun on his
limbs as he hit his stride.

His breath was steady and even, the rhythm of jogging well-
known to him and comfortable. But the wheezing behind him did
not sound easy. Glancing over his shoulder, he slowed his pace
and trotted backwards, staying on the balls of his feet as he
surveyed the motley expedition behind him.

Ophelia, no surprise, was on his heels, cheeks red, but doing
well. She ran with him in the mornings and had no trouble. She
claimed that she withered on the days she didn't run, which
seemed asinine to Tristan, but he hadn't any idea what Ophelia
was on about most times. Behind her was Bad News, who had
been training with Ophelia for some months. She still had the
uneasy gait of a beginner, still too much in the moment, unable
to get into the long mesmerism of this kind of heart-pumping
activity.

His father walked far behind them, following Eleanor and
Mrs. Cabot. Neither woman seemed prepared for this exercise,
and it made him wonder what Ophelia had told them to expect.
Had neither of them ever done such physical labor before? How
did they expect to get up a mountain if they couldn't manage to

get through a pasture?

Tristan caught his father's eye and signaled for them to trade places. He wanted to get a handle on how far behind the women truly were on their physical conditionings. Did they need to quit now before they went to Ben Nevis and ruined the ascent there?

His father ran up, easily sprinting past Bad News and Ophelia, ready to lead their crew for the rest of the trail. Tristan slowed his backwards jog to a halt, letting the three runners pass him. Finally, Mrs. Cabot and Eleanor caught up.

"How are you both faring?" Tristan asked politely.

Eleanor gasped. Ah, he noticed she was still wearing a corset. No wonder she was having a hard time. He hadn't thought to pay close attention to her at the start of the run when it was dark. As he was trying very hard *not* to pay attention to her at all.

"I think I might be able to go a bit faster," Prudence said, her voice surprisingly even. "But I didn't want to leave Eleanor unsupervised."

Eleanor nodded, her eyes wide, her breathing so shallow and fast Tristan was surprised she hadn't passed out completely.

"Miss Piper," Tristan said, hoping that he didn't sound like the most outrageous pervert. "If you are to keep up, you must remove your corset."

She shook head adamantly. "Must. Remain. Proper." Eleanor changed from red-faced to white.

Oh no, she was going to pass out. "Mrs. Cabot, Mrs. Cabot!" Tristan shouted, holding out his arms. Eleanor swayed. "Water, go get the water!"

Mrs. Cabot looked pained but sprinted off towards camp. Tristan didn't dare take his eyes off Eleanor, and good thing. She looked at him, glassy-eyed, unseeing, and crumpled.

He caught her before she hit her head and gently took her down to the ground. He looked around, panicked, knowing what he had to do, and hating it. "Fuck, I'm sorry Eleanor," he said.

Tristan would never have claimed to be an expert with women. But he could take a corset off one with surprising speed. It was handy today. He yanked open the buttons on her dress, pulling it open. He felt the worst kind of scoundrel. Disrobing an unconscious woman.

"Believe me, this is not how I imagined it," he muttered, his fingers working the laces. The cords gave a loud whirr and thwack as he pulled them from the eyelets. "But you must breathe."

Her eyes snapped open, clear and lucid. She took a look at his face, turned over and vomited next to his leg.

"Breathe," he said, rubbing her back, wincing as the acrid smell hit him.

She was gasping for breath still, and starting to shake. He set about getting that corset off of her entirely. It was doing her no favors. She rolled back again, allowing him to work.

"Having a hard time not swooning?" he asked.

Eleanor moaned incoherently.

The last eyelet was freed, and Tristan pulled the blasted thing apart. "I get that a lot. I've been told I'm rather handsome. Up you go." He pulled her to her feet, supporting the whole way. She wobbled like a newborn colt. "I need you to walk, Eleanor. We have to get your blood pumping. Let's go. Take a step."

He felt her fingers tighten around his shirt in response, and she took steps as he did. Slowly, they walked back towards camp, a little shuffle at a time. Eventually she was able to do so without hanging on to him like a newborn babe.

"I still feel sick," she said, her voice hoarse.

"You need water," Tristan said. "Mrs. Cabot should be along soon."

"I'm so sorry for ruining the morning run," Eleanor said.

"Not to worry. We all get a turn. But I do wish you'd trust me when I say that you cannot wear a corset and climb the Matterhorn. Or Ben Nevis. Or any of them."

As he spoke, Eleanor clutched at her gaping clothing, her face coloring not from her illness, but from her shame. "This is the worst thing that has ever happened to me."

"Then you've lived a charmed life, Miss Piper."

She stopped short and looked at him, gripping her clothes tightly together. "You called me Eleanor."

"You are mistaken," Tristan said. "I can still feel your surname on my tongue."

"Not now, when you were—" She gestured to her clothes.

"Ah yes, well, do forgive me. I thought you were unconscious." Tristan winced. That didn't sound like the civility he'd hoped to convey. "I only mean that we were in a crisis situation."

Eleanor abruptly went back to walking. Tristan scrambled to keep up. "We've decided to all call each other by our first names, you know. Us women. We felt that it encouraged camaraderie for us. To help us all succeed."

"Seems prudent," Tristan agreed. In the distance, he could see Mrs. Cabot running towards them holding a waterskin. She had speed, not that it would matter on a mountain, but helpful at the moment.

"What if you and I did the same?" she asked, and turning toward him, he spied the high color on her cheeks.

He was relieved to see that she had a more normal pallor but did not think this was the time to invite informality. She'd just fainted, and he'd ripped her corset off, for God's sake! "I am very flattered, but I think you should be given a chance to rescind your offer at a later date. You cannot consider yourself of sound mind at this minute."

She pulled herself up stiffly, and he realized he'd made a grievous error, insulting her pride. He was trying to be a gentleman, damn it all! "I only mean—"

"Thank you," she cut him off. "Your concern for my state of mind is considerate. I believe I see Mrs. Cabot approaching."

Tristan fell back, allowing her time to nurse her wounded pride. This was not a good first day. He was tasked with getting them up a mountain. He couldn't manage to get Miss Piper past the largest oak tree on the property.

THIS WAS NOT the sort of day Eleanor would write down in a diary, if she'd kept one. She'd made a fool of herself on more than one occasion, and half expected to be shipped back home to London. If she couldn't manage a single morning run, she certainly wouldn't be allowed to go to Scotland. And suddenly, she very much wanted to prove she could at least make it up Ben Nevis.

Servants had made a fire in a ring of stones and cooked an extremely delicious meal of sausages and root vegetables in a single large pan over it. Eleanor had never seen such an endeavor, but now that she had, she was more impressed than ever with the treats that emerged from anyone's kitchen, let alone what came from this open fire!

Eleanor's lungs hurt with a scratching cold that kept her coughing. She'd been such a ninny to wear a corset. Even Lady Rascomb had advised against it. But Eleanor wasn't as slender as the other girls, and well, not having support for herself seemed unwise as well as improper. Lady Rascomb had gifted her some extra undergarments—they were more like old-fashioned jumps, rather than corsets. Meant for support, not confinement. There was another run tomorrow, in which she'd have to prove herself.

"It's that tenacity that you'll need up on the mountain," Lady Rascomb advised after Tristan had told her how adamant Eleanor had been about her corset. "Some believe that it is all physical to climb a mountain." Lady Rascomb jabbed a finger at Eleanor's heart.

"Isn't it?" Eleanor asked.

"Your body will always want to give up," Lady Rascomb said. "Climbing a mountain, birthing a baby, washing a bathtub. It doesn't matter. Bodies are weak." Then she poked herself in the heart. "It is the *will* to keep at it. To persevere, despite the pain, despite the boredom."

Eleanor thanked her and changed into the new clothes. Prudence walked with her, cutting through the woods so that they might join up with the others by the end. Tristan had taken off running on the original path, his easy speed making Eleanor envious. She wanted her body to do that. Why couldn't her stride lengthen that way? The rhythmic breath that sustained him never made him overheat and vomit.

She'd been coddled her whole life. Who was she to believe she could add anything to a climbing expedition?

Now, seated around a fire, night having fallen, Eleanor was inexplicably tired. At home, she would have stayed up for hours longer, but now, she could barely follow conversation.

"Are there any concerns for the expedition before we turn in for the night?" Ophelia asked. They'd already talked through tomorrow's schedule—more physical conditioning, an overview of equipment, some mock climbing if they had time.

To Eleanor's surprise, Tristan cleared his throat. "I have one, but I'd prefer if my lady mother advises on this as well."

"Once you make your concern known, of course. I'd never hide my opinion from you." Lady Rascomb, lit by the campfire, looked younger suddenly. She could see how Lord Rascomb would be instantly enamored with her. She was so capable, so resilient. Two things Eleanor was not. Unless it had to with a piece of rope, and she was finding out how very little the world cared about a bit of twine.

"I am, of course, a supporter of propriety and its dictums."

"Are you?" Justine challenged. "I seem to remember—"

"—I said I am a supporter." Tristan glared across the fire at Justine. If Eleanor had ever wondered if there was something between the two of them, that glare put it to rest. "However, I am concerned about propriety getting in the way of our ultimate success."

"Which aspects of propriety concern you?" Lady Rascomb asked. "And don't say it, Justine, I know you have a snide remark in there."

"I'm very clever," Justine protested. "I usually have at least three things to say at Tristan's expense."

"Why must you pick at *me*?" Tristan snapped.

"Because it's so very easy," Justine said with absolute sincerity and no remorse.

"Children," Lord Rascomb rumbled. "I believe we were talking about the expedition."

"Thank you, Papa," Ophelia said.

"I imagine you're speaking of corsets?" Lady Rascomb asked.

"That is one, yes."

"Miss Piper and I have solved that particular problem," Lady Rascomb said. "What is the other concern you have?"

"Miss Piper informed me that the ladies have taken to using each other's given names. I thought this was very clever."

"It was Ophelia's idea," Justine said.

"It breeds familiarity and comfort, something we all must have in order to do well on our venture, for we do not have some of the other benefits that teams like Mr. Whymper's do."

"And what would those be?" Ophelia asked. Eleanor watched the furrow between Ophelia's eyebrows deepen, accented by the shadows of the campfire.

"Speed. Strength. Experience."

Eleanor felt that criticism to her very core. She had none of those things, and she felt as if Tristan was all but saying she should be sent home. She wanted to melt into the wooden stump she perched on. Could she please just go to bed?

"And you believe exchanging proper names will help this?" Lord Rascomb rumbled.

Tristan shrugged and bent forward, resting his elbows on his knees. "I think it wouldn't hurt."

"Lady Rascomb?" her husband prompted. "What are your thoughts on the matter?"

"The risk here would be for Mrs. Cabot and Miss Piper in particular." She glanced between them. "But given these circumstances, if we returned to formality when we were in town, I don't see why there would be an issue. I think we could set some of our propriety aside."

Tristan clapped his hands together and beamed a smile at Eleanor. One that she felt was unwarranted. It hadn't been her idea. In fact, it had made her uncomfortable to be so overly familiar with Mrs. Cabot on the first day they'd ever really had a chance to speak.

"Some. Not all." Lady Rascomb raised her eyebrows at her son.

"If that's all the concerns to be raised for the evening?" Ophelia looked around their group. Eleanor was impressed that both Lord Rascomb and Tristan were able to let Ophelia run discussions and take charge of their camp. It was as if Ophelia was truly in charge of their fates, which made Eleanor feel all the more uncertain.

Shouldn't she feel better about everything if Lord Rascomb was in charge? He was older, had the experience, and was well, he was a man. And men were in charge of virtually everything.

"Come, my little chickadees," Lady Rascomb said, standing and shooing them over to their side of the camp. "Our cozy blanket bags await."

Feeling utterly humiliated, Eleanor followed the rest of the women to their sleeping enclave, where blankets were laid out on the ground. Last night she'd been too exhausted from the train ride to pay much attention to her surroundings, and clouds had covered the skies by evening.

Tonight, however, climbing into her blankets sewn together to create a bag for her body, the sky was peppered with bright lights so numerous that as her eyes adjusted away from the fire, she wondered if this could possibly be correct. Surely she had seen the stars before, but somehow now, tonight, they burned cold and brilliant.

Her body was exhausted and buzzing all at once, and what with this star revelation, how on earth was she supposed to get any sleep at all? Her mind excavated the memory of Tristan ripping the cording from her corset, muttering, *This is not how I imagined it.*

The other women whispered goodnight to each other, and Eleanor almost forgot to respond. As she examined that very hazy moment again and again, she heard the rhythmic breathing of others drifting into sleep.

So Tristan had thought about removing her corset? She should be offended, shouldn't she? Or at least disgusted? Wasn't that how respectable women would think? But it wasn't as if he were some man in the park muttering it as she walked by. When Tristan said it, aiding her in a time of need, it felt completely . . . thrilling?

Because it was Tristan. Because he was nice to her, smiled at her, helped her. Which she'd repaid by vomiting on his leg. Not the best way to respond to a courtship. Was that what it was? Or would he have done that for any one of them?

She didn't know, but she did like the idea of Tristan courting her. Would he think her below him? The Pipers were not noble by any stretch of the imagination. Could he look past that, even if he wanted her father's money?

The ground dug into her lower back, so she flipped onto her side. It was silly to think so much about Tristan when she should be thinking about how she was going to conquer this challenge ahead of her. It was strange to think that only a month ago she hadn't wanted to go at all, and thought the whole adventure absurd. Now, after reading the books from other women climbing mountains, spending time with Ophelia and Lady Rascomb, even her time teaching knots at the salons, she desperately wanted to prove she could get up that mountain.

Being a novice didn't bother her, because she knew how to work hard, but she wished for less scrutiny. Humiliation was never fun, and somehow this seemed worse. Almost as if they didn't succeed, they would somehow set the cause of women backwards. While men like Mr. Fulk derided the ambition, Eleanor didn't want to give him the satisfaction of returning to

England without accomplishing something.

The idea of Mr. Fulk's droning patronizing made her tired. The nerve. But she certainly didn't want to fall asleep thinking of him. Instead, she pictured herself triumphantly putting her boot-clad foot on the very highest rock on some snowy-topped peak. That was enough to let her drop into sleep.

THE WEEK WAS challenging, Tristan would say that. Everyone had their own issues. Eleanor was still the slowest runner, but after discarding the full corset, she was able to run without fainting. They tied ropes and heaved each other over the stones of the ruins and up the sturdy oak trees in the grove. Eleanor showed them a few more knots that might come in handy.

They still observed regular mealtimes and tea time, of course. They weren't brutes. But Tristan found himself maneuvering to sit next to Eleanor at every stretch. The first few times it was to check on her health. Then it was to get extra help with his knots. She talked freely while he worked on dressing out his knots to perfection, telling him of Captain Smythe and her father's dockside office. She even confided the times she'd been forgotten by her parents, which was absolutely horrifying.

He'd never been forgotten by his parents, and he was one of four. Far more understandable for that to happen to him. In turn, he regaled her with his mountaineering stories and descriptions of snow. He congratulated himself on not thinking of undoing her corset again, or what she looked like with her thick, wavy brown hair down around her shoulders.

He had once accidentally come around the corner too swiftly in the morning and seen her still pinning up those silky, shining locks before their morning exercise. It stopped him short. Breathless. She'd caught him looking, and he recovered, poorly, but managed to say something inane about the upcoming day.

It was bad enough that he'd taken a second run in the evening while the rest of them relaxed and told stories around the fire before dinner. And it made him think as he ran through the wooded areas, jumping the now-familiar tree roots and dodging divots in the dirt, why couldn't he court Eleanor, if he wanted?

After they'd climbed the Matterhorn, of course. One did not mess with expedition dynamics, that was a given. Of course, the timeline for their adventure stretched over two years, so that might be a challenge. As the second son to a nobleman, however, his honor was all he had claim to at this point. And he couldn't very well court a lady that he was leading. That was unethical.

By the end of his turn about the woods, and the setting of the spring sun, he was satisfied with his decisions, and ravenous for dinner. He was the last to be dished up, and he greedily accepted the plate as he sat down next to his father.

"All well?" his father asked.

In between bites, Tristan answered, doing his best to slow down, knowing he'd get a stomachache later if he didn't. "Of course. Needed to think." Tristan watched as his father's eyes slid to Eleanor.

"I see," his father said, but let the matter drop.

Despite appearances, there was no real privacy here. Any conversation he might have with his father would be easily overheard by the women in their camp if the wind blew just right. He couldn't risk a discussion here, but perhaps later.

On the last day of their excursion, Herringbone arrived. He was amiable and dressed far nicer than the lot of them, who had not bathed in a week. They all smelled of sweat, ropes, and labor, but it was good. There seemed to be an easiness amongst them that Tristan was glad for. The arrival of his brother threw all of those developments into fresh contrast. Especially that bit about cleanliness.

Still, as he was in the presence of ladies, theoretically, and not the harridans Tristan knew them all to be, Herringbone doffed his hat.

"It looks as if much progress has been made," his brother said to the group.

His mother limped toward him, not bothering with her cane here. "Arthur, what are you doing all the way out here?"

Herringbone kissed their mother's cheek and continued. "I've come to invite you all to a party, in your honor."

"I love a party!" Bad News squealed.

Tristan rolled his eyes and was about to make a snide remark, but Eleanor elbowed him in the ribs. It was gentle, but still. He grinned. He knew that hitting was a good sign.

"I've already spoken to your parents, Miss Brewer, Miss Piper, and to your companion, Mrs. Cabot. You will have not only fresh baths awaiting you at our nearby Cloverbee Manor, but also your finest gowns. I've invited the best of the best from London and Bath societies, and we shall have a lovely few days of eating and dancing."

Herringbone pulled himself up straight and beamed at all of them. The women smiled—Bad News actually clapped—but Tristan knew something else was afoot. Herringbone didn't care for parties. But still. Two days of feasting after this week would be nothing short of decadent.

And sinking into a hot bath? That sounded like heaven too. If he had a tumbler of whisky, or even a nice dark wine, that would be the ticket.

"We finish here tonight, sleep, and then we'll pack up and leave tomorrow morning," Ophelia said.

"Just so, sister," Herringbone said, easily deferring to Ophelia, which Tristan knew was so very difficult for his brother to do. He was the heir, the most important of the four of them. Even though their father coached them all that this was Ophelia's project, it was sometimes hard to remember that neither Arthur's nor Tristan's interference was welcome or necessary.

Sometimes he wished Ophelia had been born a boy. An Oberon to her Ophelia. A king to her . . . drowned girl. She had such a spirit, it was rare in any gender, and to have the power a man had to go about the world as he wanted was a freedom she needed. He could only imagine how difficult it could be to have to smile as men derided her passions and ambitions. But she did so, at almost every ball.

Perhaps that was why Herringbone arranged this. It would be an occasion where none of these women would have to hide their pursuit or be made to feel ashamed of it some way. He stepped forward and clapped his brother on the shoulder.

Herringbone flinched, no doubt at how absolutely and thoroughly filthy Tristan was after running through the woods for a week.

"I wish you all good health, good luck, all that," Herringbone said, stepping out of Tristan's reach. Tristan grinned again. Herringbone's valet would give him a proper dressing down for the handprint of dirt on his coat.

His big brother set himself back on his horse, no doubt to return to the train station. Cloverbee Manor wasn't that far from here by train, so it would not be much of an inconvenience for anyone in their party to get there.

They all turned back to their work—hauling bags via a makeshift pulley over a tree branch. But none of them did well after that interruption. Even the very pleasant and hardworking Mrs. Cabot—Prudence—was distracted. Tristan started to pay attention to their chatter, only to find they were obsessing over what he too was thinking about: the bath and the food.

"Aren't you wanting to know what your maids packed for dresses? Or what gentlemen will be in attendance for dancing?" Tristan prompted.

Bad News scoffed at him and rolled her eyes. "Sometimes Tristan, I think you can't be as utterly daft as I believe you are, and I feel bad about it. Then, you say something like that, and I think, ah, I have the right of it after all. Tristan has the mental capacity of a wayward slug."

Tristan pulled himself upright. "Come now, that's not fair."

Ophelia laughed. "Brother. Please. You've spent all week

with us, seeing us in all our unholy glory. Haven't you figured anything out yet?"

Tristan looked to Prudence and Eleanor for help. Neither of them came to his aid, and in fact, both looked to be suppressing smirks. "That's precisely why I thought you'd be excited about dresses and company. Because you've been in the dirt."

Eleanor actually snickered.

"Not you too?" he asked, even if he was developing an idea of why his words were so utterly absurd. They were as exhausted and hungry as he was. Thinking about putting on formal clothing was not appealing.

"You talked me out of my corset earlier this week," Eleanor said, a playful grin toying across her pretty flushed lips. "And now you are trying to talk me back into it?"

The talk of her corset made his mind stop functioning. In fact, it stopped being a humorous situation entirely to him, only because he could think of nothing other than how she wasn't wearing a corset now.

"This is freedom, Tristan," Prudence said, catching his attention. He turned toward her, focusing very hard. "Why would I want to give it up?"

"Because you are hungry and exhausted?" Tristan guessed.

"Dear Lord!" Bad News exploded. "He gets it! It turns out, we are people. Just like him. We get tired and hungry and would like a long relaxing bath to warm up in, and some delicious food to put the meat back on our bones."

Fortunately, Tristan's mother came over at this point, checking on why the hauling of the bags had stalled out. "Are they teasing you?" she asked, as if he couldn't handle his own against a pack of feral girls. Which, it seemed, he couldn't.

"Yes, but only because I'm so unbearably handsome," he said, giving his best charming grin to Eleanor, who at least blushed. That was a point in his favor. Bad News scoffed again.

"It's because you're unbearably stupid," Bad News corrected.

"Oh, Justine, language," his mother admonished.

"Fine. Because Tristan is so unbearably backward in his thinking."

That actually landed a mark on him. He was quite forward in his thinking, thank you very much. He had no trouble letting Ophelia lead the campaign, let her make the speeches and the decisions. He was the infantryman. There to help carry bags, muscle through if needed. It wasn't particularly fashionable to tell other men that he was following his baby sister's instructions for his next big adventure. He'd gotten more than his fair share of teasing about it. "My thinking is very progressive, I would like you to notice."

Bad News rolled her eyes again. "Please."

He found himself wanting to make his mother speak up for him, until he realized just how ridiculous that was. "If you have no need of me, then, whether it be my outrageously fashionable looks, my incredibly progressive mental capacity, or even my unarguably masculine brute strength, I will go find some other occupation." Tristan turned on his heel to go seek out his father.

"Au revoir!" Bad News called.

There was a garbled hushing of her from Eleanor. Words he couldn't make out, but it was gratifying to know *someone* might be on his side. At least a little bit. And really, he was quite glad it was Eleanor, if it were to be anyone.

His father was making lists of provisions and estimated costs by the fire. Tristan sat down on the nearest tree stump. His father hadn't changed much over the years. There was perhaps a bit more gray, yes, which appeared after his mother's accident, almost overnight. But he was trim and stoic, eager to help, and kept his own counsel. A man of few words, whom Tristan admired inordinately. He was a great man, and even more so, a great father. He looked at each of his children as individuals, with different talents and different roles. It was a gift to be seen not just as the spare, as he so often was called, but as his own person, with his own wants and needs.

"Equipment all in order?" he asked Tristan absently, not

bothering to look up from his ledger. Trust his father to bring a writing desk into the woods.

"Seems to be," Tristan said. "Did you know about Herring-bone's party?"

"Mmm?" His father looked up finally. "I do wish you wouldn't call him that."

"Hard not to anymore, honestly." Tristan looked out at the land. He preferred being out here than in London. He couldn't quite figure out what he liked most, or really, even why. Because there was so much of town that he did like—the wine, the women, the clubs, the gambling. But those were the activities he engaged in while he avoided thinking about the future. What he would do with his life. Military service? The church was out of the question. A trade?

"I had an inkling your brother would get us all over to Cloverbee. He's desperate to be included."

Tristan frowned. "He is?"

His father looked up at him, blinking rapidly, as if he had dirt in his eye. "Of course. He feels that as my heir, he should not participate in these kinds of daring feats. But it does not mean he doesn't want to."

Tristan stared off to where Herringbone had made his exit on his horse, as if he might still see the echo of his brother standing there, hat in hand.

"Your brother feels his duty quite acutely. He hasn't the freedom you do."

"Freedom?" Tristan almost growled. His freedom was insecurity and aimlessness. If only his plight was that he would inherit money and lands and a purpose.

"Yes, freedom. The heir must always be concerned about what is best for his estate, his lineage, his greater family. As a second son, you have far more freedom in whom you marry, how you spend your time, what you will do with your life. Especially now that we have modern medicine. It's unlikely that you'll have to worry that you'll inherit. Arthur will marry a fine lady, and they will have children. You needn't worry. Arthur will do his bit."

Spoken like an heir, Tristan thought. He should get up and find somewhere else to be before his temper rose to the surface. He was generally good natured, but when his temper rose, he almost went blind with it. Years of practice and a few hard pummelings from the boys at school had taught him to keep it in check at all times. Few things could rattle it free, but his father talking about the difficulties of being the heir—of being *needed*—made control precarious.

He stood. "I think I'll go for another run."

"Another?" His father squinted at the sky, gauging the progress of the afternoon. "The girls still practicing with the pulley?"

"Yes, good progress, they're all familiar now. Ophelia is likely going to have them hauling each other up the trees next."

"Not a bad idea, actually. Never know if one will fall down a bergschrund."

Tristan grunted. That would depend on the season they visited the mountain. A bergschrund shifted and changed as a glacier slowly moved, widening and narrowing that gap between the ice and the rock it carved. In the winter, the snow might accumulate there, and an unsuspecting mountaineer might fall farther than he wanted. In summer, the melting of ice might cause the gaping bergschrund to grow, making forward progress impossible.

Rope work and strength would keep them all safe.

He thought of Eleanor. She was right behind him on their line, theoretically because she was the weakest of their party in strength. He could pull her along to safety if she needed. He hadn't been the one to make the assessment—that had been his father and Ophelia choosing the order. But he didn't mind. He might be the weakest in the knot-tying skills. Eleanor had introduced some that were surprisingly difficult to remember. The splicing? Very handy, if he could keep it in his head.

Going past the wooded area, Bad News decided to harass him again. "You're too good to be hauling bags, is that it?" Justine yelled, her hands on her hips.

"Must you—" He cut himself off. There was no reason to argue with her. He could pull twice the weight she could, they both knew it.

"Yes, I must. What's good for the goose is good for the gander and all that," she said.

"It's a better use of my time to run," he said. "I can already haul as much you all can put together."

"Wonderful. You'll carry the tent poles, then." Ophelia let the sandbag drop from the pulley.

"Fine," he said, setting his jaw.

Eleanor picked her way over to where he stood on the path. "I need to run as well. I haven't quite gotten as fast as the rest of you."

Normally spending an extra minute with Eleanor would be welcome, but he wanted to *run*. Doing his best to control his disappointment, he gestured to the well-trod dirt path. "You know the way."

She looked up at him, her expression questioning, but he didn't want to explain his dark mood. Between the idea of being *the spare* and Justine's constant picking, he wasn't sure how to explain his mood without sounding like a child. And he knew that, which was why he was going to go run, rather than whine.

"You don't have to run with me," she said. "I know I'm slow."

"I'll keep within earshot," he grumbled. "Go on."

She nodded and started her slow jog. It was agonizing to go at that snail's pace. He let her go ahead ten paces, and then began his own. He ran past her, his long strides no match for her much shorter gait. Still, he ran ahead, then circled back for her, keeping to his promise to keep her within earshot.

At the pond, where they often stopped, he ran an extra lap around it, waiting for her. He was feeling better, actually. A run was precisely what was needed. She arrived out of breath, as if she had perhaps sprinted the last bit. She looked relieved to see him waiting for her.

Tristan let her catch her breath, doing his best not to make her feel self-conscious. He looked out over the pond, letting the smell of the rich earth surrounding the pond fill his nose. This was a place he could find peace.

Behind him, her breathing regulated. She was already faster at coming down from her run than she had been five days ago. He was impressed with how quickly she'd taken to this.

She was gulping in air, hands on her hips. "I'm not sure I'll ever get used to this."

He smiled. "You will. And you'll be grateful for it when we go up to higher elevations. It may seem silly to run when you aren't being chased, but it helps."

Eleanor gave him a generous smile at his attempt at humor. "I feel silly."

"Did you know that in the springtime, hundreds of years ago, women would run footraces against each other for prizes?" Tristan had much of his history knowledge thanks to his mother, who took a keen interest in what women were up to in the centuries past.

This time Eleanor's smile was genuine. "I did not. I've been told my entire life that women are far too delicate for activities such as these."

"Even the nobleman's daughters would participate. It was an honor to win." Tristan smiled. He wasn't sure if that was entirely true, but Ophelia had latched onto the idea. Sometimes Tristan wondered if Ophelia wasn't driven by these old stories—wanting to prove herself worthy of their lineage.

"I wonder if they bothered wearing a corset when they ran," Eleanor said, coming to stand next to him overlooking the pond.

Tristan smiled. "They probably knew better."

Eleanor crouched down and dipped her hands in the cold water, splashing some on the back of her neck. "Thank you for helping me. I'm not sure I said that."

"I'm always available for gallantry."

She stood, a wry look on her face. "Especially if that gallantry includes undressing a woman?"

"I aspire to nobility and grace," he said. Her eyes were deep, chocolate brown, and he could gaze into them forever. As if he could tip forward and dive into her, never to surface again. "I'm glad you recovered so quickly."

"I'm grateful for you—your entire family—for including me on this. I hadn't any thoughts about mountains two months ago, but now, I feel as if I'll die if I don't try to climb one."

A breeze picked up, pushing loose strands of her dark hair into her face. She was so beautiful, and he could feel her passion and commitment mirroring his own. It was all the softness she wore on her exterior that he felt on the inside. He reached up and gently brushed her hair back, tucking the wayward strands around her ear.

"Tristan," she said, looking up at him as if she were beckoning him into her depths.

Instead of letting his hand drop, he cupped her jaw, pulling her slowly to him, giving her the chance to escape, if she so chose. But she didn't. Her hand touched his chest, over his heart. If she wanted to pull it out and keep it, he would let her, if only she would allow him to kiss her.

"Eleanor," he said, waiting for her to say something—anything—to make him stop. But she didn't.

She stood on her tiptoes, and he pulled her close, his lips brushing hers, gentle, ever so gentle. Lowering herself to the ground, she pulled away, but he didn't want to be finished. If this line was to be crossed, that could not be the end of their kiss. He followed her, wrapping his other hand around the back of her neck, pressing his lips to hers once more.

This time she softened against him, and he kissed her more ardently. She must know how often he thought of her, and how else could he show her than by kissing her dizzy? He deepened the kiss, and she did the same. She reached her arms around his neck, making him wrap his arms around her waist, pressing his body fully against hers. He felt as if time stopped here, giving him the chance to experience a heaven available only to him.

Despite the exhaustion of the week, his body went tense, wanting more than he would ever take from a respectable young lady in the middle of rolling pastures and isolated copses of trees. Still, she was so soft in his arms. The skin on her arms was like satin, her lips were sweet, and he was happy that both of their scents were only those of hard work and mud.

She pulled away from him, and he felt dizzy himself. An early afternoon drizzle had descended, but Tristan hadn't noticed the raindrops. He was lost in her lips and her skin and her hair.

"It's raining," she said.

He couldn't speak. While he'd imagined this kiss, he'd thought it would be akin to his prior encounters—breathless, passionate, yes, but lusty. This had been different—unlike the other kisses he'd ever committed to—and he didn't know what that meant. She wouldn't look him in the eye, and that didn't sit well. "Eleanor."

There was her attention. Her lips swollen from his. "Yes?"

His mouth opened and closed as he tried to think of what he should say. "Should I apologize? Because I don't want to."

Her cheeks flushed even higher, but she shook her head. "It was very nice."

That was a blow to his ego. Dogs were nice. An egg sandwich was *nice*. If there had ever been a rebuff, he knew it. "I see."

Perhaps she heard his bitterness. "I rather liked it," she added, looking up at him through her lashes.

That felt a bit better. "Would you permit me to kiss you again?"

A smile played on those imminently kissable lips. "As long as we don't take too long getting back to camp."

He sidled closer to her, moving slowly so as not to spook her. "You are known to be very slow." He closed his arms around her, and she laid her cheek against his chest, letting out a content-sounding sigh. She felt so good in his arms. So right. He let go of her on one side to tip her chin up, so that he might kiss her again.

One of her arms snaked up to pull him down to her. She took more command this time, kissing him as much as he kissed her. Sipping at him, pressing kisses. Then his impatience got the better of him and he let his tongue wend its way out of his mouth and into hers.

Another breeze kicked up and she shuddered against him, allowing him into her mouth. It was heaven. She was heaven. He rubbed her back, telling himself to keep his hands above her waist, even though he desperately wanted to cup her bottom and pull her against him.

Suddenly she launched herself backwards, and he heard it, too. Someone was coming. He heard Ophelia's laughter. They were all coming. Eleanor's eyes were wide with terror. She shooed at him, and so he did the only thing he could think to do: he took off running.

He was well out of sight before they broke into the clearing. They greeted Eleanor, and then he was out of earshot, heart pounding. What did he just do?

There was no fraternization on the expedition. That was a hard and fast rule, one that they had all agreed upon ages ago, back when Ophelia had proposed this expedition. That no matter what, they would maintain propriety.

And she was the daughter of a ship's captain. Even a second son of a viscount should be more circumspect, shouldn't he? Clearly, the best course of action was to pretend this never happened. To forget the softness of her lips, the way her body melted into his. This was going to be hell.

✦

Chapter Seven

HER LIPS THROBBED as she concentrated on looking at the pond, desperately hoping that the light breeze would cool the heat in her face. What was she thinking kissing Tristan? Oh, she was thinking about how handsome he was, how kind he'd been, and how he looked at her as if she were the entire world.

No one had ever looked at her like that—like she *mattered.* Not only could he see her, that she was physically in front of him—which, honestly, was not always the case in her experience—but he seemed to understand her. She wasn't born to a family of physical women, or adventurous ones. But he could see her try, and he accepted that effort.

Justine was the first to burst into the clearing, her face red. Prudence was on her heels, also gasping for breath. They must have been racing. Ophelia glided in not long after, looking not as bedraggled.

"Taking it easy while the rest of us are working, then?" Justine said, bending at the waist to catch her breath.

"It's fine," Prudence said. "We all have to work on our weaker skills. She was brilliant with the pulley challenge, and frankly, the best one of us at the knots."

"Physical conditioning takes time and patience," Ophelia announced.

Hoping that none of them would be able to see in her face that she'd been enjoying Tristan's company just moments before, she turned to face her friends. "Thank you, Ophelia. I am trying my best."

"Run back with us?" Ophelia asked. "I don't need a break."

Justine groaned. "Why are you like that?"

Prudence huffed out a laugh. "Because Ophelia knows that it isn't a race."

Justine rolled her eyes. "It's the only way to make it interesting."

"I'm ready if you are," Eleanor said. How exhausting it must be to be Justine, making every moment into a competition.

Ophelia nodded, gesturing to the path in front of them, so Eleanor started down the trail. They weren't far when Ophelia spoke.

"I know I shouldn't ask, but my curiosity is killing me."

Eleanor was not yet at a point where she could carry on an intelligent—or unintelligent—conversation while in hasty motion. She made a noise that she hoped sounded like she was giving Ophelia permission. But Ophelia was her superior in many ways, which made giving her permission to ask a question feel strange.

"Does my brother? Or rather, do you? What I mean to say is, are you both, or rather, will he?"

Eleanor looked at Ophelia, finally finding some joy while taking her exercise. Normally Ophelia was so calm and collected. Here she was sputtering just as much as Eleanor would. "Do you have a question?"

"Only, is he courting you?" Ophelia said, color showing in her cheeks. "Do you fancy him?"

Eleanor thought about it, his flirtatious comments, his solicitousness, the time they shared laughter over collecting the ropes, and then of course, his kisses. Those soft, wonderful, dream-inspiring kisses. But there had never been talk of intentions. And Eleanor didn't make it to being an unmarried twenty-five-year-old without savvy regarding her status. "I . . . don't know?"

Ophelia made a face. "Sounds about right for him."

Heat flushed Eleanor's system, and it had nothing to do with the quick pace. Was Tristan a scoundrel out for his own pleasure at the expense of her reputation? But the expedition was supposed to be above reproach, and here she was not only defying the rules, but being lured into sordidness by a fellow mountain climber. She felt so stupid. So ridiculous. But she couldn't afford to look that way—she wanted to stay on the expedition. "What do you mean?"

"That Justine was right—the rules we must abide as women do not apply to him. And he brazenly disregards it, not caring about what it looks like for us."

Did Ophelia know that Tristan had kissed her? "Oh." What was she supposed to say to that? She couldn't deny him doing anything improper, for that would give Ophelia the idea that something *had* happened.

"I do apologize on his behalf if he is too forward with you. He normally sticks to dancers and chorus girls and the like. He doesn't know how to behave with respectable ladies."

Eleanor felt suddenly very out of breath. At least the jogging would cover her discomfort. Did he currently support a mistress? Was she merely an available distraction when he couldn't visit his woman in London? That made her physically ill to think about. She hadn't wanted to be . . . *entertainment*.

Ophelia sighed—an activity Eleanor couldn't have managed if she wanted to at this point, gasping for air as she was.

"I'll speak to him," Ophelia promised.

"No, don't!" Eleanor managed. "Far too embarrassing. He'll think I said something."

Ophelia looked at her with pity, but acquiesced. "Then I won't say a thing. But I will give him condescending looks."

Eleanor huffed out a laugh. "Reasonable."

The rest of the run sped by, and when they arrived back in camp, Eleanor felt surprisingly good. The emotional elevation she had been promised was finally present. She grinned. Just in time to leave this place.

TRISTAN SIGHED AS he sank into the bathtub. He'd scrubbed down prior to descending into the hot soak, grateful for running water and soap, and this delightful brandy his brother kept in stock. He rolled his neck from side to side. Spending a week out in camp made him oddly appreciative of the simplest things: chairs, hot water, padded mattresses. Give him a week amongst these creature comforts, and he would long for the clear skies and campfire once again.

But this felt like its own ecstasy. The camp had gone well. He'd had time to discuss it with his father while they rode in their own train car. The girls had performed well, progressed well, and showed commitment. Tristan did not discuss kissing Eleanor in the woods, as he would not have mentioned it to anyone.

Eleanor had not sought him out again either, which was for the best. She was pretending it hadn't happened either, for which he was grateful. Was he though? He'd have liked to think his kisses powerful enough to fluster her. Make her weak in the knees. He was not unattractive, and he'd had it on good authority that he was a decent enough kisser, and a superb lover.

For the best, then, that it was only a moment in the woods, and not something more public or more permanent.

There was a discussion of a croquet game on the lawns this afternoon, preceding the ball. Some guests had already arrived, and Herringbone—argh, that was going to be challenging to not call him that—*Arthur* wanted to have entertainment available for everyone.

Arthur's valet, Matthias, had taken the opportunity to lay out a lawn suit for him, which he might as well wear. After a decent soak, finishing the brandy, Tristan dressed himself and headed downstairs.

The day was sunny and unseasonably warm—a surprising gift from the weather. Many guests took afternoon tea on the wide stone veranda, spectating and commenting on a croquet game already in full swing. He joined the table, sitting next to Prudence.

"Where are the other ladies of the expedition?" he asked.

Prudence nodded toward the lawn. Tristan followed her gaze, searching amongst the white dresses until he spotted his sister, Bad News, and finally, Eleanor. She seemed to glow. There was a new air of energy and excitement about her.

Despite his mind protesting, his body reacted. Partly because he had tasted those lips. He'd felt the softness of her body melting into his. He hadn't taken things further, but his imagination had more than enough information to make the leap of what it would be like to tumble into bed with her.

A man cleared his throat, and Tristan looked up to find Mr. Piper standing next to his chair. Oh God, he was thinking of debauching the man's daughter as he stood right there. Tristan bolted to his feet. "Mr. Piper."

"Mr. Bridewell," the mustachioed man responded. "Delightful view. Delightful place. We're delighted to be here."

"And I too, am . . . delighted." Tristan looked over Mr. Piper's shoulder to smile at Mrs. Piper who stood behind him. "Please, have a seat. My brother, Lord Berringbone, is your true host, but I don't mind filling in."

They sat, and while Tristan expected Mrs. Piper to take the seat next to him, providing the customary gentleman-lady alternating seating, it was Mr. Piper who sat next to him.

"Before I hear from Eleanor," Mr. Piper began. "I'd like to hear about how this week went from you. I trust your judgement."

That's a poor idea, Tristan thought. His judgement was patently terrible. "Everyone did well. Eleanor was the least prepared for the trials we faced, but she worked hard and achieved the same expectations as everyone else."

Mr. Piper turned back to Mrs. Piper. "See, Mary? I knew Eleanor would have no trouble fitting right in."

"But how is her health now?" Mrs. Piper asked.

Tristan gestured to the lawn, where Eleanor pitched her head back in a hearty laugh. It was unladylike, that laugh, but he'd never seen her be so unapologetically joyous before. He longed to go out to the game and see if he could make her laugh like that. "You can see for yourself."

"Seems to agree with her," Mr. Piper said, satisfaction evident in his voice.

"She's lost so much weight in one week," Mrs. Piper protested.

"We all did," Tristan said. "We worked very hard out there."

There was a disapproving sniff by Mrs. Piper, but that was soon drowned out by an appreciative one as a footman placed a tiered sandwich tower in front of them.

Tristan chatted amiably with the Pipers, wondering idly what kind of man they'd prefer for a son-in-law. Would they look for a title for Eleanor? He assumed so—that was what many of the new-money industrialists attempted. It was no secret that Mr. Piper had thought he would receive something from Queen Victoria for his civilian service during the American Civil War. But no such commendation appeared. Social elevation was still available to him should he wed his daughter to a nobleman.

Not a second son, like himself, of course, but to an heir. Like Arthur. The idea of Eleanor marrying Herringbone was . . . nauseating at best. His bulging eyes would never appreciate the softness of her warm brown hair.

"Excuse me," Tristan said, on his feet before he realized what he was doing. He couldn't just sit there. To cover his irrational reaction to his own thoughts, he drifted over to the rest of the table, greeting his brother's guests.

But there was one guest he didn't know—a lovely brunette with large blue eyes and a hint of red highlights in her hair. She was in white like all the other ladies, but there was something slightly different about her that Tristan couldn't quite put his finger on. Ah well, someone would tell him eventually.

Next to her was Lady Emily Welburton. She was plain to look at, with widely spaced eyes like Arthur, but she was well known to be intelligent and pleasant. Both of his sisters seemed to appreciate her company.

"Lady Emily," he greeted, giving her companion a pointed look.

"Mr. Bridewell, may I please introduce my cousin, Miss Sophia Perkins."

"Miss Perkins," Tristan said, inclining his head since he couldn't very well lean over the table to take her hand.

"Mr. Bridewell," Miss Perkins said, blinking rapidly at him. Oh, she was fluttering her eyelashes at him. That was unexpected. "I'm so glad your brother obliged to extend an invitation to me. I was visiting my cousin in town, and I have not quite acclimated to the fast-paced city life."

"I'm grateful to my brother as well, Miss Perkins. I do hope you enjoy your stay here at Cloverbee." The smile she gave him seemed far more than a polite one. The urge to flirt was automatic, but it somehow felt wrong all of a sudden, so he kept himself from winking or giving an overly large smile.

Ophelia, Bad News, and Eleanor arrived at the top of the stairs, flush from their croquet match. It caused Tristan to straighten, feeling caught out in talking to the beautiful Miss Perkins. Flattering as it was to be the target of a young lady such as her, it felt predatory in the same way that walking backstage at the opera did. But backstage, the give and take was clear: money for companionship. Both parties held some kind of power. Here, Miss Perkins was assessing him in a way he wasn't sure he liked. Almost as if she might ask to see his teeth next.

He saw Eleanor stop short. She was surprised to see him for some reason, but he couldn't fathom what. His brother owned the place, for God's sake. His presence at a house party was mandatory. He started towards her, only to find her sitting abruptly down with her parents, appearing to all the world as a dutiful daughter. And not avoiding him at all.

Inwardly, he cringed. He deserved that. After all, he had literally *run away* from her after kissing her. Not exactly gentlemanly. And if she knew anything of his reputation, she'd think him a proper scoundrel. Which . . . maybe he had been deserving of in the past, but not now. And not with a young lady like her. Even if he did think she was a bit beneath him, which he thought only because it was true. But he would absolutely still treat her with the utmost respect, of course. Even if they were not supposed to be fraternizing within the expedition.

This was why they separated men and women. Because sometimes, it was awfully hard to keep one's lips to oneself.

ELEANOR FOUGHT THE pounding of her heart. She'd gotten the experience of purposely trying to regulate the speed of it during the long morning runs of the prior week. She wasn't terribly good at it yet.

Standing on the threshold of the ballroom, decorated as it was with spring dogwood blossoms and hothouse flowers, Eleanor desperately tried to reconcile the different pieces of her life. The person who could run, dodge tree roots, and regulate her heartbeat, and the other who felt peculiar and small in the worst of ways, and extremely out of place at balls.

Her mother had bought her a new gown for the occasion—a striking frock of emerald green, with cream-colored underskirts draped for contrast. Gold thread glinted in the accented embroidery, which matched the golden necklace her mother had brought. The off-the-shoulder neckline kept Eleanor very aware of her posture, not wanting to hunch and strain the fabric.

All the other ladies made appreciative noises about it, even Prudence, whose cherry red dress was simple, yet stunning. Only a widowed woman could carry off a gown so daring. She looked sleek and dangerous in it, neither of which Eleanor would have ever associated with the American. She was far too friendly.

Ophelia was still in her overly feminine pale pink ruffles—possibly to counter any gossip of her masculine-seeming hobbies. And Justine was clad in a violently purple dress, bright and arresting. With her slim waist and ample bosom, she looked like a barmaid about to fall out of her corset. Even Justine noticed it, and huffed as she tried to stuff the offending anatomy back into the gown.

"It isn't my fault," Justine had said through gritted teeth. "If I could wear a sack cloth and not have cleavage, I would do it."

The four of them were quite the ensemble, entering the ballroom. All colors of the rainbow, all different styles, all women determined to conquer the Matterhorn.

"Are you excited?" Ophelia asked all of them.

"I like dancing," Justine admitted.

Was Eleanor excited? She wouldn't say that, exactly. She wanted to dance with Tristan more than anything, but she also didn't want to be disappointed when he acted blasé about their kiss. Or if he made things worse and gave a stiff apology, promising to never do it again. She wanted to dance with a man who was so enamored with her that he kept on dancing after the music finished. A man who might entreat her to introduce him to her parents, though, she supposed, Tristan had already met hers. She made a noise that could be interpreted either way. Mostly because she caught sight of Tristan.

He'd been devastatingly handsome this afternoon on the veranda, wearing a white linen suit so casual and so stunning amongst the sober colors of the other gentlemen. His flaxen hair had glinted in the sunlight, and she had stopped short, her brain short-circuiting in the face of his handsomeness. It hadn't been fair—she'd been off minding her own business, and here he was traipsing about, looking like Alexander the Great come to life.

Now in his formal evening wear, black jacket and black trousers like every other man, he managed to somehow seem extraordinary here as well. The tailoring of his suit was perfect, showing off a slim waist and broad shoulders. He was smooth and easy in his demeanor, born to this way of life. It made Eleanor feel all the more vulgar and silly.

"No time like the present," Prudence said, with all the determination of a military overture.

Eleanor steeled herself and stepped forward. Being a country house party, there was no majordomo to announce them, no formality of a receiving line. They were just . . . there. Many other guests had already come down, elegant and twirling in vibrant hues.

Two women approached, which obliged Ophelia to introduce them. They were Lady Emily Welburton and Miss Sophia Perkins. Lady Emily seemed to be a long-time friend of Ophelia, though while she and Justine were acquainted, Lady Emily didn't seem as warm with her. Miss Sophia Perkins was new to all of them, which at least made Eleanor feel as if they were on more equal footing.

They dashed off to meet the next group of guests, and Ophelia leaned over and said, "Lady Emily has been hoping to marry Arthur for ages. I'm not sure what exactly is standing in the way of it all, but she seems well-nigh desperate for it. I suspect Miss Perkins is here as a distraction for Tristan."

A sudden burst of bile came into Eleanor's throat. Someone for Tristan? Miss Perkins was far prettier than Eleanor, and being cousins with a lady definitely made her of better family than Eleanor's.

Justine snorted, given that it was just the four of them standing together. "She's no match for Eleanor. Pretty hair, but what does she *do*? Eleanor can tie knots like a sailor."

Eleanor blushed at both the praise and the idea that her *tendre* for Tristan had been caught out.

"It's fine, Eleanor. You don't have a tell. *He* does," Justine said. "That man goes around wearing his thoughts on his shirtsleeves like the bloody village idiot."

Eleanor couldn't see it, but then, she hadn't known him for as long, so she supposed reading Tristan's facial expressions would become a talent in time? "Oh," was all she could manage back.

The music struck up, and none of them had dancing partners. There weren't nearly enough men to go around, but the ratio wasn't terribly off. Surprising, considering that it was Lord Berringbone inviting guests. Though, technically, it was his mother, Lady Rascomb hostessing this party.

"Dance cards," Ophelia said, procuring them from by the door. They helped each other tie the ribbons around their wrists. Soon enough, men were being persuaded by the music to begin looking for partners, and while it was too late for this dance, soon Eleanor's dance card filled up.

But while it was lovely to have Mr. Blakely pencil his name in for a dance, when Tristan came up to request a dance, she felt as if she might begin to shiver.

"Might I sign your card as well?" Tristan asked, not at all sounding abashed or ashamed or stiff.

"Of course," she answered, extending her arm so that he might take the card from where it dangled.

He looked at her wrist—covered in gloves of course—and seemed to contemplate it in a way that heated her entire body. He did not carefully take the card without touching her. He did the opposite, dragging a finger from her mid forearm down to the ribbon. He pulled up the card and penciled in his name, but before he let it go, he looked up from his bent pose.

"You only have one space left, Eleanor."

"Miss Piper here, Mr. Bridewell." Eleanor gave a polite smile that most likely looked like a wince.

"I think I liked it better in the woods," he said. "Where I could be Tristan, and you were—"

She was so painfully aware of him holding her hand. It made her fluttery and impatient and anxious. "There are many things in the woods that are commendable."

"Many," he agreed, and she knew he wasn't speaking of trees or stars or campfires.

The heat in his eyes brought the memory of their kiss to the forefront of her mind. How could he work such magic when she was so determined to forget it?

"But we haven't danced in the woods," he said.

"There was no music."

He shook his head gently. "Not like a minuet or a waltz. So we might as well take advantage of civilization."

Eleanor jolted. Two dances was perilously close to a declaration of interest. "Are you certain?"

"I am. Are you?" Golden brows lifted in question.

She felt as if he were asking another question. Not just about a second dance, but about something bigger. Something that might look like courtship. "I'm . . . certain." She hated that she sounded breathless. She wished she could be more like Justine in her confidence, or like Prudence with her poise.

"Excellent," he said, penciling in his name.

Ophelia came sashaying over, her ruffles twisting with the movement. "I'm surprised Arthur saddled us with dance cards. It's a private ball. What's the point?"

"You know Herringbone," Tristan said, then winced. "I mean Arthur."

Eleanor smiled. She knew Tristan had a penchant for nicknames, but she wondered why he was giving up what was likely the oldest one.

"Are you finally showing some respect? Who talked to you?" Ophelia put her hands on her hips.

"Papa," Tristan said, "has asked me to be more respectful."

"Does this extend to Justine as well? You've been calling her that awful nickname for years."

"What nickname?" Eleanor asked.

"Bad News. I'm surprised you didn't know. They print it in the newspapers, after all."

Tristan shrugged, cheeks coloring. He was embarrassed. How unexpected. "I didn't realize you called her that," Eleanor said.

"He started it," Ophelia said, staring at her brother, as if he could dare him to apologize right then and there. "It's given her a devil of a time."

"It was only meant as a joke."

"It wasn't a terribly funny one." Ophelia screwed her face up, possibly trying to counteract her fury. "You haven't known the trouble it caused."

"It's just a name," Tristan protested.

"Not when it destroys a reputation," Ophelia countered.

Eleanor didn't care for hearing all of this. She didn't like how it painted Tristan—uncaring, and frankly, villainous. "Did you really?"

Tristan looked at her, and the vulnerability she saw in his face was shocking. Gone was the confident veneer of a gentleman and a scoundrel. This was a little boy who'd been caught out. "I did. It was years ago, and it was bad of me to do so. She always seemed to pick at me, saying mean things, and I didn't like it. I wanted her to stop, and frankly, her presence was always 'bad news' to me, then. I said as much to some friends, and well, it took on a life of its own."

Ophelia's eyes skated over to Eleanor's. "What you don't realize in the innocence of his telling is who his friends are. Men with power, men with connections."

"We were *boys* at the time." Tristan protested, throwing his hands up.

"You were old enough to go to war and didn't manage that, did you? No, you conspired to ruin a girl's reputation."

"Like you could ruin Justine. She's already done it herself," Tristan scoffed.

Eleanor didn't like that one bit. "She has never done anything truly ruinous. She speaks her mind, but really only in private company. She laughs when something is funny, is that so wrong?"

"Look at how she dresses, and who she dances with," Tristan said.

"You know as well as I do that a lady cannot refuse a dance,"

Ophelia snapped.

"Justine dresses at the height of fashion. She's dressing like every other woman in a ballroom," Eleanor said, feeling rather protective of Justine.

Lady Rascomb came over, her cane topped with a pretty ivory rose. "This looks like a rather heated discussion that might be best held at another time."

"Tristan is finally coming round to the idea that he may have single-handedly ruined Justine." Ophelia's hands crossed over her bosom.

"Oh dear. Not the revelation we hoped for a ballroom." Lady Rascomb did look properly shocked.

"Not in that way," Tristan said. "Just by giving her that nickname."

Understanding dawned on Lady Rascomb's face, and did Eleanor see some relief as well? "I see. Then a deep apology is in order, dearest. But now, the music is about to start, so we ought to find our partners. Off you go."

Eleanor tried to erase her troubled look as Tristan wandered off to find Lady Emily. Tristan's behavior was rather horrible. How could anyone be so callous? And to poor Justine who was so full of life? Could she really be falling for a man who would perpetrate the downfall of a young lady for no other reason than malice?

As Lord Berringbone approached her for the first dance, she gave him a polite smile. It was an honor to have the first dance with the host, and he was indeed signaling his acceptance of her by opening the party with her. She wondered how her parents had managed it.

Her parents were dancing together, this first dance, which was nice to see. Her mother's health had not always permitted her to go out, and her father was often too busy with work to find the time for social functions.

"Are you enjoying the Ladies' Alpine Society?" Lord Berringbone asked.

"I am very much, my lord," she answered, feeling oddly swept up in the moment. Here she was, in the country, dancing with a nobleman. How strange for a girl who spent most of her time down at the docks.

"You seem to have fit in nicely with the other young ladies," he observed.

"Your sister is very generous with her knowledge and her kindness. She's an excellent leader. I have no qualms about her expedition."

"So you'll be ready to climb Ben Nevis in a month's time?" He looked down at her, and the kindness she saw there made him more handsome than he'd seemed before.

Before they'd danced, he was so aloof that she hadn't known what to think of him. He was like a less handsome version of Tristan, who was so near to an English ideal that she didn't know of a man, living or dead, that could surpass him. But knowing Tristan's past behavior, and experiencing Lord Berringbone's kindness, she couldn't help but wonder if it was indeed the other way around. That the elder brother was the better of the two.

"I believe I will be. I need to keep up the physical conditioning that Ophelia has prescribed, but that shouldn't be too much trouble. Lord Rascomb is going over the packing lists for everyone. I think I'm most nervous about forgetting something."

"Understandable. It's quite an undertaking. You did not mind sleeping out under the stars?"

"The first night I wasn't sure about it—I thought we'd at least have a tent. But after that, I was too tired to care, or too enamored with the stars to be bothered." Lord Rascomb explained how heavy a tent was, and how they ought to acclimate to sleeping in the open. They wouldn't always, but in a safe place like the ruins of Berringbone Hold, they could manage.

Lord Berringbone smiled, increasing his attractiveness once again. "I do enjoy sleeping out under the stars. It feels so freeing, somehow."

Eleanor smiled in return. "I agree completely. The expectations of the world seem far away, and the stars seem so close."

"Exactly," he said.

Their connection was real, and they smiled at one another, an acknowledgment of a moment shared. Eleanor wondered if she'd allowed the wrong brother to kiss her.

$$\sim\!\blacklozenge\!\sim$$

Chapter Eight

TRISTAN ACCIDENTLY TIGHTENED his grip on Lady Emily's hands, only realizing it when the lady made a squeak of pain.

"My apologies," he said, glancing back at her for a moment. It was difficult to tear his attention away from Herringbone and Eleanor, dancing. Dancing and *smiling*. He didn't like that one bit.

It was bad enough that Ophelia had all but painted him as the worst kind of villain in front of Eleanor, but now Arthur was out there charming the woman? It wasn't exactly fair to have his family conspire against him.

"Are you quite all right?" Lady Emily asked.

She was the human equivalent of plain porridge. She was the color of dishwater, all over. Her hair, her skin—even her gowns were the most tepid and sober colors. Really, her only recommendation was her status—the daughter of a marquis. That kind of pedigree was excellent, even if their family had no money. "Fine," he bit out.

"Ouch!" she yelped. "Sir, please pay attention. I'm afraid my toes cannot support us both."

Tristan winced. This was the behavior that Ophelia was complaining about, wasn't it? His single-minded focus on his own wants and needs? "My sincere apologies, Lady Emily, I am distracted."

"I can see that well enough, and my toes can feel it."

That was a bit sharper than he expected from plain porridge. "I will make an effort to do better. You deserve my attention as my dance partner."

Lady Emily narrowed her eyes at him in contemplation. "You know, you'd be quite handsome if you'd stop being such an arse."

Tristan missed a step, and barely missed Lady Emily's toes. "I beg your pardon?"

"If I wasn't well-acquainted with your personality, I would mistake you as the better-looking brother. But as it is, Arthur has you soundly beat."

"*Arthur?*" he asked. When did this woman get leave to speak of his brother so intimately?

"He's very kind, and if I may say so, much funnier than you."

Tristan didn't like this conversation at all. "My jokes are excellent, I'll have you know."

She looked at him with something like pity. "If you want to win the heart of the girl Arthur is dancing with, which is what I assume has you so preoccupied, I think you'd better rehabilitate yourself."

"I need no such thing," Tristan said, his pride doubly insulted.

Lady Emily shrugged. "Then you will love to have the attentions of my cousin, Miss Perkins. She's very pretty, but I will tell you from childhood experience, she is as mean and selfish as they come. I have the scars to prove it."

Tristan scoffed and let his mouth open and close as if he had any reasonable comeback of his own. He did not wish to be seduced by the beautiful and mean Miss Perkins. Part of why he liked Eleanor so much was that she wasn't mean. She was nice. "Oh," he said, when he began to realize what Lady Emily was really saying. "Ohhhhh."

She was saying *he* was mean and selfish. And if he pursued Eleanor, she would either reject him outright, or he might scar her for life. Or would she turn mean and selfish too? None of those outcomes were acceptable. But wait. "When did you start calling my brother Arthur?"

Lady Emily gave him another pitying smile. "Many years ago. I had hoped we would marry, but alas, my family hasn't the money."

"Hasn't the money?" Tristan repeated. Hang on, wasn't that what he had been thinking to himself earlier? When was his cynicism remotely acceptable?

"Arthur made it clear that he needed to marry a woman with a good dowry, which is something I cannot promise. We decided to wait, as my father had some investments he thought might come to fruition. But sadly, they did not. My dowry is virtually non-existent."

"But we don't need money," Tristan sputtered. Did they? He knew nothing of the family finances because it wasn't his business. He was the spare, off to do the lofty business of finding himself.

Lady Emily raised her eyebrows. "Don't you? I can't name a single aristocratic family that is flourishing. Owning land worked before the industrial revolution. Now what do we do? Give parties to fundraise? Sell our homes? The modern world is not built for the system created."

Tristan winced. He hadn't ever bothered thinking about any of this. Because he'd been busy feeling sorry for himself, and about how limited his choices were. When in fact, his father had the right of it: he had the most freedom out of all of them. Wasn't that an awful realization to have in public?

"Mr. Bridewell, I would normally be a bit more circumspect, but your mouth is hanging open."

Tristan shook himself out of his reflective stupor. "My deep apologies, Lady Emily. I only now realized the absolute depth of my selfishness. It can be troublesome at times to find the correct perspective, since we cannot see outside ourselves. We only see our own hardships, and not the hardships of others."

Lady Emily's eyes seemed to soften. "I believe they call it maturity."

"Rarely has anyone accused me of such a state."

Lady Emily said nothing, but continued to watch him as they danced.

"I assure you this is a painful realization for me." Tristan became aware of how absurd it might be to say such a thing while dancing, as it did not seem to show it as painful. But he hoped Lady Emily would understand.

"I imagine." Lady Emily's eyes flicked over his shoulder, no doubt to where Herringbone and Eleanor danced.

"Are you in love with him?" Tristan asked, blurting out the words before he could think better of it. He hadn't meant to be so forward, but then, so much of his life was happenstance and reactions, and not the product of thought and intention.

Lady Emily gave him another assessing look. "I suppose it doesn't matter."

"I rather think it does."

"Are you in love with her?" she challenged right back.

Tristan turned them so he could once more gaze at Eleanor, and her regimental posture, the beautiful dark tresses braided and tucked and curled this way and that. "No, but I think I could be."

"That's quite an admission."

"Is it?" It felt nowhere near enough. He wasn't in love with her—for that seemed too large of an idea for how he felt. But he respected her, thought her beautiful, and if he were to marry any woman, she would seem a good personal match, even if they weren't a terribly good social one.

"Your reputation has never been one of a poet, prone to flights of fancy."

Tristan chuckled. "Yes, my love affairs have all been very transactional."

They danced on, each smile on Eleanor's face a stab in Tristan's stomach. Every interested raised eyebrow of Herringbone's felt like a blow to the head. They shouldn't be getting along so well.

Lady Emily sighed. "To answer your question, yes."

Tristan's attention drew back to his dance partner. "Yes?"

"Have you already forgotten your question?" Lady Emily chastised.

Also, yes. He had forgotten. He'd forgotten because Herringbone's hand was on Eleanor's waist. Because they spoke and conversed and enjoyed polite conversation. Because Herringbone could smell her perfume and Tristan could not.

"I am in love with him," Lady Emily confessed. "I have been for years."

"Oh," Tristan missed a step, ruining the dance. "I hadn't realized."

"Why would you? What is the point of my *tendre*? I can pine all I like, but it will bring us no closer."

"Does he feel the same about you?" Tristan asked. It wasn't as if Herringbone shared his feelings with him. Or anyone, for that matter.

"I used to believe he did. I'm not so sure, anymore."

"It doesn't seem that impossible of a situation to me," Tristan said. "You are both titled, of the same class, and we are not in need of money, so what would be the difficulty?"

"Spoken like a second son," Lady Emily said with a dark laugh.

Tristan bristled. "It isn't as if you are a merchant's daughter."

Lady Emily's eyes narrowed. "No, rather, the other way 'round. Why should a daughter of a marquis marry down? Why marry a viscount when I could marry an earl, or a marquis, or a duke? They have money also."

Tristan did not like this conversation one bit. "Are you saying my family is not good enough for you?"

"I'm saying that the considerations of family are larger than one person. A second son may think of love, but the heir must think of the family legacy as a whole. As a woman must as well, since she will enter into a new family, raising the next scion."

"You make it sound like my existence is such a waste," Tristan said, not bothering to keep the bitterness from his voice.

"Not at all," Lady Emily said, her voice measured and kind.

"I'm saying that you have a freedom that Arthur does not. If you wish to marry the merchant's daughter, then by all means, you should."

They turned on the dance floor, and he caught sight of Herringbone and Eleanor again. Lady Emily had a point. What did it matter if his wife was not of the aristocracy? Especially if she came from money, that would excuse a great number of trespasses.

The set ended, and Tristan bowed to his partner. "Thank you for the conversation, Lady Emily. It has been most enlightening."

"Likewise," she said, rising up from her curtsy. Tristan escorted her back to her mother and wandered off to the terrace to get some air. He sat in the dark, thinking about wealth and class, adventure, and future. Seriously courting Eleanor would have to wait until after the expedition completed, which would be several years. They weren't even planning on going to the Alps until next year. But if Eleanor wasn't a part of the expedition team, it wouldn't matter. He could court her in the manner she deserved.

The cold seeped through his trousers, and he knew he should get up and go back in. He had promised a dance to someone, though he couldn't remember who, since it wasn't Eleanor. Ophelia was the expedition leader, and therefore, the person who could get Eleanor off the team.

This wasn't the moment to go to her about such a personnel change.

"Oh!" A feminine voice exclaimed.

Tristan was on his feet before he squinted against the light of the house. "My sincere apologies, Eleanor."

"I didn't realize you were out here," she said. Her face was shadowed by the light of the ballroom spilling out behind her.

"I'm glad that you allowed me to call you Eleanor," he responded. His body warmed, whether that was from no longer sitting on the stone wall or being in her presence, he didn't care.

She stepped closer to him. "I'm surprised you aren't in there, charming everyone."

"You think I'm charming?" He liked that idea. He also liked how she sputtered and backtracked in the face of his confidence. She was adorable when she was on her back foot. He crept forward as she stuttered out a confirmation.

"I mean that it is a room full of your friends."

Tristan nodded. "And yours too, now. But you aren't in there either. And I know for a fact that your dance card is full."

"It is," she admitted, her fingers twisting the ribbon that dangled from her waist.

"Are you tying a knot right now?" he asked.

She snatched her fingers away. "It's an old habit. I do it when I'm nervous."

He stepped closer, trying very hard to keep a grin off his face. "Are you nervous right now? With me?" Because that was a very good sign.

"Well yes," she said. "Last time we were alone together, you kissed me and then ran away as fast as a racehorse. I'm afraid if you took that speed through the ballroom, you'd run over Mr. Moon's aged mother, and I don't think she can take the excitement."

Tristan laughed. "So are you nervous for me to kiss you, or for the health of Mrs. Moon?"

"Frankly, both." Eleanor smiled wide enough that he could see it despite the shadows.

Tristan didn't care who saw or what might happen. He took the last two steps towards her and tilted her head up, roundly kissing her. It was heady embracing her, the softness of her body melting into his. Catching her gasp as it escaped her soft lips was sheer delight. He gathered her up, encircling her waist, trying to pull her ever closer. Because he was wild about her, and it didn't need to be a secret.

She was funny and capable. She was intelligent and kind. She was beautiful and soft. What was he thinking, putting off a woman such as this?

Her hands pressed against his chest, clutching his lapels. She kissed him back with as much fervor. Her lips crushed against his, and when he tested her willingness with his tongue, her mouth opened.

He gripped her tighter, taking small steps back. His body was aflame, and all he could think was sitting down on that cold stone wall and pulling her on top of him. He explored her mouth, consumed by her scent and her taste.

Abruptly she pulled away, her eyes dark, her chest heaving in the most tantalizing way. If his body hadn't already gone hard a minute ago, the sight of her would undo him now.

"But—" she panted.

Tristan loosened his arms. As much as he'd have liked to smother all her protests with more sweet kisses and exploratory hands beneath her skirts, he was not the sort of gentleman who pressed on in unwanted circumstances. "May I court you?"

She stared at him, obviously startled at his question. "What?" She pulled away, out of his arms, which he did not care for at all.

"May I court you? I think we would suit." Tristan watched like a starving orphan as she licked her swollen lips.

"I'm sorry, I—" Eleanor took another step backwards, putting her hands on her hips.

Terror pinged through his body. Had he misinterpreted the signs? She had been kissing him most enthusiastically.

"I'm surprised, that's all," she said finally. "I thought you were a bit more of a rogue."

Tristan winced, remembering how his sister had protested his nicknaming habits. "I was a rogue. I would like to think of myself as—currently—mature."

Eleanor chewed her bottom lip, and it was challenging to leave her to the endeavor alone. She folded her arms across her chest, giving him a display of her very excellent breasts that were very difficult to not pay attention to. "You were a boy when you thought all of them up?"

Tristan looked up to the sky, for he certainly could not look at her while he thought. "All the ones that stuck, anyway."

"Justine does pick on you something terrible." Eleanor's arms dropped.

"She does," he agreed, swaying closer to her.

"But. . ." Eleanor looked at him, her eyes dropping to his lips.

"But you'll kiss me twice and just leave me out to dry? Use me up? Tarnish my reputation?" He couldn't help but smile as he once again closed the gap between them. "Love me and leave me?"

She gave him a schoolmarm's smile and shook her head, acknowledging his teasing. "I thought you were perhaps kissing me out of boredom."

"How utterly insulting." A thought occurred to him. "Wait. You weren't kissing *me* out of boredom, were you? As an experiment, I can understand. Being irresistibly drawn to me, also, very understandable."

"You do have a high opinion of yourself," Eleanor said.

"*I* don't have a high opinion of myself; these are all things people have told me. I'm merely repeating gossip. Well, gossip and empirical facts."

Eleanor laughed softly and shook her head again. "You're incorrigible."

"I'm dogged," he said, trying to catch her eye, but the shadows made it difficult. "I'm serious, Eleanor. I'd like to court you. We'll be proper about it and everything."

She considered him, and it made him want to straighten his spine and pull down his waistcoat. Prove he was worthy of her scrutiny. "I think I'd like that."

"Excellent!" His heart leapt. This was the future—Lady Emily was right. By God, what a smart girl. He should really recommend her to his brother. "I will take care of everything."

"May I tell people?" she asked.

"Why would you not tell people?" he asked. "Are you ashamed of me?"

She laughed, and dear God, it sounded like tiny silver bells tinkling. "No, I thought you might be ashamed of me. I am a merchant's daughter, after all."

"No, Eleanor. You are an heiress. There's a difference. An heiress has power. A merchant's daughter is . . . I don't know. Something else entirely." He reached out and squeezed her hand. "Let me speak to your father formally before we say anything. Give me the evening to sort it?"

"I can wait that long," she said. "For you."

ELEANOR PASSED THE rest of the dance in a daze. She would stare at Tristan from across the room, and he would look up, as if feeling the heat of her gaze, and smile. It melted her completely. Could this be what happiness was? She couldn't even remember what they discussed when he danced with her. She was no longer herself—she was far too dreamy for her practical self.

Even her mother remarked on her demeanor.

"I don't believe I've ever seen you this at home in public." Her mother leaned in and took a discreet sniff.

"I haven't imbibed, Mama," Eleanor said, wanting to swat her away, wondering if she would smell Tristan on her clothes. His distinctive scent of fresh air mixed with Cloverbee's clean lemon verbena soap.

"One would hardly blame me for suspecting, given how you're acting."

"It's the fresh air, Mama. It does one a world of good." And it did. She would climb Ben Nevis in a month. She would marry Tristan next year. Then they would climb the Matterhorn as a married couple. Adventurers together! It sounded so delightful. Right out of an adventure novel itself.

How her life had changed as a result of Ophelia's ribbon distress! She should send that modiste a note of thanks.

Tristan danced with her and escorted her into supper. They talked about mountains and knots, London and horses, dockside and Grosvenor Square. He was adept at conversation, making her laugh and parrying back when she managed to squeeze in a joke as well. Her father caught her eye from down the table, raising his eyebrows. When she nodded, he broke out into a wide smile. Her father would be associated with an aristocratic family after all. He wouldn't get to be his own earl, and neither would she be a lady, but it was close enough proximity that her children might be eligible to marry nobility.

Oh, their children. A whole new idea for her to fantasize over. She decided to not tell anyone officially until Tristan had a chance to speak to her father. Or his father. Or whomever he needed to in order to make their courtship proper.

What did that mean for a man like Tristan? Carriage rides in Hyde Park? Chaperone-approved balls? She couldn't believe that at twenty-five, she finally had a suitor. After being ignored for so long, someone finally saw her. And he was handsome and accomplished and an aristocrat on top of it all. She felt like she was in a fairy tale.

When the ball concluded, and Ophelia, Justine, and Prudence swarmed her, whisking them upstairs to bed, Eleanor didn't even feel tired. Her feet didn't hurt, and she could have danced for hours more.

"What's going on with you?" Justine asked, poking her in the ribs as they ascended the stair.

"Me?" Eleanor repeated, because she couldn't think of anything to say.

"You seem very . . . happy." Prudence observed, a secretive smile on her face.

Did Prudence know? "I had a lovely time. That was the best ball I've ever been to," Eleanor said.

"Private balls are much better than public ones," Justine agreed. "Don't you think, Ophelia?"

"Hm?" Ophelia asked. It was then that Eleanor noticed a troubled look on Ophelia's face. "I'm sorry, I wasn't listening."

"Tired?" Prudence suggested.

"Yes," Ophelia said, perhaps a bit too quickly. "Just tired. I'll see you all down at breakfast in the morning."

"But—" Justine called as Ophelia peeled off from their group and went to her room. Ophelia's door shut behind her before Justine could finish her sentence. "But I thought we were all going to undress together, save the maids some work."

"I think I'd like to go to my room as well," Eleanor said. She wasn't tired, but she didn't think she could keep her mouth shut about Tristan asking to court her if they began talking about the evening.

"Well." Justine huffed. "Breakfast it is."

Eleanor gave a weak smile as they all entered their own rooms, one by one. Breakfast might be very enlightening.

—◆—

Chapter Nine

Eleanor crept downstairs, wondering if the meal would even be set up this early. Perhaps she could bother someone for a cup of tea, at least. She hated to make a fuss. But as she approached the corridor, she heard the sounds of a whispered argument.

She didn't know what she should do—she certainly didn't want to be accused of eavesdropping, but she also didn't want to suffer the embarrassment of walking into a fight. Perhaps it was merely two servants having a disagreement over where to place the chafing dishes. Eleanor squared her shoulders and continued on to the breakfast room.

"—oh! Miss Piper, you've arrived!" Tristan swanned over, all smiles, his hand outstretched.

Eleanor's stomach flipped, knowing that he would soon be courting her properly, and they would have a chance for yet another kiss. But she looked behind him, seeing only Ophelia. In fact, it was only the two siblings in the room. They were the ones arguing? She hoped they weren't arguing over her. Did Ophelia object to Eleanor joining their family?

"I have wonderful news, by the by. Oh, where are my manners? Did you sleep well?" Tristan looked at her with such joy he was radiating.

"I did, thank you." Eleanor allowed him to guide her to the table.

"Do you take tea or coffee or chocolate in the morning? This seems like something I ought to know."

"Tea, please. And you?" Eleanor sank into her chair, feeling her head might be spinning a bit. He was so very much, right here. She thought she would have a moment to sip at a cup of tea and stare out the window, but instead he was barraging her with questions and information and looking like Apollo.

"Oh, tea, of course. Can't call oneself a proper Englishman if one doesn't support tea. Coffee is for the Americans, the unruly blowhards."

Was he referring to Prudence? Eleanor would never be so cruel. "I beg your pardon?"

"You know, the Boston Tea Party? Dumped the tea in the river? Not a part of Britain any longer after that stunt?"

It was too early to be assaulted by history. "Oh, yes. Of course. Forgive me."

"Eleanor isn't a morning person, Tristan. Let her have a moment." Ophelia sat down opposite, studying Eleanor's face.

"Oh, is that what it is? You do seem a bit stunned." Tristan pulled back from her.

"Did you not notice when we spent an entire week together in the woods?" Eleanor managed.

"I thought that was just because we went running first thing in the morning," Tristan said, frowning. "You seemed fine after that."

"I was anything but fine, but it was barely morning after we were done." Eleanor accepted the small pot of tea from the footman, relieved to have the balm for her slow mind at the ready.

"Touché," Ophelia said, accepting her own cup. "So you see, Tristan, Eleanor is fine for running, that isn't a concern."

"Is it a concern?" Eleanor asked, feeling as if the rug was pulled out from underneath her. She hadn't known that there was a problem with her performance. She'd improved towards the end of the week. Even went on that extra run. The one where

Tristan kissed her—not because he was bored or restless, rather because he *wanted* to.

"Don't worry about it," Tristan said. "It'll all work out."

"Will it?" Ophelia challenged.

Tristan gave his sister a hard look. "Yes. It will."

Eleanor had a feeling a discussion was being had in front of her, and she didn't like it. Shades of her childhood were projected here, and she wasn't having it. "I'm sorry, I would like to know what's happening here."

"Yes, Tristan, why don't you tell Eleanor what you asked me." Ophelia crossed her arms.

Now Eleanor was very confused. It didn't sound like Ophelia was against Eleanor at all. Rather that she was defending her.

"I'd rather wait until everything has been figured out," Tristan said, his voice firm, but no match for his sister.

"No, no. This is quite important. Eleanor needs to know."

"Needs to know what?" Eleanor asked, looking between the two siblings.

Tristan looked down at his hands, so Eleanor looked to Ophelia.

"He's asked me to take you off the expedition."

Disbelief settled into Eleanor's mind. "That can't be right. Tristan, tell her what's really going on."

"Yes, Tristan, I would hate for Eleanor to be kicked off the team for a misunderstanding." Ophelia's voice was flat and unforgiving.

Eleanor couldn't believe what she was hearing. She worked so hard for this. Maybe she wasn't very good at running, but she believed that once on the mountain, she could push herself as well as the other women.

"I did ask her to release you from your obligations to the expedition." Tristan kept looking down, not meeting her eye.

Eleanor looked in her own lap, his words reverberating in her head. She couldn't believe it. Why would he ask to court her one night, and then kick her off the expedition the next day? There was no explanation. He was toying with her. Tears formed in her eyes. Who would be so cruel? She stood up.

She wasn't the sort of person to have a waspish thing to say, or a slap to the cheek for impudence. The only grace in a moment such as this was dignity. She turned to leave, but he grasped her arm.

"Don't go," Tristan said.

She looked back at him, not knowing what was going on. Tears were about to fall, and she certainly didn't want to suffer the embarrassment of such a display in front of him. Not when it was his cruel sport that caused them. "Why?"

"Because you must understand why I asked you to be off the expedition. It isn't for whimsy. It's because you *must* be off the expedition. So that I may court you. Properly. As you agreed."

Ophelia gasped.

Justine and Prudence walked into the breakfast room at this moment. Spying Tristan's grip on her arm, and Eleanor's tear-filled gaze, they must have concluded something quite big was afoot.

"I didn't know I had to choose one or the other," Eleanor said, straightening herself. She could handle this with dignity.

"Why didn't you just tell me, you nincompoop?" Ophelia asked.

"I still need to speak with our father and her father." Tristan searched Eleanor's eyes.

"Why did you ask me last night? I had the very devil of a time sleeping because of it!" Ophelia said. "And why does she have to choose? Why not both?"

Tristan threw an exasperated look at his sister, giving Eleanor a moment without his intense gaze on her. She blinked hard, trying to will away the tears. She didn't want to choose.

"Because this expedition must be above reproach! You can't have a courting couple on a remote mountain. That's scandal, and then you won't be able to make a decent match, nor Miss Brewer, and if you think women's mountaineering can survive upper class scandal, you haven't been paying attention."

"What are you even talking about?" Justine asked, her arms crossed.

"The queen wants to bar mountain climbing all together, thanks to the death of Lord Francis Douglas. Throw in some ruined young noblewomen, and you've set back mountaineering for decades."

"I don't believe you," Justine said.

Tristan got to his feet. "You can't possibly not have thought about this."

"About what?" Ophelia said.

Tristan gripped his palms together, his frustration palpable. Eleanor didn't like it. Most of all, she could understand his point. The women who had gone before them, who'd climbed lesser peaks, had done so with respectability intact. There was discussion of all-female teams for this very reason.

"You want to continue mountaineering, yes? After the Matterhorn?" Tristan asked Ophelia.

"Of course. Climbing mountains is the only thing I want to do with my life." Ophelia stood now as well.

"You won't sell any books or guides or essays if you are thought of as a ruined woman. Men won't take you seriously because you are a woman, and women won't take you seriously because you are ruined. The only way to make this gambit successful is if you maintain the expedition's pristine reputation."

Eleanor looked at Ophelia, her expression stunned. Then she shifted over to Justine and Prudence. It was sinking in. But Eleanor suddenly knew her mind. All of what Tristan said was true. But if she had to choose, she would choose the mountain.

She might be lonely, she might never marry, but her father would settle money on her so that she'd never want for anything. And when she was an old and doddering spinster, she could at least point to her footnote in history. She could say she was a part of the women to first climb the Matterhorn. That was far more important than being a wife.

"I choose the mountain," Eleanor said, enunciating each word clearly. She didn't want to be misheard or have to repeat herself.

"What?" Tristan rounded on her. "But you agreed with me."

Justine chuckled softly, and Ophelia hissed his name in disapproval.

"No one yet knows you've asked to court me, so we shan't mention it. And no one needs know. I trust everyone here can keep a secret?" Eleanor looked at the other women, who all nodded. Justine had a devilish smile on her face.

"We can, but he can't," Justine said, pointing her finger.

"Then it will be on his head if his sister's reputation is ruined." Eleanor looked at him coolly. She didn't want to marry a man who would take her hard work from her. To live a life smaller in scope seemed not just unpalatable, but impossible. To give in to men like that awful Mr. Fulk was beyond comprehension.

She thought swiftly through the consequences. If they married before Ben Nevis, there would be scandal that Eleanor was pregnant, which would be the reason for the fast marriage. If they married after Ben Nevis, he could, in his husbandly wisdom, forbid her from going up the Matterhorn. She hadn't thought that last night, but his betrayal this morning certainly proved otherwise.

"But—" Tristan's hurt and disappointment was writ across his face.

She couldn't bear to witness it. She fled the room, hearing Prudence advise everyone to leave her be. The American seemed to be the wise one after all.

Chapter Ten

TRISTAN RETREATED TO the bathtub. Nothing a good soak and a dram or six of whisky couldn't fix. He'd been so sure about Eleanor. He'd never been sure of any woman—not ever. Not any of his actresses or dancers. Not any of his noble dance partners at the chaperone-approved celebrations. Eleanor had been different than the other women he'd met. She was patient and smart, interesting and witty. And she chose the mountain over him. A stupid fucking mountain that she'd never climbed.

Granted, if he were honest with himself, he would have done the same. Chosen the mountain over her. But he'd been outdoors his entire life. It was his identity. The only thing he was good at besides shallow conversation. To be rejected so roundly hurt like the devil.

It wasn't as if she'd been traipsing around mountains her whole life. This was her first taste of it, and she was going to give him up before she even knew if she liked it?

Perhaps he was easy to give up. He'd thought she was teasing last night when she'd accused him of kissing her out of boredom, and he turned the question back on her. Was he not good enough for her? Would she have given up the mountains if he'd had a title? If he'd been Lord Berringbone, would that have been enough?

He took another sip of his whisky, letting it burn down his throat. How was he supposed to face her after this? How were they going to be roped together, side by side, when he knew that he ranked below a pile of rocks for her affection? Would she even be able to be professional, given her inexperience? Or would he be the object of her scorn, and thus the object of all four women's scorn?

He knew how female friendships worked, having been at close proximity to Ophelia and Bad News for so long. What one despised, the other despised even harder on her friend's behalf. He groaned. But he'd be damned if *he* gave up the expedition! He was here first! In fact, he was far more necessary to the mission than Eleanor. She'd taught them some lovely knots, yes, but now they all knew them, so her worth was already spent.

She *should* stay home, out of harm's way. Yes, that was really it. Not only was her staying home better for the propriety of the mission, it was also for her safety. He ought to tell Ophelia and get her to understand that Eleanor had no business going to Ben Nevis, because she had absolutely no business going to the Matterhorn. The logic was flawless.

The whisky glass slipped from his hand and shattered all over the floor.

"Oh, damn it all," he said, peering over the tub. That was good whisky.

"Are you well, sir?" called Matthias. Now that they were back in civilization, he had a valet. Sometimes handy, other times, nothing but a nuisance.

But drunkenly surveying broken glass in his bathing chamber definitely constituted a lovely time to have a valet. "Matty! I've dropped my tumbler! Can you come sweep it up?"

There was a subtle banging, and then, "I'll just get the implements to do so. One moment."

Tristan sunk lower in the tub, allowing his drinking hand to drift below the surface. The water had started to feel cool, but to that one arm felt very warm indeed. That's what it was like being around Eleanor. He'd only gotten accustomed to her, having spent the week in the woods with women. Had he been in the woods with different women, well, he'd probably think he was in love with one of them, instead.

Because if he'd truly been in love, or rather, had truly wanted to *marry* Eleanor, well, then, he'd be much worse off than he was at the moment. He'd be . . . drunk in a bathtub? Ah yes. Touché, self.

No, he was infatuated with her, nothing more. Swept up in the emotion and excitement of an adventure. Beginner mistake. Perhaps that's why the Alpine Society didn't admit women. They'd all end up in love with their climbing partners. That would be the real tragedy.

The best thing he could do was leave. Well, the best thing to do would be to get out of the bathtub without cutting himself on the scattered glass. Then, the leaving. Jot off to London, hole up in his bachelor's rooms, find an actress or a singer to occupy himself for the month until Ben Nevis. Simple. Lacking in humiliation. Imminently doable.

First step: where the fuck was Matthias and a broom?

"I can't believe he would do such a thing," Ophelia said to Eleanor, giving comfort and support where it could be given.

"Thank you," Eleanor said, trying very hard to find her voice when Ophelia and Justine had talked without pausing for breath for the last few hours.

They'd excoriated Tristan the entire time, listing the arrogance and hubris needed to assume a woman would choose a man over an adventure. But it wasn't that which bothered Eleanor. It wasn't his idea that she might choose him over the Ladies' Alpine Society. It was that he'd thought to make her choose at all.

She had believed Tristan saw her. The real her. Not Captain Piper's pipsqueak daughter. Not Mrs. Piper's dutiful daughter and companion. She had thought he'd seen *her*, Eleanor. The girl who had sat in dusty rooms down by the docks, tying knots blindfolded and behind her back for the amusement of Captain Smythe's wife when she came to pick up his wages while he was at sea. Or even the Eleanor who played by herself because her parents didn't want her associating with the girls of the merchant class, hoping they could elevate themselves socially. But not having access to noblemen's daughters, there were no peers to befriend.

She'd been stuck in an odd place her whole life, and then she'd been swept up by Ophelia and Justine and Prudence, and there was Tristan: beautiful, shining, golden Tristan. A fairy tale prince.

A fairy tale prince who wanted her to give up the only place she'd felt welcomed. Once again, she'd become attached to a person who wanted her to be something she wasn't. To work for some unattainable status she couldn't do anything about.

Prudence put her hand on Eleanor's. "Would you like to go for a walk?"

It was hard to cut through Ophelia and Justine's well-meaning and persistent chatter, but Prudence was so much wiser than her years. Perhaps that's what America did to a girl. Eleanor nodded, and Prudence managed to cut through the conversation.

"Eleanor and I will take a turn around the gardens. Ophelia, can you please check with your father about departure tickets to Scotland, just to make sure Tristan didn't manage to get Eleanor kicked off the expedition already?"

Ophelia paled at the words and shot to her feet. "Of course. Oh, how clever you are, Prudence."

"And—" Justine stood.

Prudence interrupted her. "You might want to go with Ophelia. You're awfully observant. And persuasive to boot! If anything has gone amiss, I'm sure you can convince Lord Rascomb to keep Eleanor on our team."

The two women set off towards Lord Rascomb's study, while Prudence took Eleanor by the arm to the garden room, which opened into the fenced rose garden. Once the door closed behind them, Eleanor took the biggest breath of fresh air she could manage.

"You looked a little besieged," Prudence observed, her arm still through Eleanor's.

The sun was bright through the clouds, warming her cheeks despite the chill in the air. "Oh, shouldn't we get our bonnets?"

Prudence shrugged. "I think our sanity is worth more than a pale forehead at this point, don't you think?"

Eleanor smiled. "Of course. But this might be the first time I've been outside without a hat in ages."

Prudence gave her a little shove with her shoulder. "We're living dangerously."

The clutching sensation in Eleanor's stomach eased. The pebbled dirt crunched under her feet, and a sense of normalcy returned. "I'm not used to so much . . . talking."

Prudence smiled. "I grew up with my mother and her sister together in the house, so there was always chatter. I don't mind it, but I'm like you—sometimes I prefer my solitude. Especially if I need to think."

Eleanor let out a shaky breath. "Perhaps that's my difficulty. I don't need to think. I am feeling far too much to think."

"Also a very reasonable course of action."

They walked in silence amidst the thorny stalks of would-be roses. It was impossible to tell now what all the garden held. The clouds covered the sun, cooling the air even further. Eleanor began to wish for a hat again.

"It's only that—" Eleanor's voice cracked. She was grateful that Prudence didn't urge her onward, but rather waited for Eleanor to collect herself before she continued. "It's only that I got my hopes up."

Prudence let the words sit in the air before commenting. Eleanor liked that she had space to breathe when she spoke with Prudence. Things felt less . . . anxious, with her around.

"Hopes for what exactly? For marriage? Or for Tristan in

particular?"

It was time for Eleanor to employ the casual gesture the Americans seemed to favor, and she shrugged. "I'm not sure. Perhaps him. Perhaps it was because I felt like he really knew me. Understood that I needed to be a part of something like this expedition. And then when he tried to take it away from me, it felt like a—a—" Eleanor faltered, tears threatening again. She blinked them back.

"Like a betrayal?" Prudence suggested.

"Precisely," Eleanor said. "Like he hadn't known me at all. For if he had, he would have realized that these few months with the Ladies' Alpine Society have changed me irrevocably. I'm working so very hard to be worthy of the trip, to be capable like Ophelia. To be strong like you and Justine."

Prudence tugged Eleanor closer. "Do you know, I feel the same way? That I have to work so very hard to be seen as worthy? I haven't the knowledge of knots like you do. I haven't the experience like Ophelia. I haven't the sheer willpower of Justine. I'm just little old me, Prudence, from Minneapolis, Minnesota. Not that I would recognize it. I haven't been there in years."

"But you are extraordinary, Prudence. Me? I'm just no one. From London. Do you know how many people are from London? Millions. I haven't been anywhere as interesting sounding as Minneapolis." The word stumbled on her tongue, but she liked saying it. The place sounded strange and wonderful and full of possibilities.

"Then, Eleanor Piper, you are one in a million. Or possibly more. I haven't the slightest idea of the population of London." Prudence's soft smile bolstered Eleanor.

Eleanor sighed. "How can you be so wise and motherly when you are my age? I wish I could be like that."

"You don't. Not really, anyway. I had to grow up far too fast and far too soon. But I wouldn't trade it. I'm twenty-five with a widow's freedom. What could be better?"

Eleanor nodded. Soon, she would be considered on the shelf. And she would have the freedom of a lifelong spinster, as long as her parents agreed to it. But she hated being at the behest of others. Prudence had no one to answer to but herself.

"Listen," Prudence continued. "We have a few more days here in the country to relax and prepare without anyone saying, 'Where are your corsets?' or 'Why are you running?' so we ought to enjoy it while we can. Maybe we can even sneak some extra desserts while we're at it."

Eleanor laughed. Tristan frowned at them all when they ate scones. He wanted less weight—less weight on the packs, less weight on their persons. He explained that it was all the physics of going up the mountain. The less to carry, the easier it would be on all of them. Eleanor understood the point. But now she wanted to be like Justine and eat an extra scone while staring Tristan down, if only to spite him.

"I would eat three scones every day if I could manage it. If only to see the look on Tristan's face when I slathered cream on them," Eleanor confessed.

"That's my girl!" Prudence said with a laugh. "But for now, what would you like to do? We have some time before Ophelia and Justine are free."

"Would you mind if I taught you some knots? It's oddly relaxing for me." Eleanor knew she was a strange person, and that might put Prudence off. But instead, Prudence accepted with a nod.

"I would love to know more. Let's get our practice ropes and order some tea. All will be right with the world."

⇥⇥⇥⇤⇤⇤

LONDON WAS MISERABLE. Certainly, there were Tristan's usual haunts and games. But he hadn't the focus for cards or gambling. Even Jacobs took his money one night. He drank too much, and his morning runs were nothing but the smell of spirits coming up through his pores.

He avoided the last few sessions of the Ladies' Alpine Society salons, which earned him beleaguered looks from his mother and outright disdain from Ophelia. His father said nothing. It made him wonder if the man knew. His father was by nature reticent and might not broach a subject for years if he deemed it uncomfortable. Tristan kept his head down, but still attended the weekly family dinners.

He also attended a few parties and balls, but only the ones he was fairly certain the Pipers would not be able to secure an invitation to. These were parties of the rich and the titled. He saw Lady Emily and her cousin, Miss Sophia Perkins. Miss Perkins was very pretty, and he didn't mind dancing with her one bit. Her interest was obvious. And he was fairly certain that she was more than game for a rendezvous in a dark library or garden maze.

But he never asked.

Lady Emily tried to discuss Eleanor with him during one of the assemblies, but stopped when she could see Tristan's reluctance. He didn't dance with Lady Emily again after that. He didn't want the reminder. Nor did he want the shame of thinking of her encouragement. If it hadn't been for her, Tristan would have never thought to throw caution to the wind and ask to court Eleanor. It was a truly ridiculous idea. A merchant's daughter? Not to mention the complete lack of responsibility it was for a man who had a hobby of climbing treacherous mountains to have a wife back at home. No, he needed to remain unattached. That was clear.

As long as he supported his sister's climbing career, which he intended to do for as long as possible, then he should not have attachments. It wasn't fair to keep someone waiting for months on end, wondering if he'd lived or died.

Ophelia called for another expedition meeting two weeks before they were set to depart for Scotland. Tristan contemplated not attending, until his father pulled him aside after the weekly meal and explained that he needed to participate in the planning, or he would be struck from the expedition.

Chastened, Tristan appeared on the Thursday as directed. He sat in his mother's drawing room, waiting for the rest of the company to descend. He was met first with thin and angular Mr. Leopold Moon, the young financier who was tracking the finances and investments of the expedition. The man was like a walking letter opener. He was sharp and pointed, and while normally that didn't bother Tristan at all, right now he was feeling much too raw to risk a cutting remark.

Tristan selected one of his mother's books to leaf through as they waited for the rest of the company to materialize. Ah, drat. It was sonnets. He really didn't care for sonnets at the moment. They were too curly for his taste. There was something about the Bard's poetry that felt like a curlicue, or something else equally baroque. He couldn't exactly put his finger on what made it so challenging to like them, but he was fairly certain the shape of it in his mind was enough.

Eleanor entered with Prudence. They seemed thick as thieves now, laughing and talking. Eleanor stopped short when she spotted him.

It gutted him to see her. She was stunning, with rosy cheeks and her hair shiny and lustrous. There was something else about her as well, that he couldn't quite place. She was clearly doing well without his interference. Pride pricked at him. He was barely getting through his days, and she was happy and hale, giving no thought to his suffering.

He should have known, really, that any woman allowing herself to be kissed out in the woods wasn't the type to be respectable. Even if he had been the one to initiate the kiss. He had, hadn't he? His very ego depended on him having some semblance of control, so he definitely must have been the person to start the kissing. Both times.

His body tightened in response to the memories of her. The feeling of that soft skin pressed against his. The silken texture of her lips on his. The gripping of her fingers on his chest. He swallowed and turned his attention back to the sonnets. The damned curling sonnets.

He glanced up at her. She was sitting next to Prudence on the sofa near the door. Likely because it was on the opposite side of the room from him. But it gave him a direct line of sight to her. Or perhaps she wanted to look at him, and examine his obvious distress.

Ophelia entered with his mother. Thank goodness. That meant the meeting would start soon. For wherever Ophelia was, Justine was not far behind. Tristan concentrated on his sonnets. His mother approached.

"Shakespeare, is it?" she asked.

Tristan made a very enlightened noise.

"I thought you hated Shakespeare." His mother tilted the book with her finger so she could see what he was reading.

"Only the sonnets," he said.

"Which," she observed, "is precisely what you are reading. How interesting."

"I enjoy pain." Tristan watched as Justine entered and flounced towards Ophelia. All the while he studiously avoided looking at Eleanor.

"Clearly." Tristan watched as his mother's gaze drifted to Eleanor, who was as pointedly not looking at him as he was not looking at her. "Tristan, perhaps—"

"Please, Mama." He closed the book. His father appeared, which signaled the start of the meeting and would prevent a humiliating conversation.

She held up her hands, her cane dangling from her thumb, indicating she would let him be for the moment. Tristan wished the whole thing with Eleanor could be erased from his memory. As if it never happened. What was worse was that nothing *did* happen. Flirtation and a few kisses did not a love affair make. So why was it so damned difficult to get back to some semblance of normalcy?

Ophelia stood and called their meeting to order. They discussed Scotland, as it was now only two weeks away. There was inventorying of equipment to do, the last checks for each item to ensure they were still in pristine condition. Ophelia handed out a packing list for each of them.

Tristan looked his list over, frowning when he looked at the clothing section. "Fee, why did you include petticoats, and what is this? Rags? Rags for what?"

Justine tittered. He shot her a look. That was something that hadn't changed.

"This is a standard packing list for our expedition. Since we are six in number, with the majority female, I standardized our list according to our needs. You may not take petticoats as you so desire." Ophelia spoke as if she'd practiced this speech. She likely had.

"This is not how other mountaineers pack." He couldn't resist a parting shot.

"We are not other mountaineers. We are these mountaineers," Ophelia shot back, gesturing to herself and the other women seated next to her. "May we move on? Or do you need more clarification of the packing demands?"

Tristan grumbled his assent, knowing he'd lost face. Frustration boiled inside. He felt stepped on. He felt dismissed.

Ophelia prattled on about a few more details. Mr. Moon stood and reported on the finances and the investments. Tristan didn't bother to listen. It wasn't anything he cared about. Second son, and all that. He was the drone in this hive of bees.

"Are we done?" Tristan asked, straightening himself from against the bookshelf.

Ophelia frowned at him. "I suppose so. But I'd like to remind everyone to keep up their skills and fitness levels. The weather reports are showing that Scotland is experiencing a rather cold spring. We may have a bit of a slog ahead of us."

Tristan crumpled the packing list and threw it at the fireplace, stalking out of the room. Why did he sign up for an adventure like this, when he could be a part of a real expedition? He was a member of the Alpine Society, something that only his father could boast being a part of. Those were the real explorers. The real mountaineers. Instead, he was babysitting his sister and her frilly debutantes.

He walked directly to Blakely's flat, not far from his own. The man was just getting up, but ready for mischief.

ELEANOR CHECKED OVER the trunks. She had run through her packing list and the trunks three times. Her heart beat faster at the thought of tomorrow's journey. Tomorrow would be the farthest she'd ever been from home. And also the farthest she'd been from her parents. And the start of a new piece of her life that was hers and hers alone.

"I don't understand," her mother's voice carried down the hallway. "Haven't they been working towards this for months? Why would it take so long in Scotland to climb that silly hill?"

Her father's grumbly voice didn't carry through the walls as clearly, but he made some kind of response. They both appeared in her doorway shortly.

"I didn't realize you would be gone so long," her mother said, carrying a handkerchief in her hand, as if she might actually have been crying. Had she?

"I gave you the itinerary weeks ago," Eleanor said. "Ophelia is very thorough."

Her mother waved her hand in dismissal. "Oh! It was so long, I couldn't be bombarded with so much information all at once! Nor do I feel that it's fair for you to ambush me with this kind of extended vacation." She sniffed and dabbed with her handkerchief.

Eleanor smiled at her histrionic mother. This was her way of saying Eleanor would be missed. "We need to be closer to the mountain so we can observe weather patterns. Not to worry, we are meeting up with a local man who knows the area. The Bridewells have been corresponding with him for months. He'll be another member of our expedition."

Her mother sniffed in disdain.

Her father looked between his wife and Eleanor, and then took the opportunity to change the subject. "I'm impressed you'll be on the Special Scotch Express! What an achievement! London to Scotland in one day. My, oh my, that's technology! Industry! Innovation!"

She loved that her father would rather talk to fill the void of his wife's emotions than actually display any of his own. "It is. From Edinburgh, we'll travel to the Highlands. Then a few days to acclimate and adjust our equipment, if necessary. It's a decent plan."

"Do you feel ready?" her father asked, real concern showing in his eyes.

Eleanor almost felt like squirming under this much attention from her parents. So unusual. But she also rather enjoyed it. Her waist was trimmer, her arms more shapely. She'd finally figured out the burst of joy and energy one might find at the end of physical exertion. "I do. I'm stronger than I've ever been. It's remarkable how much more capable I feel than I did a few months ago."

Her father looked at the ground and shuffled his feet, clearing his throat. She suspected it was to avoid showing the tears in his eyes.

"I always wanted to do something like this," her mother said.

Both Eleanor and her father rounded on her.

"Why are you both looking at me like that? Of course I did. Something big and extraordinary. Make my mark on history."

"Like climbing a mountain?" Eleanor asked.

"If it had been presented to me, I would have taken it. The best way to get out of Kent was to marry your father. So I did. It was the biggest adventure offered." Her mother gave her father a doe-eyed look of flirtation.

A bittersweet twinge filled Eleanor's heart. That was how love was, or at least, what she'd thought it was.

"Well." Her father cleared his throat and turned back to Eleanor. "I hope you have everything prepared."

Eleanor surveyed her trunks again. "I believe so. I've gone over the luggage three times."

"Well, just in case you need something to distract you from your companions," her father said, fishing something out of his coat pocket. "Here is something I thought might be diverting."

Eleanor took the brown paper package from her father. It was clearly a book, but when she ripped the paper open, she couldn't help the quizzical look on her face. "*The Ingoldsby Legends?*"

Her father shrugged. "It's a new edition. Besides, it was that or a biography of Mary Queen of Scots. This one seemed more optimistic."

"Thank you. I have no doubt it will be of great benefit." Eleanor hugged it to her chest. Any distraction from Tristan would be welcome.

She'd hated seeing his perfect golden mane at the last meeting. He was surly and rude, not bothering to greet any one of them, let alone look at her. It made her heart sink.

Mistakenly, she'd hoped there was a way out of this mire with everything she wanted. They could have a secret courtship, and if they suited, they could marry between the Ben Nevis climb and the Matterhorn. There was so much time between the two that it wouldn't be seen as scandalous in the least.

And she would marry him as long as he promised that she would be climbing the Matterhorn. If only the guarantee were there, she could take the leap. Perhaps they could put it somehow into a contract. But his face had made it clear; there was to be no reconciliation. His regard was clearly lost forever. And she'd done it to herself. It was a modern world, and she was the architect of her future, for better or worse.

Her father had asked her once, in the morning after Lord

Berringbone's ball, if he should expect to hear from Tristan. Eleanor hadn't managed to keep her tears to herself at that moment. Her father had given her a pitying tap on the shoulder with a bit of a squeeze. The height of his paternal affection. It was the best he could do, and she knew it.

"Well," her mother breathed, as if nothing more could be done about any problem in the world. "I must be off to my garden group. It meets in less than an hour, and I'm sure I look ghastly from this horrid display of emotion."

"Your garden group is an excuse for ladies to drink alcohol out of doors in the afternoon," her father grumbled.

"Yes," her mother agreed. "And I quite like it."

They left, doddering down the hallway, bantering back and forth as they'd always done, so wrapped up in each other that there was no room for Eleanor. Their sudden absence gave her a pang of loneliness. She'd hoped to find her person that would be the answering partner to all her witticisms. But at twenty-five, with an adventure pending, it wasn't likely.

That must be the thing about growing up: learning to put certain things behind oneself. Understanding that some doors close forever, whether one is ready for them to or not.

Sometime later, a maid delivered a large box. Inside was a beautifully tailored traveling costume in a dark mauve. It was sleek and serviceable, not garish, but would set off her complexion wonderfully. A small felt hat was nestled in the box, a matching color. It would be the envy of her friends. Eleanor smiled. Her parents were strange, but they did support her. They tried their best.

⁓◆⁓

Chapter Eleven

TRISTAN STILL TASTED the bitter black coffee in the back of his throat. He was hungover, and it was loud, and the heavy urine smell of the train platform was nauseating. Not that he would admit such to his father or anyone. It was merely the tattered star on top of the last few weeks—which had been an epic display of debauchery that he was now not particularly proud of. Partially because while he'd *meant* to debauch women, had even found his way to a brothel with a few good friends, he couldn't manage to get his body to agree.

The women in very little clothing lounging about the brothel's parlor had absolutely appealed to him. But the thought of Eleanor twisted him into so many knots, he didn't want to so much as feel a feminine hand on his shoulder, let alone his cock.

So he'd drunk instead. And drunk. And drunk. Even Blakely noticed, and he wasn't the sort of bloke who noticed much.

The sound of the trains rattled his head, building up pressure, and while the steam might exhale on the train, it did nothing of the sort in his brain.

"Quite all right?" his sister shouted at him. Justine stood by, looking off in the distance, clearly bored.

He winced a response that he hoped was an affirmative. The porter had taken care of their trunks, so there was nothing for him to do but stand there like a complete idiot. His mother, along as the chaperone for the young women, straightened her gloves

152

once more. They bunched up on her cane, a sensation he knew she disliked.

Their train would arrive shortly. Ophelia had told them all to arrive twenty minutes early, and then told them the departure time was earlier than it truly was, to make sure they were all accounted for. Tristan wanted to believe that trick was for Justine, who was chronically late, but it was likely more for him, who was more often chronically later than Justine.

Prudence and Eleanor arrived, their low-heeled boots clacking through the station. It was an early hour, but Eleanor looked refreshed and ready in a deep reddish-hued traveling costume. It made her hair look as deep and rich as the mahogany banisters at his childhood home. She looked him square in the eye, purposeful.

It made him stumble back a step, as if she'd struck him. He swallowed, tasting that burnt coffee flavor again.

"Mr. Bridewell. Good morning." Eleanor greeted him, and it seemed as if he'd swallowed his tongue. His tongue covered in fur.

"Miss Piper. Mrs. Cabot," he croaked. Mrs. Cabot looked at him with such pity, he thought perhaps she was a mind reader.

They went on to greet the rest of their party. The train screeched up at the station, the hiss of steam clouding the platform. The rest of them made idle chatter, discussing the stop in York for lunch, and what they'd all brought to keep them occupied during the journey.

Tristan hadn't brought anything for the train car. It honestly hadn't occurred to him. Thoughts of Eleanor had kept him busy the entire last month, and he'd done everything to distract himself from them, unsuccessful as he'd been. His mind felt like a slate that had been erased, but the chalk imprint of those moments on the garden balcony lingered, the image still hauntingly visible. His joy a hollow echo taunting him.

Eventually, they boarded the train. Tristan picked up a newspaper to eventually read, sitting across from his father. He felt the judgment from his father's gaze, but he cracked open the newspaper with flair, blocking his view.

Tristan read the first paragraph over and over again. He still wasn't sure what the article was about. His body buzzed with nervous energy, and his mind kept drifting to beautiful Eleanor, clad in her perfectly tailored traveling costume, sitting in the car behind them. There wasn't even a coherent thought he had about her—no lewd images, at least not ones he'd entertain in a public train car, no dwelling on past conversations or kisses—it was his inherent awareness of her that kept him agitated.

The train began to slow. They must be getting into York—the one stop for a meal on the long ride to Edinburgh. Tristan lowered the paper.

"Is it the news of Singapore, or the editorial on Mill's motion to give women the vote that has you so occupied?" his father asked.

"Pardon?" Tristan blinked rapidly, trying to cover the fact that he was so startled by his father's speech.

"I didn't dare interfere with your reading, but we have a few more hours to go. Might as well discuss the current events."

"On a full stomach," Tristan said, hoping he'd be able to glean something from the paper he'd stared at for five hours.

"Naturally," his father said. "On a full stomach."

Their quick meal of sandwiches wrapped in paper and hasty mugs of over-steeped and under-sugared tea was wildly unsatisfying. But the tea was warm, and that was something. Tristan stole glances at Eleanor, who seemed subdued. Was she nervous about climbing Ben Nevis? Was she sick from the rocking motion of the train? Or was she as aware of him as he was of her?

They boarded the train again, Tristan lingering to watch the last swish of wine-red disappear into the train car behind them. He turned to board the train, finding his father watching him.

"We are going to have a talk." The tone of his father's voice was clear; he would tolerate no arguments.

Tristan felt that same fear he'd had as a boy—the icy feeling of disapproval that seared him in ways he couldn't explain. He trudged up the steep train steps, trying to ready himself for what could only be a searing set-down.

His father's gaze had the weight of an iron anchor. The train lurched forward, trundling them towards Scotland. Tristan wondered how the machine could move when a force such as the Viscount Rascomb was onboard.

"You might as well come clean about it."

Tristan did his best to keep all the clever barbs he had in his mouth. "About what?"

"Ophelia has told me already."

"Really." Tristan knew this tactic. He'd employed it several times himself with his friends over the years. Usually it had to do with winnings from card games or who nicked the best bottles from his liquor cabinet. "What all has she told you?"

"That you are very likely in love with Eleanor Piper."

Oh, bollocks. She had told him. "I wouldn't say love. That's a bit extreme."

"But you'd requested to court her." His father narrowed his eyes.

Tristan shook his head, as if he could deny it. He wanted to deny it because he was embarrassed. It had been a foolish, impulsive desire, born out of an inappropriate passion. "Yes. I did."

"Is she compromised?"

Tristan's head snapped up. "Of course not! I would never!"

"You would never with Miss Turner, two years ago."

"That was different. She was an actress."

"And then the next one, I can't remember her name."

"Mrs. Fitzroy."

"Ah, yes. And I do believe I paid a bill for emeralds at the end of that affair." His father leaned back in the seat, still watching him closely. "Girls like Eleanor Piper won't settle for a bauble. Fathers like Mr. Piper won't settle for a bauble, either."

"I know that," Tristan said.

"And you understand that I cannot have you tomcatting around on this expedition. Your sister's entire future is at stake."

"I understand that. I was trying to do the proper thing, but—"

"But you cannot keep your hands in your own pockets? You know what will happen to every single drop of Ophelia's dream to become a mountaineer if she gets branded a harlot? Even by association?"

"I do, yes." Tristan had been trying very hard to protect that very thing, which is when everything went absolutely sideways.

"She'll lose all credibility. Not just the marriage prospects, but all of her writings that she has promised. It all goes away."

Tristan glared at his father. "I know."

"If you know, then why would you let your prick do the thinking?"

"What did I do?" Tristan flung his arms out, forgetting he was on a train momentarily and rapped the cold glass of the train car window with his knuckles.

"You kissed a girl and fell in love with her!" his father said, his face flushing temporarily red.

"I tried to make Ophelia remove her from the expedition. That way, I could properly court her, and there would be no issue about Scotland or the Matterhorn, or any of our preparations out in the countryside. Every woman's reputation would have been safe, if Ophelia had gone along with it." Tristan slumped back against his seat. "But then Ophelia got mad and demanded to know why I wanted Eleanor off the team, and then she told Eleanor what I'd asked, and then Eleanor broke the whole thing off! She chose the adventure over me. There. That's my humiliation. Would you like to rub my face in it a little more? I'm not sure I've got many more details for you to savor."

His father was silent. Tristan looked up, wanting to know the tone of his silence. His father turned his weighty gaze out the window.

"Do you not have another chastisement for me?" Tristan asked.

"No." His father heaved a sigh. "It makes a damned mess of everything. We'll have to work hard to build trust back up."

"I know."

"You asked the girl to pick which dream she wanted. The mountain or a marriage."

"Because I did not think she wanted the mountain in the first place." The shame that shot through him was foreign and altogether miserable. His father was silent, so he continued. "And she told me she wanted me."

"Everyone should be given a chance to follow their dream. Miss Piper included. Should you have a dream, as Ophelia has hers, as Arthur has his, as Portia had hers, I will give you all the backing you want."

Tristan felt the flush of shame for his lack of ambition. "I know."

"I know that it hasn't been easy for you, not being the heir."

Tristan shrugged. It wasn't that he wanted to be the heir. But sometimes, wasn't it nice to have a direction already laid out to follow? Instead of starting from nothing?

"But times are changing rapidly. While being a viscount is a heavy responsibility, I fear the job will only grow more difficult in the years to come. Arthur knows this. You, however, have the opportunity to start anew, free of the confines of the estate."

Tristan did his best not to wince. This was the speech he hated the most. The *how lucky you are, Tristan,* speech. Where his future was shiny and bright and open. And not a yawning pit of nothingness that he stared down every time he heard this.

"But perhaps you are more like Portia, and less like Ophelia and Arthur?" His father kept up his gaze out the window. "All Portia wanted was a family. She married a man she loved, living in the house of her dreams. Her ambition was simple. Perhaps that is more akin to what you want?"

Tristan shifted uncomfortably in his seat. He didn't *know* what he wanted. Not until he'd met Eleanor. And then he wanted her, by whatever terms she'd have him. But then, those terms weren't acceptable to her, so here they were.

His father continued when Tristan didn't answer. "I thought because of your dalliances that you were not a man who wanted a family. But now I'm not so sure."

A family? That seemed a leap of logic. "I believe that doesn't work with what I've been branded as."

An amused look graced his father's face. "And what is that?"

"Feckless. Irresponsible. And of course, devilishly handsome." He couldn't help tacking the joke on the end. The bravado he used, the only positive thing anyone ever said about him. Herringbone was the smart one; Ophelia was the driven one; Portia was the nice one. Tristan was the good-looking one. What did he have when the only asset he had was skin-deep?

Unexpectedly, his father frowned. "That's not what people say."

"It is. I've heard all of those," Tristan assured him. "Especially that last bit."

"It isn't a bad thing to be an attractive man."

"Indeed, it has served me well." Tristan looked out the window. "But what else am I?"

"You're the son of a viscount is what else," his father said, his tone sounding insulted.

Tristan nodded. Another tick of a box that had nothing whatsoever to do with him. His looks, the circumstance of his birth. He was lucky, not good.

"Not that I would ever condone this sort of compliment hunting for anyone else, but," his father said, staring him down as if they were adversaries, "but you are generous and thoughtful towards your sister, which not all men could be. You are excellent at putting aside your ego and letting her shine. You are strong, loyal, and determined."

"Determined?" Tristan laughed. "I could hardly say so. What have I done in my life that was determined? I have no ambition, I have no career or legacy to show for my twenty-six years on this earth."

His father looked down at his hands. "You saved your mother's life. And that only could have happened if you coupled your strength and determination. I'm not sure I could have saved her as you did."

Tristan scoffed. Who would not go to the end of one's strength to save their mother? Who would not risk it all for the person who loved them without conditions? "Anyone would have done what I did."

"Anyone might try, but not many could. You have a special streak of stubbornness that others don't. I've seen it in the mountains more than once. But that day—" His father choked, emotion winning out.

Tristan shifted uncomfortably. He didn't like thinking of that day—when his mother was caught in an avalanche. When they almost died. When she became crippled and he robbed her of the ability to climb a mountain forever. "If I'd been better, she'd walk without a cane."

His father shook his head, regaining his faculties. "No, if you hadn't done so well, she wouldn't be here at all. The cane is her blessing, not her curse."

Tristan hung his head. His father hadn't been there. Hadn't seen Tristan's fatigue. Hadn't seen when he'd had to stick his hands in his armpits because his fingers felt like ice. If he'd been stronger, if he'd been better, his mother would have been out sooner, they could have gotten down the mountain sooner, they could have gotten to a physician sooner, everything would have been better, and her leg wouldn't have been so mangled.

"The snow is what broke her leg. No matter what you did, her leg would be broken. But what you managed made sure it didn't kill her. You performed an extraordinary feat, and I thank Providence for you every day."

"It's not enough," Tristan said. "I'm not enough."

"It may feel that way sometimes. I've certainly felt that during seasons of my life. Especially when I became a father."

Tristan looked up. "What are you saying? You're a wonderful

father. Every single one of my friends wished they belonged to my family and not their own."

"I've worked very hard to be a good father, and it wasn't easy. Fortunately, you all have been exceptional, most of the time. But I think that's how I failed you. The others didn't need guidance for their lives. Not really. But you seem to need more than the others, and I don't know how to give it."

"That's not true at all," Tristan protested. "You haven't failed. It's me. What am I supposed to be doing? I haven't a clue. I don't have a head for numbers, or writing articles like Ophelia. It's too much of a chore for me. I'm not good for much other than hauling bits and bobs up a mountain."

"Plenty of men are trying to explore the remotest points of the earth these days. Perhaps you can attach yourself to those men. Help haul their bits and bobs. And soon you'll have even more training. You'll have done the Matterhorn. Only a handful of men living can claim that."

Tristan frowned. "But that's not a job. I can't say, 'Here, Eleanor. I've a life waiting for us. I'll be climbing mountains, risking my life for another man's glory. See you in six months. Have fun in London, all alone.'"

His father seemed amused again. "That doesn't seem like much of a selling point, I admit."

"See? I can't very well offer for her when I've nothing to show for myself."

His father's eyes rounded, and Tristan realized what he'd said. He hadn't meant to; it just came out.

"You want to marry Miss Piper?" his father asked.

Tristan's leg began jiggling out of control. It was a nervous habit he'd managed to suppress over the years, but sometimes it still happened, no matter how much he tried to stop it. "I'm not sure."

"She's a lovely girl."

Tristan nodded. "But she's not aristocracy."

"That might matter for some, but does it matter for you?"

Tristan felt like this was a trick. "Does it matter for you?"

"If you were wanting to marry a widowed dancer, then perhaps. I would worry about social climbers or fortune hunters. But Miss Piper has a respectable dowry. She doesn't need our wealth."

"But what about social climbing? Isn't that obvious? I've heard that's what Mr. Piper has been after for quite some time."

"They aren't gaining anything by marrying a second son. They'll be closer, of course, and any offspring you have might one day marry into nobility, but it isn't as if you are a viscount in your own right."

Tristan blushed. "No, but I went to school with the boys who will be."

His father nodded. "Do you think that matters to Miss Piper?"

Tristan thought for a moment. "I don't think so."

"Does she feel the same about you as you do about her?"

The only thing he could do in response to that thought was to heave a sigh of such magnitude his lungs ached. "I thought she did."

"But?"

"But the look on her face when Ophelia told her she would be kicked off the expedition—I don't think she'll ever forgive me."

"Did you tell her that was the cost of your courtship?"

Tristan shook his head. "I did not make that clear. I thought that if we were courting and Eleanor wasn't on the expedition, her father would still support our venture. But if I ruined her, then he might not only pull his funding from us, but also not give her the dowry she deserves."

His father nodded. "That's possible. But it wasn't up to you to make that choice. It was hers."

"I know."

Knowing he'd made his point, his father turned his gaze out the window, at the bleak countryside rushing by. Tristan did the same. It made him feel queasy, seeing the scenery rush past at such an appalling speed. His leg stopped jumping.

"Perhaps after this attempt at the Ben," Tristan said, not wanting to finish his thought because he had no idea what he planned.

"After the Ben," his father agreed, not needing a full plan to be supportive.

Tristan felt better. And warmer. And stronger. Perhaps he *was* more like Portia, and less like Ophelia. He didn't need big, giant, life-changing ambitions. He could have smaller ones that included the revolutionary ideas of being happy, and finding someone he could grow old with. Or climb a mountain with, for that matter. He considered it. Perhaps Eleanor had a passion like Ophelia. Perhaps he could support Eleanor's dream, if she had one, the way he supported Ophelia's ambition.

The idea of it appealed to him, and then he thought of telling such an idea to Blakely, who would tell him how he was the man, and how he needed to be in charge. But what if Tristan wasn't good at being in charge, and rather, was really good at carrying out other people's ideas? That was a talent, wasn't it?

He was fairly certain Eleanor would prefer a man like that—a man who didn't have to be in charge every minute of every day. Where the marriage could be a partnership, and not him charging ahead, expecting her to keep up, never looking at what she needed. It certainly wasn't that he would turn into a milksop over night. He had plenty of ideas of his own. And definitely certain places where he would take charge. He just needed to convince her to take a chance on him.

SCOTLAND WAS DARK and wet and miserable when they arrived.

"I thought this was supposed to be Scotland's summer," Justine grumbled, putting her shoulder against the wind. A carriage was waiting for them, and they huddled together as they moved through the station, porters rushing back and forth to get all of their trunks.

The amount of luggage for their party was comical. Not only did each person have a trunk of personal items, there was an entire trunk of ropes, and an entire trunk of sewn-up sleeping blankets, tents, and other camping essentials. They weren't sure of the conditions at the base of Ben Nevis, since the English army had pulled out of Fort William over a decade ago.

Ophelia and her father corresponded with several men who knew the mountain, but they'd been evasive about the conditions and available amenities. So they overprepared, which Eleanor appreciated.

The rain was cold, coming in at her face sideways. She kept herself shielded, but when she heard, "Allow me," she glanced over.

Tristan was beside the carriage, handing them up, as the drivers and porters secured the luggage. It was the first time they'd been so close since the morning after the ball. He'd left for London without telling anyone, and Eleanor had somehow felt abandoned. Not that it was a new sensation, but rather disappointingly familiar. Nor had he been present much at the Ladies' Alpine Society salons. Ophelia told her that he had to be threatened into coming to the planning meeting. Eleanor had assumed it had been because of her. Even the way he'd stared at her at the train station this morning had that same tinge of disapproval.

But now, in the rain, instead of sulking and averting his gaze, this time he looked at her with a new clarity. His Tristan-ness had returned.

Eleanor felt taken aback. His blue eyes were so arresting, she couldn't help but meet his gaze. Her lips parted, wanting to say something, anything, but nothing came out. Cool raindrops fell on her lips instead, which she licked off. His eyes flickered down, watching her mouth, and she suddenly felt embarrassed.

He smiled at her, a polite one, not one of his stunning, all-encompassing smiles, and she stepped into the carriage. He handed up Prudence and closed the door, leaving the four girls and Lady Rascomb crammed into the conveyance.

"I'm exhausted," announced Justine.

The smell of wet wool and felt filled the small space.

"I think we all are," Prudence said, and even though her tone was soft, it still felt like a rebuke. They sat in silence. Long minutes later, the carriage lurched forward, and all the women swayed with the motion. The small window was streaked with rain.

They reached an inn somewhere near Edinburgh. When they got out of the carriage, the coachman attempting valiantly to use an umbrella to keep them dry against the pelting cold rain, it was so dark that it seemed they were miles from another building. A doorway opened, spilling light into the mud, and a shadow dashed out to the carriage.

"I'll get the girls inside, thank you." Lady Rascomb took the umbrella from the coachman and ushered them all out, instructing them to dash across the mud and find safety inside.

A round woman with skirts practically belted at her chin ushered them inside. She wore a mob cap, and Eleanor couldn't figure out if it was part of an older style or perhaps worn at night here in Scotland. But it largely covered the woman's brown and silver hair as she ushered them in, dripping wet and shivering.

"There's another carriage on the way," Ophelia said. Lady Rascomb limped inside last, shaking out the umbrella and leaning it against the doorframe, as if she were a maid and not a viscountess.

The woman nodded. "I figured as much. I'm Mrs. Gordon, owner of this here establishment. We've the whole place for you tonight. If you like, I can show you up to the second-floor parlor. That's where I've put all you ladies, as it's far warmer up there."

"Please," Lady Rascomb said, gesturing for her to lead the way. Somehow, she was in complete control of all her limbs, whereas Eleanor and the other girls were shivering with the cold.

Eleanor had to keep her teeth clamped shut to keep them from chattering.

"I've got stew and fresh baked bread at the ready. We'll get you settled in, and I'll have Beverly bring up trays."

The steps were wooden, but a well-worn rug was tacked along them, which Eleanor was grateful for. Her traveling boots were muddy from the dash in the rain, and the polished floor was slick. Up another staircase was their floor, with a lock on the main parlor, and individual rooms off of that.

The rugs behind them were wet from their passage, a trail of sodden fibers. Eleanor did not envy whoever must clean them.

"The rooms all have keys in them for you, and this door locks from the inside. I have a key to it as well, but no one else. It keeps the gentlemen at bay." Mrs. Gordon gave them all a sharp look as if any one of them might arrange a clandestine meeting. "Lady Rascomb, I give you the key to the main door, and thus you can be responsible for all your charges."

Lady Rascomb accepted the large brass key, and Mrs. Gordon eyed Justine, despite the fact they were all wearing full-length sodden traveling gowns. "Not to worry, Mrs. Gordon. I will keep the girls safe."

"See that you do, if I may be so bold as to give advice. This parlor here is the only one of your rooms with a fire. I have bed warmers for each that I will bring up at nine o'clock on the dot, not a minute later. If I may, I'd suggest you lay out your wet clothes to dry on the racks, and enjoy your dinner out here in your dressing gowns. You'll warm up faster and won't be as likely to catch cold."

Eleanor longed to get out of her wet clothes, take off her sodden boots, and unpin her hair. The day had been long, and while she hadn't moved her body much, the jolting noise of the train had exhausted her.

"Thank you for the sound advice, Mrs. Gordon. We look forward to the dinner trays." Lady Rascomb walked Mrs. Gordon toward the door, effectively ending the interaction.

The innkeeper left the room, and with it, all the girls sighed. Immediately Eleanor began picking at the buttons of her traveling costume. Her nails were bluish purple, and not at all adept at getting her free of the wet clothes.

They'd managed to get their wet outer clothing off when there was a knock at the parlor door and the porter delivered their trunks. Lady Rascomb assigned rooms, and the porter pulled the trunks to the appointed doorways. When the man left, Justine flopped onto the settee and pushed off her boots, groaning.

"I love you all very much, and as such, I'm taking off everything," Justine announced.

"That's why you have a reputation, Justine. I understand what you mean, but you can't just say whatever's in your head," Ophelia chastised.

Justine groaned again in response. They picked at each other when they were tired, Eleanor noticed. Justine grew more flamboyant, and Ophelia grew more judgmental. What did Eleanor do, she wondered? What was her tic?

Eleanor opened the trunk in her room. They were to stay here for a week, resting, gathering information about weather, obtaining a guide, and arranging for transportation to the Highlands. She wondered if they would get to see some of Edinburgh's sights, given how much time they had. Would they visit the castle? Holyrood Palace? Surely, for someone like Eleanor, who had not traipsed around France or Italy or America, they might indulge her here in Scotland?

Eleanor was cold in her little room, with its small cot-sized bed, nightstand, and dressing table. She stripped off her dress and her boots and, with relief, peeled off the woolen stockings. There was something immensely freeing in removing those. She took out the pins in her hair, running her fingers along her scalp, finding sensitive spots to gently massage. Digging around in her trunk—which she promised herself she would unpack later—she found her nightdress and dressing gown.

Clean clothes felt like heaven. She finger-combed her hair and walked out into the parlor, braiding it as she went. Prudence was already there, ensconced in a book. Refreshed in her dry clothes, Eleanor felt the inn was taking on the cozy atmosphere of a vacation. There was a knock at the parlor door, which made Eleanor exchange looks at Prudence. Did they dare risk the wrath of Mrs. Gordon by opening it?

"Dinner," a young voice on the other side of the door called.

Prudence snickered, and Eleanor hopped up. Why was she so hungry? She hadn't done hardly anything but sit on a train, and yet she was hungrier than the nights they'd spent out at Berringbone Hold. It was a different sort of hungry after a jostling train ride. One born out of a desire for warmth, for comfort, for ease.

A young woman barely out of childhood bustled in with a large tray. She set down the tray and without a word efficiently put together a table that had been sitting in pieces against the wall. Eleanor hadn't even noticed it.

Once the table was erected, it was set, complete with linens and proper place settings. Eleanor watched, completely speechless. She'd never seen anything like it in her life. Such efficiency in this little inn.

The expression on Prudence's face, wide-eyed, with a downturned mouth, conveyed her surprise as well.

"I'll be back up in a moment with the stew and the bread." The girl curtsied as efficiently as she'd done everything else and hurried from the room. She must be the Beverly that Mrs. Gordon mentioned.

"Is that dinner?" Justine called, emerging from her room in her shift.

Ophelia drifted out of her room at the same time, then noticed Justine in her shift. "Honestly, Justine. You must put on a dressing gown or at least a wrapper. I can see right through that."

Justine rolled her eyes. "Who's going to see me? I didn't put anything on because no one is around to see but you all, and none of you count against propriety."

"It isn't the done thing, Justine," Ophelia reminded her.

Ophelia was wearing a dressing gown that cinched around the waist, making her the picture of nighttime modesty.

Justine groaned. "One of these days, I will do something that actually *is* shocking. Something that really ought to ruin my reputation, and then you'll see how very modest I've been my entire life." She stomped back into her room.

Lady Rascomb emerged, looking lovely and proper. Her long pale-golden hair was brushed out, cascading over her shoulders. Her loose dressing gown flared at the waist, concealing any nightdress or shift she might be wearing underneath. Even the cane, which she leaned heavily on, did not detract from her regal promenade to the fireplace.

"We have a proper dinner, by the looks of it." Lady Rascomb smiled at all of them. How she could be in such good humor, with grace and politeness, despite the obvious pain she was in, was beyond Eleanor's understanding.

Another light brush against the door, and Ophelia hurried over to open it. The girl came back in with the tray once again laden. She set out bowls of stew, a board with fresh sliced brown bread, a pot of honey, and a crock of butter. There was a small basket of apples and a knife to cut them with.

"It may not look like much, but I tell you, it's the best you'll have." The girl looked down at the floor.

"It smells wonderful," Prudence said, bestowing a bright smile on the girl.

Hearing Prudence's accent, the girl's head snapped up. "You're an American!"

Prudence chuckled. "That obvious?"

"I've cousins that went years ago. They send letters back, but I've been dying to know how it really is."

"I'm happy to answer whatever questions you might have," Prudence eyed the table. "But perhaps it could wait until after dinner?"

The girl nodded, her excitement palpable as she gripped her tray and nibbled her lower lip. "Of course. My apologies, ma'am.

Ladies." The girl curtsied again and left the room, closing the door ever so softly.

None of them stood on ceremony, and they fell upon their meal as if they hadn't eaten in a week. They washed down the hearty stew, dotted with large chunks of potatoes and carrots with ale, and sopped up the bottoms of the bowls with hunks of brown bread smothered in butter and honey.

By the end, all the girls were reclining on the couch. Lady Rascomb cut the apples into pieces slowly, handing them down the line so that each girl got a slice to dip into the remnants of the honey at a leisurely pace.

"Do you think the men got this good of a meal?" Prudence asked, her eyes glazed over as she licked honey from her fingers.

"I think it was exactly the same," said Ophelia, staring into the fire. "That's what we've requested for this entire trip. The same for us as for them."

Eleanor thought of Tristan, one floor below her, in his shirt-sleeves, collar off and shirt unbuttoned. The fire would light up his golden features, playing with the shadows of his perfect cheekbones and tender pink lips. Just as he'd looked around the fire at Berringbone, so at ease, so perfectly fit into the landscape.

"But we aren't the same, Ophelia. We're women. They're men. We're different. Shouldn't we have different accommodations?" Prudence asked.

"That's just it, Prudence." Ophelia leaned back, propping her head up with her hand. "That's how men belittle women. We have to prove we can do it as they do it, for any variance causes them to judge us even more harshly."

Justine sprang forward, an unexpected fierceness on her face. "And which of us will determine what women need? You? Me? Eleanor? Because we are individuals. I need less than any of you. Any of the men, as well."

Shocked by Justine's outburst, the room fell silent. Eleanor watched as color bloomed on Justine's cheeks, and she sat back with her arms folded. It was then that Eleanor realized something so bloody obvious that she felt like an idiot for not knowing it sooner: everyone dealt with adversity differently.

Eleanor hung back and became quieter. Justine planted herself in the middle and challenged whatever was to come at her head-on. Prudence massaged and comforted. Ophelia became more and more rational. And Tristan ran away.

And yet, they were about to go climb a mountain that was chock full of adversity. She'd learned only a little about it so far, trusting Ophelia and Lord Rascomb in their planning. The last thing Eleanor wanted to do was doubt the abilities of their expedition, but would they be able to overcome themselves on this adventure? Let alone the mountain and the weather.

"I daresay I'm tired after such a long train ride," Eleanor said, giving a weak smile to them all. "Early to bed for me."

"'Early to bed, early to rise, makes a man healthy, wealthy, and wise,'" Prudence said, unfolding her legs from underneath her.

"I beg your pardon?" Lady Rascomb said.

"Benjamin Franklin. It's one of his sayings. You must have heard it at some point." Prudence scanned their faces.

"It does sound dreadfully American," Ophelia said, hiding a giggle. Eleanor twisted her lips to hide a smile. The idiom did sound a bit overzealous.

"I don't see how it all depends on when one sleeps," Justine protested. "It's a bit limited, don't you think?"

Prudence put her hands on her slim hips, her expression teasing. "Well. I can tell none of you every grew up on a farm."

"Is that the only way to be healthy, wealthy, and wise?" Lady Rascomb asked, as if she might be affronted.

The teasing eased the tension from Justine's outburst, and soon they slipped off to their rooms, one by one, tucking themselves into bed.

$$\sim\!\!\blacklozenge\!\!\sim$$

Chapter Twelve

"WHAT DO YOU mean Mr. Alistair isn't at home?" Tristan demanded. The morning was bitingly cold. He rubbed his hands together, as his leather riding gloves didn't keep out the pervasive damp chill.

The wizened old man squinted at him, as if he must be hard of hearing. "Mr. Alistair has been called away." This time the old man spoke the words slowly. "There's an illness in the family. I don't know when he'll return."

Tristan took the news like a blow on the chin. "Did he not leave us a note? No correspondence?"

The old man stared at him some more. "If he did, I would've given it to you straight away."

"Of course," Tristan said, backing away from the steps of the small house. "Thank you. I apologize for disturbing you." Tristan set his jaw. What were they supposed to do now?

Mr. Alistair was supposed to be the Scottish aide-de-camp. When he didn't show up for their morning meeting or respond to notes, Tristan was dispatched to fetch him.

But now what? There was nothing for their expedition. No transportation, no mountain experts, no supplies. They'd have to start from scratch and blunder through themselves, and hopefully not be taken for all their money by some Scot with a grudge against the English. Though it seemed they all had a grudge against the English.

Tristan swung back up on his horse. Normally he would return and report his findings to Ophelia. But they were in a strange country, and women couldn't be wandering around sorting this. He turned his horse and rode to Edinburgh. Surely he'd find an outfitter hoping to land a company such as theirs.

He spent all day walking the streets, popping into shop after shop, asking questions, and looking for maps with no luck. It was well past time for an evening meal, and Tristan was starving and soaking wet. Defeated, he returned to the inn—not far from Mr. Alistair's humble abode and where he started his odyssey. Indeed, it had been on Mr. Alistair's recommendation that they'd taken over the small establishment. The London Alpine Society had referred Tristan to Mr. Alistair last year, when they'd begun to plan this absurd trip. Their correspondence had been filled with attention to detail, planning expertise, and knowledge of local terrain. They could not have asked for a better guide. And now that guide had vanished!

They had to find somebody new, somebody trustworthy. Some families had Scottish heritage and contacts, but theirs was not one of them. They were Southerners, through and through.

He hated being the bearer of bad news. He handed his horse off to the stableboy at the inn and found the rest of the expedition assembled in the downstairs public dining area, waiting for him. Ophelia's eyes darted behind him, looking for the lost Mr. Alistair. Her mouth thinned into a grim line that matched his own. He caught his father's eye next and shook his head. His mother caught the movement and excused herself.

Eleanor was seated next to Ophelia, and it was easy to let his eyes drift over to her. She looked soft and cozy in a brown and yellow woolen gown, a small scarf covering her neck for warmth. He wanted to scoop her up and cuddle in front of the big fireplace, listening to her stories of the sailors that wandered through her father's office.

But the warning in her eyes, the guarded mistrust, kept him at bay. He took a seat next to his father, and Prudence poured him a cup of tea.

"Tristan, would you like to share your news?" Ophelia prompted.

He sipped the malty black brew, which he rather liked, truth be told. It was heaven for an exhausted man. "Our Scottish guide is in the wind."

"When will he return?" Ophelia asked, beating their father to it.

"Unknown. Family illness elsewhere. No note or instruction was left for us."

His father grunted, no doubt mentally flipping through the names of men who might have contacts up here. But those would all take letters of introduction, which meant time. They wanted to climb Ben Nevis when it had snow on it, as the Matterhorn surely would regardless of the time of year they climbed. If they waited too long, the snow on the Scottish peak would melt and they would get bogged down in mud.

"Does anyone have a connection here in Scotland?" Ophelia looked around, hopeful.

None of the young ladies said anything. It was a moment Tristan wished for another man at the table. A man could network more easily, go to places of business and make inquiries, arrange for travel and provisions. As it stood, it would end up all on his shoulders. Already, Tristan was starting to feel resentful. What would they do without him to do the drone's work while they sipped on their nectar?

His mother entered the room, conferred with Ophelia first, then briefly with his father. Tristan narrowed his eyes. She had a triumphant look about her.

"Mama, I think you should be the one to announce the news," Ophelia said.

It was right at that moment that Tristan realized what good graces truly were. That this sort of elegant sharing of authority is what young ladies were trained to do when they knew they would marry into nobility. His mother was every inch a noble lady, and he felt confident that Ophelia would do well, too, should she concede to a traditional life.

"I've spoken with Mrs. Gordon, and it turns out that young Beverly is from the Highlands. One of her brothers runs a small carriage service and can arrange for transportation in Fort William. Young Beverly also says that her father and uncles know Ben Nevis well and have climbed it many times. They would be able to guide for us, or even suggest the best routes for this time of year."

Tristan frowned. All this had occurred where? A conversation in the kitchens? After he had spent hours being rained on, and splattered in mud? "How are we to know that young Beverly is telling us the truth?"

"Mrs. Gordon vouched for her. And it is well known that her brother runs the carriage service. It was mentioned to me upon arrival, long before they knew we were in need of aid." His mother gave him that look that made it seem like she could read his mind. He didn't like it.

"This sounds like an excellent solution," Prudence said. "Thank you, Lady Rascomb, for your quick thinking and versatile conversation skills."

"This isn't the first time I've been in a tight spot, climbing a mountain in a foreign country."

His father patted his mother on the hand, congratulating her. Tristan still felt like he had a hornet flying 'round his head. This was too easy. This was—well, it didn't include him. And a realization hit as he scooted his chair back, ready to storm away in a huff: it didn't matter if he topped out the Ben or not. He'd wanted to be included, to be valued and wanted. He wanted to be necessary. His mother had solved the problem in her usual elegant way, instead of his way, spending a frustrating day pounding on doors all over Edinburgh.

Instead of being angry, he should be grateful. And proud. His mother was so capable, regardless of a cane or a limp. Then shame seeped in. Shame that he'd thought she wasn't this capable. That somehow, that avalanche had robbed her of everything. But it hadn't. She was here, in Scotland, with them. She was cheering them on, celebrating their successes, and helping when there were issues.

Dear God, what else was it that he couldn't see? That was his own mother that he'd thought so poorly of. He wished he could be out in the woods alone. His head was clearer there.

He stole a glance at Eleanor, who had been silent during the entire exchange. She was looking at her hands, a demure posture. Had she learned that at finishing school, or was it a habit learned from being ignored so frequently? She'd told him about feeling extraneous at her parents' dinner table. About how she'd been forgotten at her father's office, an afterthought for everyone.

Her confessions had come naturally as she'd taught him knots, overseeing his practice. The others were all there, doing the same in his mother's drawing room, chattering as they tied the same knot over and over, committing it to memory.

Eleanor must have felt his eyes on her, and she looked up. Instead of glancing away, as she had every other time since that terrible breakfast, she locked eyes with him. Those soft, deep brown eyes that he could lose himself in. He understood now, he was fairly certain anyway, what had gone wrong. Why she'd rejected him so wholeheartedly. Did she understand why he'd pushed to remove her from the expedition?

It wasn't because he wanted her to not be with them—no, of course not. But she'd said in the beginning that it was foolish for her to do this. Why would he think she would mind being off the team? And still, he did need to protect Ophelia's reputation, and really, Eleanor's as well. He wasn't certain he was ready to marry her—that seemed like a bit of leap. But to court, to really see if they would suit, that seemed reasonable. Manageable. And if they'd gone public before coming up to Scotland, even with his mother and Prudence Cabot along, it was too easy to slip away. Going out to the Berringbone ruins was one thing, given they'd brought plenty of staff, but to Scotland? That would make anyone think twice.

Besides, they'd needed Eleanor's father's investment in the expedition. If they were courting and Eleanor wasn't going, her father would still likely give them the money. If Tristan ruined Eleanor's reputation before they got to the Matterhorn, he doubted Mr. Piper would feel generous.

But Eleanor's gaze was making his mind falter. He wanted—and that feeling of wanting overwhelmed him. But he couldn't let something as trivial as wanting distract either of them. Not now. Not with the mountain so close. After Ben Nevis, he would beg, or grovel, or plead—whatever it would take for her to give him another chance. But now? He needed some air.

He pushed back from the table and was out in the cool air before he could think.

ELEANOR FELT UNMOORED. The days passed more quickly than she expected, each member of the party charged with obtaining different items or scheduling services. Eleanor had been charged with finding maps, along with Prudence, and together, they tripped along in Edinburgh, not doing nearly enough sightseeing for Eleanor's taste.

In the evenings, they ate together in the downstairs dining room, attended by Mrs. Gordon and Beverly. The men working at the inn seemed to all be outside caretakers, and Eleanor wondered if that was another reason this particular establishment was chosen for them. After dinner, they separated and retired to their respective parlors. Eleanor and the other women changed into dressing gowns, took the pins out of their hair, and talked and chatted while indulging in cups of tea. It built camaraderie for them, but she always wondered how Tristan fared, downstairs, with only his father for company.

He hadn't spoken directly to her, but he gave her meaningful looks across the table that confused her. The hurt of his betrayal hadn't lessened. If anything, it had increased as they sat in close quarters, planning for an adventure he hadn't wanted her to go on.

Seven days after their arrival, they boarded an early morning train for the Highlands. They left most of their luggage with Mrs. Gordon, as climbing the Ben, as the locals seemed to call it, was a one-day affair. They would be back in just a few days. Armed with a small trunk, shared with Prudence, they boarded. It was a surprisingly luxurious affair, but when they reached the end of the line, they had to collect their belongings and board a ferry, which was a decided downgrade in experience. The air grew colder and wetter. She drew her coat and scarf around her tighter to guard against the cold.

The scenery was breathtaking. Despite the fact that spring was barely noticeable, and the cold pervasive, the impressive, rugged landscape bewitched her.

"Climbin' the ol' Ben, are you?" the ferry master chuckled at them. Eleanor didn't know how he knew, but the ferry master had a comment for every single one of them. He clearly didn't believe women had any business climbing a mountain, and men only did so because they were, as the ferry master said, his bushy white eyebrows raised, daft.

"Positively raving," Tristan said with a brilliant smile. Eleanor felt herself smiling in response, even if it wasn't aimed at her. She looked away before he caught her at it, embarrassed that she could be so swept up by him.

They passed by what looked like a ghost town, buildings left in place, but absolutely no people in sight. White sheep dotted the landscape, looking like bits of cotton strewn about a yard.

They arrived in Fort William, cold and tired. Beverly's brother met them at the shabby dock, much to their collective relief. It was twilight, and they were all cold. The thin-walled shelter of the boat had kept them out of the wind, but was not warm. Instead of meeting them with a carriage and strapping trunks in intricate puzzles about the conveyance, Beverly's brother had an open-air wagon. They all climbed in, their trunks laid at their feet, and off they went to the inn, run by another of young Beverly's relatives.

As expected, Eleanor and Prudence roomed together, while Ophelia and Justine took another. Lord and Lady Rascomb took the master suite and Tristan was bunked alone. The rooms were spare but clean, and now, having arrived in the Highlands, the idea of staying indoors seemed absurd. It was freezing outside, but the light lingered, so Eleanor grabbed her cloak and climbing gloves and went outside, not bothering to unpack her portion of the small trunk.

It had rained earlier in the day, and the air was crisp enough that it felt like skating on a knife's edge. The water was nearby, and the mountains loomed in the distance. The sky, dotted with white and gray clouds, was turning a soft lavender, a different color than she'd ever witnessed in England. The world felt different here. The air was better. She felt unlike herself, and also completely herself for the very first time.

Rough footsteps crunched behind her on the stony path. She didn't bother to turn, as she could already tell who it was.

"This is beautiful," Tristan said.

Eleanor didn't want to look away from the grandeur and the beauty of the loch and the mountains and the sky, even for the beauty that made up Tristan's delightfully symmetrical and golden face.

"I never knew places like this existed," Eleanor said, her breath curling into steam as it left her mouth.

"The world is vast," Tristan said. "There are things no one can imagine, and yet they exist."

Eleanor smiled and couldn't help but tease. "Then how do you know they exist if you can't imagine them?"

Tristan looked deep into her eyes, pinning her in a way that surprised her. Was it this place? Was it him? What made this pull between them feel like a slip knot that cinched tighter and tighter, never loosening? "Because some days I look up to find something I've never seen before. Felt before. Wanted before."

Eleanor swallowed hard.

"Eleanor, I know what I did was—" His perfect face creased, the worry spilling out into his expression. "I shouldn't have assumed you didn't want to climb. Of all people, I should know not to force a woman to choose between adventure and a man. But I was so—well, giddy at the thought of you. I apologize. It was boorish and unforgiveable."

Heat flushed through her. No one had ever apologized to her. She didn't know what to say. Her mouth opened and closed. Was this still possible between them? Could they—

"Hallooo! Come inside! Supper is going to be served shortly!" Justine yelled from the entrance of the inn.

Eleanor broke away from his gaze with effort, her heart pounding. "We need to go in."

Tristan nodded and turned, not offering his arm to her. She was glad. At this point, she wasn't sure she could trust herself with his touch.

Inside, their crew was assembled at the dining tables with a number of men who could not be anything but locals. The proprietress served stew and fresh bread, with more of that delightful Scottish butter. Eleanor didn't care if she had to eat stew for every meal if she got bread and butter with each bowl.

Their group discussed weather conditions, routes, snow, and wind.

"Women got no business on the Ben," one man said, tugging his hat down low.

"Storm's coming tomorrow anyhow," a man at the next table said, eyeballing their group. He'd clearly been eavesdropping. The whole room had seemed to be.

"Bit of a walk from here." Another man leaned back in his chair. He had his cap off, unruly red hair fluffed in every direction, as he smoked a pipe. "I've a barn, sits at the base of the Ben. You camp there overnight, well, you're that much closer.

Beat the storm on the way down."

"If we sleep in the barn tonight, we can make good time by starting before dawn," Ophelia said. "We won't have the time we planned to acclimate, but if not, we're stuck until the next clear weather window, and according to these gentlemen . . ."

They all glanced about at the room full of men who pretended to not listen.

"It may be some time before we can climb." Ophelia looked to each of them, and Eleanor appreciated how Ophelia handled them. "This is a safety issue, and I won't press on unless we all agree to climb tomorrow morning. That means no comfortable bed tonight. It's blanket bags in a cold barn tonight and a grueling climb tomorrow morning before dawn."

Eleanor looked across the table to find everyone nodding. Excitement buzzed through her like a live wire. Tomorrow they would climb the Ben. The prospect of a storm made her nervous, but given their preparations, Eleanor was sure they could ascend and descend in plenty of time.

"Are we agreed? Raise your hand if you will not climb with me tomorrow." Ophelia looked around, as did Eleanor. No hands were raised.

IT WAS STILL dark when they awoke. Eleanor shivered as she pulled on the extra layers that she hadn't slept in. She glanced at the others, all the same, all shivering or rubbing their hands or arms to warm up.

Ophelia's voice pierced the silence, scratchy and coarse. "This is what we've waited for. The sooner we move, the faster we'll be warm. I'm bringing a pack with a bit of supplies so we can breakfast halfway up. Take care of your business outside, and then we'll rope up."

They shuffled about in silence, rolling up their blanket bags, popping outside in the cold and dark to go about their business. It wasn't long until they were ready.

"Must we rope up this early?" Prudence asked.

"You heard what Mr. Campbell said. The visibility comes and goes. We don't know this mountain well, and there are a thousand paths up and down. It's a safety precaution we can reevaluate when we break halfway up."

Four hours. They would walk for four hours, then stop and break their fast with whatever had been hastily packed up for them. Ophelia led them out of the barn, their overnight things tidily stashed in the corner of the barn. Lady Rascomb would be waiting for them at the bottom, she said, with hot water bottles and whisky, and a cart to take them all back to the inn.

But this climb was the proof Eleanor needed to show herself. She could do difficult things, test herself, push herself. And she would see the world from atop a volcano. They filed out of the barn, the air crisp and cold in a way that almost hurt inside her lungs.

"Breathe through your nose," Ophelia reminded everyone. "Warm the air."

Eleanor wished for the hottest cup of tea in the world right then. She watched as Ophelia put in her figure eight knot, their leader, ready to ascend the tallest peak in the United Kingdom. Then Justine. Then Tristan, who, even in the dark, was somehow a smudged shape that made her stomach do somersaults. She had taught them this skill, and she hoped her recommendation of the safest knot would prove worthy. Her fingers were clumsy as she took her turn. They were cold despite the fur-lined gloves and felt thick. After tying in, she settled woolen mittens on over them.

She felt the pull of the rope as Prudence tied in behind her and Lord Rascomb yet behind Prudence. Her heart pounded awfully hard, suddenly nervous, as they were about to embark. She looked at the mountain, but it was another indistinct looming shape in the dark. Either it was cloudy or it was moonless. But it didn't matter. Not yet. One foot in front of the other. Breathe easy and rhythmically, and they would be done before anyone realized it.

"Tied!" Lord Rascomb called, and one by one they went up the line, checking their knot and confirming their status. When the cries reached Ophelia, she shouted, "Thus we climb on!"

Eleanor felt it was a bit theatrical, but this was ultimately Ophelia's expedition, and Eleanor wouldn't be the one to rob her of her enthusiasm. They squelched through some mud, but, as Mr. Morrison claimed, the barn was directly at the foot of the mountain. They started to ascend almost immediately.

And for some time, Eleanor was blissfully at peace, her mind free of its constraints. With nothing to look at in the dark, and the rope slack in front and behind, she walked on, almost as if she were once again asleep. Just not as warm. The ground crunched beneath their boots as the frost broke and shattered beneath their feet.

Light soon spilled over the mountain, and the effect of the warmth was almost immediate. The ground began to steam, and the sight of it made Eleanor smile. It made the whole mountain look magical, as if it might suddenly dislodge and rise with the mist. She could see why people said the landscape felt alive. It hadn't been bent to man's will, as places like London had, where the Thames was another avenue of commerce, and the streets were lined with paving stones.

Here, nature was free to breathe, to exercise its own will. Humans were too beneath Mother Nature's regard. Eleanor liked that. Nature as a force unto itself. Others knew that—Prudence knew that, having grown up on farms. It was city people like her that needed the revelation.

She knew she was grinning like an American, but she didn't care. This was beautiful: the mottled green and brown carpet of the hillside, the wisps of steam in the early morning sun. Already the long hours of training, hardship, and heartbreak had been worth it.

These short months had changed her, forced her into a realization that the world around her was far bigger and stranger than she'd realized. That she was more capable than she'd believed. That she too had her role to play, and that she had some choice in it. She longed to be more outspoken like Justine. More driven, like Ophelia. More worldly, like Prudence. More elegant, like Lady Rascomb.

But she also acknowledged that she liked herself, too. That she was capable and careful, meticulous and intelligent. And all of those things were acceptable, and even desirable in a woman. In a woman like her, specifically.

She wasn't sure how she felt about Tristan anymore. But she felt that he admired her. It still stung that he'd assumed she wouldn't mind being kicked off the expedition, after all of those long runs around the meadow at Berringbone! She'd worked so hard to prove herself. And to have her work summarily dismissed had been painful. It was as if everything that horrid Mr. Fulk had said during that dance was also what Tristan thought, never mind her own dreams and future.

But Tristan's apology seemed sincere. After this mountain she could take time to speak with him. Perhaps he wanted to try again, after this mountain. Her foot faltered, slipping a rock loose, leaving it to careen behind her. "Rock!" she called, not knowing if it was big enough to warrant a warning.

But what if they didn't suit, and Tristan ceased his pursuit of her before the Matterhorn? Would she not be allowed on the expedition then? How Ophelia reacted to this mess, it seemed to Eleanor, showed that she would be welcome on the team, regardless of her status with Tristan. Because it was Ophelia's expedition, not Tristan's, ultimately.

The ascent grew steeper, and her breathing quickened. This portion didn't allow her to daydream, focused as she was on her body. Her pinky toe went numb, which she thought was a poor sign. Then the plane at which they climbed levelled off slightly, and her foot regained blood once again. That was good to know about her boots, and there were adjustments she could make before they climbed another mountain.

Fortunately, today was a one-day affair, and she could do anything for one day. Of that, she was certain. The fog had not yet descended, and Eleanor admired the grass and streams. The rocky hillside was blanketed in green, and she drank it in, hungry for nature having spent a lifetime amongst brick buildings and wrought iron fences.

"Look," Prudence called from behind her, pointing up ahead. "Snow!" Gathering up the rope, Prudence caught up with her. "I grew up with the snow. First in Minnesota, and then when I moved to New York. But you wouldn't believe the differences in the stuff."

"Really? I've never really been in much snow," Eleanor said. "There was a Christmas season we went a bit north to a holiday house party, and there was snow on the ground, but it was little more than a carpet that crunched beneath our feet."

"That doesn't count," Prudence scoffed. "In Minnesota, the snow would come down for days at a time, piling up against houses and berms. The rivers and lakes froze over, and after we swept the snow off, we would ice skate. I'm quite good at ice skating, if I can be so bold to brag." Eleanor smiled at her American brashness. "Please do."

Prudence flashed another smile—larger than the ones Eleanor had seen before. This woman was glowing with happiness. "That snow wasn't good for snowmen or anything like that. The cold froze all the moisture out of the air, and so the snow was more like a fine powder. It didn't clump much. So it was easier on the dogs and other animals."

Eleanor shifted her head to the side. How would not-clumping snow help a dog?

Prudence must have seen her confusion. "Dogs can get ice clumps in their paws, poor things. It bunches together, and it can be painful for them. At least until it melts."

Eleanor nodded. That she could understand, even if she'd never had a dog. Or any pet of any kind. For a while she had thought she wanted a bird, but her mother talked her out of it.

"What are you two talking about?" Tristan stood still, gathering up the rope that dragged between him and Eleanor.

Eleanor involuntarily licked her lips at his approach, almost immediately feeling the wind chap them. She and Prudence trundled up to him and he fell into step, looping the extra rope around his shoulder.

"I'm telling Eleanor everything she never needs to know about snow," Prudence announced.

"Sounds delightful. I'd say we've got another six to eight hours of walking, so please, do go on." Tristan was so gentle and kind. That was something she enjoyed about him. He did give everyone space to be themselves. He might give them a silly nickname, and sometimes those backfired, yes, but ultimately, he didn't mean any harm.

He even looked adorable in his stocking cap and jaunty scarf. How come the rest of them looked like anthropomorphic mushrooms, and he looked as if he were the star of some play about winter sports?

"As I was telling Eleanor, the snow in Minnesota is dry and powdery, on account of how dreadfully cold it gets there. But when I moved to New York, the snow was much better for building things by hand, like snowmen and such."

"Fascinating. So what about all this building ice homes and what-not that I read about it exploration journals? Those come from places that are very cold indeed."

Eleanor looked between her two friends, watching them debate snow. She was surprisingly entranced, and the current low angle of the mountain made the walk pleasurable.

"Ah, very good observation, sir!" Prudence said, her finger coming up as if she had a point to prove. "Yes! That kind of very cold snow is good for building if you have tools and access to water that allows you to freeze over certain blocks, solidifying them. But with one's bare hands, warmer snow is preferable."

"You little mountain goats, what are you chattering on

about?" Justine called, no doubt feeling the pull of the rope as Tristan fell into step with them.

"Snow!" called Prudence. "And how much I love it."

The morning was crisp and clear, and the sun was shining through the clouds. It did feel glorious, Eleanor had to admit. She felt more than happy, she felt pure joy. In this air, she was invincible. Everything felt right and perfect.

Justine fell back, which pulled on Ophelia, who then joined them. They all coiled the extra rope around their shoulders.

"Ugh, Ophelia. Must we remain roped together? This is too much." Justine shifted the coils from side to side.

Ophelia laughed. "Do you not like this extra practice? The extra weight? Was it not you saying you required less comfort than any one of our party?"

Justine rolled her eyes. "I am prone to hyperbole. Everyone knows that."

"Fine. Our resting point is just up ahead, above that rise. It's the loch, where we can settle for a moment. We're far ahead of schedule, so I see no reason to burden ourselves further. You lot are quick!"

"Mountain goats," Eleanor reminded her.

"Maaaa," bleated Tristan.

They picked through the melting snow, sometimes slipping, but still in good spirits and good time. They reached the plateau with the loch nestled low in it.

Tristan took off the pack he was carrying and handed it around. Inside was a packet of food for each of them. When Eleanor unwrapped her waxed paper, she found oatcakes with crowdie piled between them, a bit of honey stuck in for good measure. Dried apple rings stuck to the sides of it. They shared a water canteen between them. The stones were cold to sit on, and the breeze that came up chilled her now that they had stopped moving.

Still, it was the best breakfast Eleanor had ever eaten. She grinned like a maniac at her friends in the circle, even at Lord

Rascomb, who still intimidated her. He gave her a kindly nod, as if he knew precisely how she felt. She wanted to kiss each one of them on the cheeks and tell them how much she loved them. But since she was still English, she settled for her munching on the delightfully crumbly crowdie cheese.

Prudence finished her meal first and scooped up snow to cleanse her hands before slipping her gloves and then mittens back on. "I feel as if I could just run right up the rest of this mountain."

Ophelia nodded, sharing her enthusiasm, but still rife with pragmatism. "We still have at least another four hours to go. There are many false summits."

"Slow and steady wins the race, right Fee?" Justine said, smiling with a mouthful of cheese squeezing between her teeth.

Ophelia scoffed. "Your manners are the worst."

Justine cackled, choking a bit as she swallowed her mouthful. Eleanor laughed then, the joy bubbling up out of her at the antics of her friends.

Tristan's swiveled towards her. "I've never heard you laugh like that."

"I am free," she said, happily. "And so are they. It's intoxicating."

Tristan eyed her appreciatively. "As are you."

Justine cooed, mocking him.

"You weren't supposed to hear that," Tristan said, pulling himself up straighter.

Eleanor looked as openly at him as he did at her, unguarded and affectionate. She liked him. She liked him so very much. Between his apology and this mountain, she had little resistance left. "This is already the best day of my life."

"High praise," he said.

"I can't wait to get to get to the top." Eleanor drank in the chilled spring air.

"Neither can I," Ophelia said. "Five more minutes to eat and take care of your business, then we'll be off."

They were ready in less than four.

"I don't mean to question you Ophelia, but should we not continue to rope?" Eleanor asked.

"Give how quickly we are moving, and based on what the men at the inn said yesterday, I think we should be fine. We'll make even better time without the weight, and be snug back at the inn before the storm hits." Ophelia squeezed her shoulder.

Eleanor eyed the heavy rope coiled at the banks of the loch as they picked up the trail. They would pick it up on the way down in a few hours, along with the rucksack Tristan had carried.

The sun was out in full from behind the clouds, warming the day as they ascended. The mountain became far more steep as they climbed, and Eleanor began to sweat beneath the layers of her clothes. She pulled off her mittens and shoved them in her pocket, which helped.

Each step gained altitude and better views of the surrounding Scottish countryside. They crossed an invisible line on the mountain, and there was snow. Behind her, Prudence let out a girlish giggle. Eleanor turned to see Prudence lifting her skirts to prance through the untouched patches between the rocks. Lord Rascomb had a delighted look on his face, watching Prudence caper about. Eleanor laughed. It was the first time she'd seen the American act anything but the proper widow.

Prudence looked up at Eleanor with a wide grin. "I can't help it. I love the snow." And she did what looked like a dance step and then kicked a bit of snow into the air. The snow caught the low morning light, and it looked like a pale rainbow as it fell.

"It would make someone believe in fairies," Eleanor said. "It's beautiful."

The fog descended upon them, and they could no longer see the views that had helped sustain Eleanor's spirits.

The morning turned into midday, and still the fog remained. It was the fame of the peak, she supposed, the mountain with its head in the clouds. Still, the snow stayed firm beneath their feet, which Eleanor appreciated. She did not have Prudence's skill on ice. She looked up toward the peak, even as her woolen skirt weighed her down. The snow had wetted the hem, and the dampness worked its way up the skirt.

Ahead, Justine shook snow from her skirt before it had a chance to melt. "I hate this."

"Clothing in general, or just that particular piece?" Ophelia teased, seemingly unperturbed by any discomfort.

Eleanor suspected that her boots were likely also about to fail in the face of the dampness of melting snow.

"See? It isn't me," Justine insisted. "It's everyone else twisting my words to make them scandalous."

"I believe you, Justine," Prudence announced. She was in the same boat as Ophelia, gleefully tromping along.

Compared to Eleanor, she was practically running. Indeed, her lack of fitness was showing as she lagged behind the rest of the company. Lord Rascomb took his position as last seriously, but it meant he would stop and let Eleanor pass him before starting up again. She felt less like the invincible woman from earlier and far more like a wayward duckling.

"Not much farther," Ophelia called from uphill. She'd stopped, her hands on her hips as she rested, waiting for Eleanor and Lord Rascomb to catch up with the group.

Eleanor wondered what "not much" meant. Did that mean two more hours? Two more yards? Two miles? Lord Rascomb fell into step with her, matching the rhythm of her steps. Her ankles began to ache from the unfamiliar exercise.

Clouds covered the sun, and the relief from its brightness was at first welcome. Then a chill set in, once they lacked its powerful rays. On Eleanor plodded. She knew she couldn't stop to rest, for if she did, her protesting ankles would not want her to begin again.

"May we chat as we climb?" Lord Rascomb asked her, using his walking stick to help pole him upwards. Eleanor should have requested one but had wanted to fit in with the others, who hadn't wanted any aid for the Ben.

"Of course, my lord," she huffed, her throat dry as she choked out the words. She willed her observations to tunnel in, so that instead of thinking of the mountain and their party, and the snow and sun, all she thought about was the next step, and all she listened to was Lord Rascomb.

"You seem reluctant to speak with me," he said, not unkindly.

"To be fair, m'lord, I can't speak at all right now." Eleanor should have been embarrassed by her impertinence, but she was too busy trying to breathe.

He chuckled. "And I suppose the rest is merely intimidation?"

She nodded, not wanting to waste her energy on talking.

"Do you think that is something that could change when you marry my son?" he said the words so casually, as if it were a known quantity.

"Pardon?" Eleanor squeaked, almost stopping in her shock, but managing to push forwards.

"Well, once we are family, we have Sunday dinners together when we are all in London. It's a lovely time, and I would be most disturbed to know if you wouldn't attend for some reason; I dearly hope it wouldn't be because of me."

Ahead there was a whoop. Eleanor's head snapped up. There were just a few more steps and they were there. Ophelia and Justine were already there screaming at their success. Tristan was there too, unslinging the water canteen. Prudence then achieved it, clapping her hands at their victory.

Eleanor looked over at Lord Rascomb, who wore the most impish grin she'd ever seen on a man over the age of thirty-five.

"I had to distract you somehow so you wouldn't give up," he said.

Eleanor shook her head. "I wouldn't have," she croaked.

"Then it's still a valid question." He winked and pulled himself up to the plateau of Ben Nevis, extending his hand to her.

She shook her head. She didn't want a hand up. With the final push, the backs of her legs burning with the effort, she reached the top.

$$\sim\!\!\blacklozenge\!\!\sim$$

Chapter Thirteen

T HE WATER CANTEEN had made its rounds, and Eleanor got her hands on it, greedily drinking down the ice-cold water. Ophelia and Justine approached the edges of the plateau on all sides. Some approaches were steep, others were not.

Ophelia oriented herself with a compass she had looped around her neck. Eleanor wasn't sure, but she believed it to be south. South towards London, towards their families.

Then Ophelia screamed wordlessly, her fists balled at her sides. Eleanor startled, but then listened as Ophelia's voice echoed in the valleys below. Justine ran over and screamed too.

"Take that!" Ophelia screamed again, her face red. "You cheese-faced donkey-fuckers!"

Justine laughed, but then yelled the same.

Eleanor was shocked at the language, looking to Lord Rascomb to see if he would reprimand his daughter. But his face was as placid as if Ophelia had curtsied to the queen.

"I told you we could do it, you arse-faced fart machines!" Ophelia yelled.

Justine doubled over in laughter.

Prudence walked over to the edge facing south and yelled wordlessly, just as Ophelia had. And then, in the most American way possible, she screamed, "Fuck you!"

Despite the fact that Eleanor had grown up very nearly on the docks of the Thames, she had not said these types of invectives in her life. Still, she felt compelled to join the other women.

As she came up, Prudence grabbed her hand, and then Justine's. Soon, the four of them were linked, and Eleanor felt that urge to scream. She hadn't understood it at first. But now, there was a power to them, standing side by side. So she let it out. She screamed. She screamed her frustration and confinement. Her invisibility and undesirability.

And then the words came, unbidden. Those years of hearing the rough words of sailors from every nation, sometimes in English, sometimes in the rough or melodic languages of their homelands. "I hope the world scars you and your brethren, you stupid maggots burrowing in piles of your own shit and monkey piss!"

She said it, picturing every man that had told she couldn't do something. Every woman who judged her as lacking because she couldn't paint or draw. Every stitch in the fabric of society that kept her from the joy of using her own two legs, and making her believe that was best.

There was silence as the word *piss* echoed in the valleys below. The other women stared at her. It was quite a long obscenity compared to the rest of them. And then the others broke out laughing. They hugged each other.

Lord Rascomb began to sing a song they'd heard at the inn, a folk song that sounded ripe for dancing. Ophelia joined in, looping her arm through Justine's and twirling around, taking them back to the middle of the peak.

Prudence swung her around, and they danced an impromptu jig, laughing, singing the tune as Lord Rascomb clapped to keep the beat. Soon, she was twirling with Tristan, and it felt like love was bursting out of her every pore. It was beautiful. And Eleanor felt so alive, and big, and free.

TRISTAN HAD CLIMBED many mountains. French ones, German ones. This day on the Ben was far from difficult, but it was clearly his favorite. Mostly because of the company. It was sheer delight to watch his sister and her friends experience this joy of accomplishment. The conditions had been ideal, and lacking the extra weight of packs, they were free to scamper up unburdened.

Eleanor was glowing. Whether it was a trick of the light filtering through the clouds, the exhaustion from the climb, he didn't care. She was perfect and looking at him as if she belonged to him. And he dearly wanted her to. This wasn't the right moment, with everyone gathered there, and every word carried across to each other and down the mountain, but soon he would ask her not for courtship, but for an engagement.

During the climb, his mind had cleared. If they announced a long engagement when they returned to London, complete with reading of the banns, all scandal would dissipate. While scandal-mongers might claim Tristan was after her dowry, it wouldn't matter.

All the doubts he'd felt before about whether or not he could commit to marrying her, or marrying anyone for that matter, had seemed foolish when examined. Because he came to realize that marriage not a pretty thing to be put on a shelf and admired. It was a living commitment, and like contracts that were amended and signed, so too was a marriage a dynamic agreement that moved and stretched as each person aged and became more than they were before.

They could be together as his parents had, adventuring the world together as experienced partners, not a man leaving his wife in London, nor as a man dragging his wife to accomplish his dreams. Tristan would be delighted to help her accomplish her dreams, because his dream was simply to live free. And being with Eleanor made him feel free.

If he had changed so much in his years from the boyhood trickster, why would he not imagine he would continue to change? And Eleanor as well. She had blossomed in the months since Ophelia found her at that party. She'd given classes to experts, spoken in front of crowds, danced with nobility. And now—climbed a mountain. Not just any mountain—the Ben. The highest peak in Great Britain. One would have to travel to Scandinavia to find another peak this high. And here they were, dancing on top of it.

God, he wanted to kiss her. But he didn't. Instead, he picked her up and swirled her about, her heavy wet skirts shifting awkwardly around her legs, slapping at him.

She whooped loudly as he did. He put her down, and she held his arms, not letting go.

"We did it," she whispered.

He let his forehead lower to hers. "We did."

Ophelia jerked Eleanor's arm away from him and engaged her back into the twirling jig. Finally, his papa stopped his singing and the girls stopped.

"We've got to save some of that energy for the way down," he said.

Ophelia caught her breath, and Tristan watched her change from the exultant girl to their pragmatic leader once again. "Quite right. Last drink of water, then we'll head down."

The canteen was passed around once more, and Tristan drank last, emptying it, savoring the cold, metallic-tasting water trailing down his throat. He thought of being back at the inn, ensconced in front of the large fireplace and cradling a dram of whisky. Not a bad ending to a day.

"Come on, then. Let's go pick up our rope. It won't take nearly as long to get down as it did to climb up." Ophelia led the charge, picking her way down. Tristan knew he'd be the one to carry the rope while his father would shoulder the now-empty rucksack that Tristan had hauled up when it held their breakfast. As it should be. The torch was passing, and despite not inheriting his father's title, Tristan was stepping into his role as a husband. Perhaps one day as a compassionate father.

"Do you know how to glissade?" Prudence asked.

"That sounds like something that happens in a ballet," Tristan said.

"You should know," Justine snorted.

Tristan glanced at Eleanor. Did she know about his previous affairs with dancers? But she didn't react to the barb, one way or the other. He hoped she wouldn't think poorly of him for his past indiscretions.

"Anyone? Because it will make this go so much faster," Prudence said.

"I think we should stick together," Ophelia said.

"I agree," his father said, breaking his rule of not speaking after Ophelia. Perhaps he just wanted to emphasize how important it was not to lose sight of each other. A lesson they had learned the hard way.

It was a day that had felt like this, even if the terrain and weather and season were completely different. The similarities were in the joy he felt with the warm sun on his face and the cool breeze brushing the back of his neck. The crunch of snow. The fact that he could look at any one of their party and smile.

And then the avalanche buried his mother. No, they would stick together. He examined the rime ice that encrusted a stone. It looked like a newspaper being held against a lamppost on a particularly blustery day.

Ophelia stopped short and surveyed the path down. "I think I'd rather us walk the ridgeline. I'm worried about a slide."

"Good thinking, my girl," his father said to her, below the hearing of most everyone. Ophelia stood noticeably taller after one of his compliments. And she deserved it. They had hit a snag when they arrived in Edinburgh to find themselves without a guide. But Ophelia had kept morale high, and expectations were met. They were on time, doing better than expected. No one could ask for a better leader.

They hiked over to the east, lining up with a ridge that would keep them above the snow fields. It was a safer route than their way up, especially now that the temperatures were dropping quickly.

Ophelia led the way, cutting into the sides of the snow with her boots, creating a staircase for the others to follow as they climbed up the ridge. Justine and Prudence followed in Ophelia's footsteps precisely, and it was then that Tristan figured out that they were out of order. Even when not roped together, they should have followed their chosen order for safety. That way, no one could get left behind. Tristan waited before climbing the stairs, gesturing Eleanor in front of him so he could speak to his father, who maintained his position of rear guard.

"Should we not maintain our positions?" Tristan asked his father.

The older man looked surprised, realizing, no doubt, that no one else was in their assigned slot. "I suppose we should. Once we get up on the ridge, we'll be able to adjust."

"I don't want to be the one to tell that to Ophelia. She'll think I'm butting in where I don't belong."

His father sighed and pushed past him. "I'll talk to her. Stay in the back until I return. We can't let any of our little chicks wander off."

Tristan agreed and followed his father up the now well-packed steps in the snow. When he reached the top, he looked over the snow that lay before him. He wasn't an expert in the stuff by any stretch, but he knew the men who were. The men who would peer up to the peaks in the mornings, judging whether or not a party should be allowed to climb, given the risk of avalanche. He wanted to become a man who could read the snow, understand the weather conditions with the certainty they'd had.

But they'd taught him the little they could, given their language barriers and his rudimentary scientific knowledge. He was not, he would confess, the best of students.

The snow here was crusted and old. Given how warm it had been that morning, he wondered that it hadn't started to melt. His father made his way up the line, passing Eleanor, and then

Prudence, catching up to Justine and Ophelia. His tracks in the snow widened where he'd walked around someone.

Tristan swiftly caught up to Eleanor. She was breathing rhythmically as she looked down at the steps in front of her. "Are you well?" he asked.

She hummed her agreement but didn't look up nor change her breathing. He noticed she looked a bit pale under the bright spots of pink in her cheeks.

"You don't look it," Tristan insisted. Did he need to insist she chew some snow in order to get some water in her system?

"I don't like heights," she said, slowing her pace.

That was news. And perhaps something she should have mentioned before. "But you just climbed that mountain. You've already been higher than you are now."

"I mean that drop over there," Eleanor said, motioning to the other side of the ridge that looked far sharper of a slope than the side they'd climbed up.

Tristan nodded. "Then perhaps you should walk closer to this other side and I can talk to you in order to distract you. What do you think?"

"Your father did that on the way up. He was very distracting." Eleanor looked pleased with his trick, and Tristan wondered what his father could have said to make her look so thrilled.

He offered her his arm, which she took. "Then that settles it. A successful plan."

Tristan took one step, and the world broke apart. His feet were in the air. His stomach was in his throat. He was falling, still holding Eleanor. He looked to her, her eyes rounded in terror, and he felt his back hit the hard ground, the snow shattering around them. But he was again in the air, still falling, hearing shrieks from above ringing out.

He thought he would die. And it was an oddly calm thought, full in its certainty. Then he thought of Eleanor. He couldn't accept her death.

He hit the ground again. This time, he was ripped from Eleanor as he tumbled down the mountain, hitting his face and arms against the rocks. He shifted to his back, pulling in his head to protect himself. And then he hit a rock. His body stopped.

A second later, something slammed into him.

He didn't know what had happened to him. His mental faculties opened back up. He opened his eyes, his eyelashes crusted with ice. He lifted his arm to brush the snow from his face, and his hand brushed against the solid form embedded into his. He peered down, discovering that it was Eleanor. Her distinctive hat was huddled against his chest.

"Eleanor?" he said, terrified that she wouldn't answer back. He touched her shoulder with his mittened hand. "Are you all right?"

Her head moved. Slowly her body shifted as she no doubt went through the same body checklist that he had. Was everything intact?

The chill at his back suddenly demanded his attention. The icy plaster against the rock dug into his back, working its cold through his layers.

Eleanor shifted, pushing herself away from him. She blinked up at him, her enormous brown eyes wide in fear. "I think I'm in one piece. Are you?"

"I think so." He wiggled his toes, testing to see if anything was broken. His legs seemed to work. So did fingers on both hands. He was sure there were other problems, but the surge of panic and instinct throbbing through his veins was keeping the pain at bay. He struggled, squirming to sit up. "Can you move?"

Her teeth chattered as she nodded, moving to a sitting position also. She brushed the snow from her sleeves. He shivered, doing the same.

"What—what was that?" Eleanor asked, her whole body beginning to shake.

Tristan looked up, hoping to see where on the ridge they'd fallen from. But he couldn't find it. They'd fallen quite far. He tried to get his bearings. The path of the fall was obvious. "My guess is a cornice."

The frozen fog was thickening noticeably, and the wind was kicking up. They had to get moving. Tristan groaned as he picked himself up to standing. His whole body ached and screamed at him to lie down, but he couldn't.

"Eleanor," he said, about to warn her that they must move or risk their lives to exposure.

She got to her feet, her body moving slow and hunched, as if she were decades older than she was. "I know." She met his gaze, the understanding clear there.

They were not near the path the others had been on. He hoped they would continue down and wait. Indeed, the safety plan was to reconnoiter at the location of their basecamp. In this case, the barn. If it were another mountain, Tristan would feel comfortable in his skills navigating them down. But that was because he knew mountains and snow from a different part of the world entirely.

This place, the Ben, it was different. The moisture in the air, the changeable mood of its weather—he didn't know how to read it. He peered down the path ahead of them. Patches of scree were visible underneath snow, which meant they were nearing the snow line. If they could get to the tree line, they could have some kind of shelter.

"We must—" Tristan started, ready to explain his entire plan.

Eleanor put her hand on his arm. "We must. You lead. I will follow."

He nodded, grateful for her serenity. Anyone would be forgiven hysterics following a slide such as that. But they didn't have time for such antics. They needed to move, and Tristan felt his heart swell with pride at her forbearance.

Each step jarred his bones. He checked behind him, watching Eleanor stumble but follow faithfully. He could tell by the way her upper body swayed that she felt as bruised as he did, perhaps more.

The fog made it impossible for him to tell how late in the day it was, or how close the tree line might be. The wisest course would be to hole up somewhere and recover. They could finish the walk down in the morning, when they were rested. Perhaps. Rested, but also possibly frostbitten.

No, they would continue. The wind seemed colder, icier than it had on the way up. Was the wind picking up? He couldn't tell.

Down they stumbled. His ribs turned from just sore to fiery pain. But they needed warmth. It was his single thought. The snow disappeared from beneath his feet, replaced with dark scree. He took a moment to watch Eleanor. "We're past the snow."

She looked up, sweeping their surroundings, nodding numbly. Tears filled her eyes.

"Are you in pain?" he asked, wondering if it was her spirit or her body that pained her.

"Let's keep going," she said, ignoring his question altogether.

Puzzled, Tristan turned and pressed on. They found sheep grazing the fields, and it was another benchmark. They were getting closer. Suddenly, an idea struck. "Do you think there would be a shepherd's hut somewhere here?"

"Pardon?" Eleanor asked, her breath coming faster than it ought. Damn it, she was hurt and she was hiding it from him.

"A shepherd's hut," he repeated.

Eleanor shook her head. "I haven't heard anyone speak of such a thing. With these winds?"

Tristan curled his fists in. She had a point. They hadn't yet reached tree line, so there wasn't any wood, and a shelter of any kind would blow over in the high winds the locals had described. They had to find something, though. He didn't think either of them could get to Fort William on foot tonight.

But gullies were everywhere. He scanned the landscape. The fog wasn't helping, but he saw one that might be deep enough to serve as decent shelter for the night.

"Come on," he said, veering off the path they'd been on. Once again, she didn't question, only persisted. Her faith in him was unnerving. He hoped he was worthy of it.

He continued downhill, cutting across the hillside toward where he'd spied the deep ravine. The dark scar down the hill was evident as he moved in the opaque fog. He glanced behind him, scared that Eleanor had lost him. But no, she was there. He huffed out a breath. He could keep them alive. He would keep them alive.

He waited for her to catch up a few more steps, as he didn't want to lose sight of her, and the fog seemed to be thickening. "Good?"

Eleanor nodded, seeming not to mind that he hadn't truly asked a question. But her eyes were still downcast, scanning the ground. It was then he noticed she was trying to conceal a limp. He'd be damned before he let her be permanently hurt.

Walking through the evening and pushing through to the bottom was out of the question. They would have to hole up, dry off, inspect any wounds. He wished they had food. But it was supposed to just be a day trip. The mountaineers he knew didn't bother taking any food whatsoever. It was extra weight to carry. And the mountaineers who did carry food had porters who carried it for them.

He reached the gully, a crack in the ground, running up as far as he could see. The seam made it obvious that this had once been a volcano. He ran his hand along the rock, but it didn't seem volcanic. It didn't snag and catch his skin.

Above him, it seemed to narrow, which made him wonder if lower it widened. Could he risk scouting it while Eleanor stayed here? He doubted she would allow it. But he certainly didn't want to make her walk any further than she had to, brave as she was. The wind was whipping against him harder now, burning his cheeks and making his eyes water.

"Not much further," he told her as she came up behind him, her breath coming in short pants. She was in pain. He offered his arm, which she seemed grateful to take. He supported her weight as they picked their way down, him eyeing the width of the gully as they went. Finally, it seemed to widen enough for two people.

"I think we've found it," he said.

"Found what?" she asked, her voice reedy and thin.

He gestured at the rocky hole in the ground. "Our hotel for the evening. Let me get us checked in."

Eleanor smiled, and he felt like he'd won a prize. At least she still had a sense of humor.

"Stay here," he said, disengaging himself from her. "Let me make sure the other guests have checked out."

He lowered himself into the seam in the ground. It was dark, but that was the least of his worries. He stamped his foot and brushed his hands across the sides of the rock. Moss and grass grew in fits and starts, making it slightly more hospitable. The gully was about five feet deep, so his head stuck out in the elements, but it should make a decent enough place to sleep and rest until morning.

The rest of the expedition might return with a search party tonight, which would be helpful. But the locals had told tales of the wind up here. Wind that could carry off a sheep, or even a full-grown man. He didn't know if he believed the stories, but he certainly didn't want to disbelieve them to his and Eleanor's detriment.

He shuffled up the gully, trying to find a patch of level ground. Finding nothing, he turned around.

"And? Any stragglers?" Eleanor asked, her teeth chattering.

"I think our room is ready," Tristan said. "Let's get you down here."

She looked doubtful.

"I'll help." Tristan boosted himself up onto the opposite embankment. "Have a seat." Eleanor sat on the other side, clearly favoring her left side. "Put your hands on my shoulders, like we're about to dance."

She obeyed, leaning forward, and he did the same, putting his hands on her waist. "This is the most awkward waltz I've ever done."

Tristan flashed her a smile. "It's about to get worse. I'm going to lower you down. Scoot off the edge slowly."

She inched forward, and when she came off the side, he gripped her waist, to help cushion her transition. His hands slid up her torso, and his stupid brain wouldn't stop noting that she was not wearing a corset. Or that his hands were so very close to her breasts. Or that his hands now safely under her arms, her hands rested on his upper thighs.

Not the time, he thought through gritted teeth. But whatever animal or base nature he had threatened to make it worse. He tamped it down.

He slid down the side and landed next to her. Very close next to her. This would be a tight space indeed.

"Cozy," she said.

"I would have preferred some furniture, maybe a chaise longue, but I'll complain to the management later."

"At least we're out of the wind."

He could have kissed her. Well, again. He would have kissed her again. For being so resilient, for not complaining, for not making a difficult position even more so.

"I'd like to explore a little more downhill. See if there's a flat spot where we could rest."

Eleanor nodded. "If you don't mind, I'll stay here."

Worry overflowed in him. She would be fine sitting here, he knew that. But the idea that something dire could happen to her, it flattened him. "Right. I'll be back soon."

ELEANOR KEPT A smile on her face until Tristan was disappearing down the narrow gully. Then she sagged against the rock, picking up her right foot. The hot, shooting pains didn't subside, but at least it didn't make it worse. It had been agony to get as far as here after the fall. Her whole body was sweating with the effort it had required.

A rock big enough to let her perch on it was nearby. She hobbled over and began unlacing her boot. Did she even want to know what was wrong with it? Or should she just keep it as it was and hope for the best? The boot was tight around her ankle, tighter than it should have been. That must have been the swelling from whatever was wrong. She laced the boot back up. Best not to worry until they had a permanent place to rest. A flat place where she could lay down and put her foot up.

It was dark and cold, and she was wet from being tumbled in the snow. It didn't smell like an animal was using this as a burrow, and she didn't see any evidence of an animal visiting recently, either.

She didn't know much about the animals that roamed Ben Nevis, but one thing she did know: they were lucky not to be dead. They should be dead. She was still trying to wrap her mind around what happened. The only thing she could come up with was that in walking side by side, one of them strayed onto a snow cornice. She'd read about them in one of the alpine journals Ophelia had foisted upon her in the beginning. A snow cornice was where the snow built up on the edge of land, but had no support underneath. So one could fall right through the snow, off a cliff. Which was what they'd essentially done. It must not have been that far of a fall, but it had certainly hurt like it had been.

Eleanor wondered if Tristan had any injuries he was hiding from her. He had a face that looked open and honest, but she knew from experience that he could keep a secret with the best of them. How else to explain his desire to kick her off the expedition? He could have given her the choice—told her that to accept his courtship meant that she would no longer be able to be a part of the Ladies' Alpine Society.

And, well, she would have answered accordingly. That was to say, she would have declined.

She shivered. The smell of wet wool was starting to surround her. She winced. How were they supposed to keep warm and stay alive when the temperatures were going to plummet, and they were both soaking wet? They had no food, no blankets, and she wasn't sure she would be able to walk much more.

"Eleanor!"

She started at her name, called from deep in the gully. "Tristan?"

"Come down here! You won't believe what I've found!"

If it weren't a steaming hot bath, she didn't care. But she got to her feet, using the walls to support her weight so she could hobble down to meet Tristan. When she could make him out in the low light, she shifted to only using one hand on the walls and attempted to walk normally.

His blonde hair was unruly now that he'd taken his woolly cap off. She wondered if this was how he looked when he first woke up. His blue eyes were bright, trying so hard to give her hope. Honestly, she wanted to just fall into a heap and cry. She couldn't walk. She was cold.

"Good news," he said.

She winced. Unless that news was a horse that could take her back to the hotel, no thank you. It wasn't good news.

Tristan pulled up a gray-brown tarp that for all the world had blended into the ground. "We've found a love nest."

Eleanor stared at him in shock, then let her eyes drift to the ground, where indeed, in a deeper natural crag sat a thick folded blanket, a cask of some kind of liquor—knowing the Highlands, that was whisky—and some wax paper folded around what might be food. Actual food.

"And this?" Tristan shook the tarp that had hidden the stash. "Is oilskin. We can secure it above us to keep us dry."

Eleanor felt the wave of so many fears and emotions and physical exhaustion and pain overwhelm her. Tears sprang from her eyes without any semblance of control.

Tristan dropped the tarp and ran towards her. "Eleanor, no, this is good news. We can survive the night, get help in the morning, try to help whatever you've done to your leg."

"What do you know about my leg?" Eleanor was quite good

at being invisible, keeping all her pain hidden.

"You're not a terribly good actress," Tristan said with a wince, as if he were telling her she her feet were too big, or her hands were too rough.

"I am so," she insisted, but allowed him to guide her to a shelf of rock to sit down.

"Then I am preternaturally perceptive," Tristan said, ducking his head to meet her eyes. "Rest here, and I will set up our own nest."

Eleanor couldn't help but let out a wet, hollow laugh. Their very own love nest. Here on delightful Ben Nevis, in a craggy volcanic gully, in high winds, that which she couldn't leave if she wanted to because she had likely broken something.

The pain was still hot and sharp, but there was nothing to be done. So all she could do was accept Tristan's help and comfort.

"Well, I wouldn't overstep and say love nest," Tristan said. "I mean, I would love to say that, but I haven't been properly introduced to any of the sheep we've passed."

Eleanor laughed in spite of herself, wiping her eyes with the back of her mittens.

He grinned and busied himself making them a burrow. He draped the oilskin tarp just below the edge of the gully, so that the wind might sail above it and not disturb them. He secured it with rocks. On his knees, he took out the packets in the hole in the ground, inventorying them. Then he set up the blanket just beyond the hold on a smooth bit of ground that was likely why this place had been chosen as a secret rendezvous spot.

"It's quite a climb for an assignation, don't you think?" Eleanor asked.

He looked at her with an inscrutable look on his face. "Some people would do anything for love. Even hike the tallest mountain."

She didn't know if she should feel chastened or honored. Was he referring to him climbing the mountain, or accusing her of not believing in love because she did climb the mountain? Should she be bold and challenge him, or meekly look away, which was her instinct?

Tristan busied himself with uncorking the unlabeled bottle. "Whisky," he said, and took a sip. His eyebrows went up in appreciation. "Good whisky." He eyed her, sitting perfectly still, and came over with the bottle. "Take a big drink. You need it for the pain."

Eleanor didn't like that he knew she was hurting. She was accustomed to being able to explain herself, make what she wanted to show visible, and hide everything else. How dare Tristan see every bit of her? It made her feel positively nude. Still, she accepted the bottle and took a drink, as instructed.

It burned fire on the way down, made her think of the campfire at Berringbone, and grass, and the top of a crème brulee she'd had once at her father's birthday celebration. And then she coughed. And every spasm of her chest sent pain shooting down to her toes and up to her skull.

"Careful. Maybe not so big of a dram all at once." Tristan took the bottle and went back to his position on the blanket, unwrapping the other packets.

The whisky continued to burn, and it made her flushed and lightheaded. A pleasant diversion from her foot. It made her bold. "And what would you do for love, Tristan?"

He was halfway to finding the contents of the wax paper packet when her question landed, and he froze in response. Was he going to run away this time too? Just as he had after he'd kissed her in the woods at Berringbone?

"I don't know," Tristan said, diving back into his inventorying. He unwrapped the first parcel, the stench of molded-over cheese unmistakable. "I think this has been here for quite some time."

Eleanor nodded. Yes, let's talk about cheese when she'd just asked him about love. Why should she have expected any different? She stood and hobbled over, not bothering to hide her injury. "I'm very cold."

Tristan nodded, a frown creasing his forehead. "That and your foot should be addressed. Let's get the outwear off, and maybe we can hang it to dry?"

Eleanor nodded, shedding both her big mittens and the gloves underneath. She worked at the toggles at her woolen greatcoat. Tristan took them from her as if he were a footman or a valet. While she slowly sunk to the ground, the agony of her boot throbbing against her leg, Tristan hung her wet coat and long woolen scarf along the rocks, ostensibly drying them, but also creating an insulated space.

"Too bad we don't have our climbing rope. The things I could do with that and our coats to make a wind shield." Eleanor pointed up-gully, where the wind still found them.

Tristan made another unreadable expression and sat down, unlacing his boots at the edge of the blanket. "Let's keep the blanket as dry as possible, shall we?"

Eleanor winced, her muddy wet boots dirtying the corner. Once Tristan had his boots off and stowed to the side, he sat looking at her with an intensity she didn't understand.

"Eleanor."

She looked around, trying to understand the context of his blinding attention. "Tristan."

"I need to look at your foot. Or your leg. Wherever you have injured yourself."

She was already shaking her head in the negative. "Absolutely not. Unnecessary at best."

He placed his hand on her right knee, the pain of even the gentle touch enough to make her want to cry out. "Eleanor."

There was no way she could walk on it anymore. No way to get out of here. He might as well look. "Do you know anything about injuries? Are you staying in Edinburgh to get your medical degree unbeknownst to the rest of us?"

He gave her a look of bemused patience. "I only want to play doctor with you."

Oh, she hated him right in that moment, making her blush.

"Fine." She bent forward to take off her left boot, which was no trouble, with crusts of icy snow stuck in the rivets for her shoelaces. Then she bent towards the right one and pain burst out. When she opened her eyes, Tristan was looking at her with a cold assessment. This was not the flirtatious man who was playing doctor.

He handed her the whisky bottle. "Drink up, lassie."

"That was, unquestionably, the worst Scottish accent I've ever heard." Eleanor still uncorked the whisky.

"But you took the bottle, so that's all I care about. I'll take off your boot, you keep at the bottle."

Eleanor winced before he even touched her, knowing that this removal would be excruciating. Tilting the bottle back, she rested her head against the outcropping of rocks. To her surprise, Tristan didn't pull against her boot. Instead, he unlaced the entire boot, the laces making a whirring sound and ending with a thwack as the waxed ends hit the metal grommets. So far, no pain, and that was something.

With the boot unlaced, Tristan peeled the tongue back, making as much room as possible. He looked up at her. "How's the whisky?"

"Surprisingly tasty," Eleanor said, feeling every drop of alcohol she'd imbibed.

"Do you know the moment we first met?" Tristan asked her.

"Just outside the women's lounge at a ball?"

"The very one. I thought, 'This is the most beautiful woman I've ever seen.'"

Warmth spread through Eleanor's chest.

"I wonder what she'd look like naked."

As she was on the way to outrage, Tristan yanked off her boot. The pain screamed through her, but all she uttered was a grunt. "You absolute arse," she said through gritted teeth.

"Distracted you, didn't it?" Tristan smirked. He bent to one knee in front of her, and it was something romantic to have a man do that. As if he were a knight of old, and she his lady love.

Except, his lady love had a repulsively huge ankle.

"Did you really think that?" she asked, still wanting distraction as she noticed the swelling. It looked bad. He was holding her ankle on his knee, moving her foot gently from side to side. She waited for his response, but he didn't give one, as if he were concentrating too hard.

"Does this hurt?" He pushed her foot flexed and then pointed, and when she said no, he moved it from side to side. That smarted and she yelped. He lowered her foot. "Good news and bad news."

"Is there good news in this?" Eleanor had to wonder.

"Of course there is, which I will enumerate for you after we get through the bad news." Tristan moved back to the stack of wax-paper-wrapped packets.

"I'm ready for bad news," Eleanor said, trying to hold back on realizing that she always thought in terms of bad news.

"Your ankle is sprained, I believe. I'm no physician, but I don't think anything is broken." He lifted his hand as if he were serving her something. "See? Good news."

Eleanor shook her head. "Not terribly good."

"Bad news is that the winds keep picking up. I don't think we can go anywhere tonight."

"No," Eleanor said, having realized this almost as soon as she'd gotten her wits about her after the fall.

"Good news is," Tristan grinned, "you're with me."

She laughed. "Is that good news?"

He looked around the small space, barely wide enough for the two of them across. "Obviously it is the best possible outcome. You're terrified of my father, Prudence would be exhausting with all that toothsomeness, Bad News complains every moment she is conscious, and Ophelia could convince you to walk all the way back to London on a broken leg, let alone a sprained ankle. I'm the best option."

The wind picked up and howled overhead. The tarp did its job and kept them from feeling it.

"Then be of service and tell me what kind of supplies you've found." Eleanor fell back on haughty language, clipping her vowels to a diamond point, as if she were the high-born and he the lowly merchant's child.

"My lady," Tristan bowed low, even though he was seated. His voice dropped to a droll baritone. "In this first packet, we have expired cheese of some sort. I've told the maids to take it to the groundskeeper for fertilizer. In this packet, we have dried fruits. They are, in fact, indistinguishable from pebbles, but that is what makes them a delicacy."

He handed over the packet of dried fruit, which indeed, was cold and hard. Apple rings perhaps? Maybe an apricot? It was hard to tell.

"For the second course, we have a packet of nuts. They have been aged for possibly a decade."

She put down the packet of fruit and accepted the packet of nuts, which made her wonder how they would split the shells. Perhaps with the dried fruit?

"And for the pudding course, whisky." Tristan displayed the bottle as if it had a label.

"Very good, sir." Eleanor gave him a dismissive nod. Dropping the game for a moment, she said, "I'm not sure I'm suited for this, Tristan. I'm cold, I hurt, I'm wet."

Tristan handed her the whisky bottle. "Welcome to mountaineering. Discomfort is all it is."

"Isn't it making it to the top of the peak? Seeing incredible vistas few humans will ever glimpse?"

Tristan shook his head. "That's the reward. Mountaineering is frostbite and shoe failures. It's losing toenails and being hungry. It's the cold, the wet, the smell of wool rotting while you wear it. It isn't glamorous. Mountaineering is the single most hardheaded, idiotic thing a person can do, short of wrapping oneself in raw steaks and parading into the London Zoo to see a tiger."

"But this is miserable," Eleanor exclaimed.

Tristan laid himself out on his side, as if he were at a Hyde

Park picnic in the height of summer. "The question is, is the pain worth the reward? Only you can answer that." He gazed up at her, his blue eyes full of questions and calm that took her by surprise.

He was asking her about more than the mountains, she knew that. Was the mountain worth the swollen ankle? Was love worth the inconveniences, the sacrifices?

Without meaning to, Eleanor slipped into the worst-case thoughts. What if she and Tristan didn't suit? What if he resented her? What if she resented him? What if they died on this mountain tonight, and there was no point in asking these questions at all?

"People die mountaineering," Eleanor said.

Tristan nodded, picking at the packet of dried fruit. "Constantly. Ask Lord Francis Douglas. It's a risk."

"Do you think we'll die tonight?" Her voice came out as a whisper. The exhaustion she'd felt earlier returned, and tears welled in her eyes. Her ankle hurt, her back felt bruised, and she was so tired. She didn't know how she'd get down the mountain tomorrow any more than she knew how to get down the mountain today.

In a flash, Tristan was up, sitting next to her, his arm around her. "As my nanny said, 'Whisht now, child.' We're going to make it. We are."

Eleanor hiccupped as she agreed with him, but tears came flooding out of her. Tristan folded her into his chest, rocking her slightly, cooing at her. It was the best thing she'd felt in ages. She leaned fully into him, letting her body melt. She couldn't hold herself apart any longer. It was too taxing. All of it was too much.

"We will be fine," Tristan said. "And I'm not just saying that."

"Why would anyone just say that?" Eleanor asked tearfully, hoping to rein in her childish weeping. But it was dreadfully wonderful to be encased in his arms.

"To make you stop crying." Tristan tightened his embrace. "It's bloody unnerving."

"But—" Eleanor sniffed and sighed. "But if I stop crying, you'll stop holding me. And I need you." She could feel the shift in his body as he realized it.

"Let's make a deal, you and I. You stop crying, and I won't let go until you tell me to."

She heard his voice rumble through his chest as much as she heard it in her ears. "Deal."

"Good," he said, and his approval did strange things to her.

Her weeping ceased, yes, but she was painfully aware of his hands on her back, fingers splayed wide. They breathed in and out, Eleanor's ears straining to listen for something that she couldn't name.

"May I ask you a question?" Eleanor was bolder when she didn't have to look him in the face. Instead, tucked against his chest, she looked at the woolen fibers of his sweater. His coat was hung behind them, next to hers.

"Of course."

"Did you really think we'd suit, or did you only want me off the expedition, and that was the easiest way?" Again his body shifted, tensing against her words.

"Eleanor. I never *wanted* you off the expedition. It was a condition to be with you. And honestly, the first time we'd met, you told me you didn't want to climb a mountain, so I thought I was doing you a favor."

"But didn't you see how hard I was working at Berringbone? How much I tried?" Eleanor sat up now, looking him square in the face. "I even told you how much I wanted to get to the top of this sodding volcano."

"I saw it. And I didn't know if you enjoyed working so hard. Like I said earlier, mountaineering is about endurance and pain and cold and inconvenience." He searched her eyes. "I wanted to be with you, and I did whatever it took to make that happen."

It was Eleanor's turn to scan his features, to see what his cracks and fissures lay. "You were willing to let *me* make the sacrifice for us to be together. That's not terribly convincing."

Tristan slid his hands to her elbows, letting her go and letting the cool air brush against her. "I did not think it through."

"Is that all you're going to give me for the last month's worth of agony?" Eleanor didn't know if it was the whisky or the exhaustion or the feeling of his hands on her, but she was unwilling to let him not acknowledge what had happened between them.

"As if I had a bloody smile on my face this last month. Seeing you was torture."

"Tristan Bridewell, my goodness." Eleanor pulled away completely, folding her arms over her chest.

"I have the bewildering feeling of disappointing my nanny. What?" His face was different now, gone was the open expression of moments ago.

"Is being unable to apologize bred into the nobility, or is that something you pick up at Eton?" Eleanor demanded.

"I went to Harrow, I'll have you know," Tristan said with a toss of his head.

"Is that for boys who are better or worse at evading personal responsibility?"

Tristan put his hands at his heart. "You wound me. I would have expected that sort of barb from our expedition team, not from you."

Feeling pushed, she gave him a shove at his shoulders. He rocked back at her meager effort. "Because I'm tired, Tristan. I'm tired!"

"Of course you are, as am I."

"It isn't the mountain. It's you." Eleanor shoved him again, harder this time, and he rocked back even further, but stayed upright. "Why can you not even admit you were wrong? That you behaved poorly?"

"I did. I behaved poorly. I apologized, and I apologize again." The words spun out as fast as he could say them, leaving them empty and incorporeal.

She shoved him again, tears once again springing, unwanted

and unbidden. This time he fell to his back, unprepared. "That's not good enough! You tried to rob me of my dreams. How dare you?"

He looked up. "I didn't know this was a dream of yours, Eleanor."

"So bloody apologize to me!" She whacked his arm with the back of her hand. She was not a violent person by nature, but she hadn't been able to get his attention any other way.

He sighed and drew his legs up, resting his feet flat on the rocky floor. "You scare me, Eleanor."

"I'm sorry," she said automatically. As soon as the words escaped her, she hated herself for it. She didn't want to apologize to him about anything, and without even thinking, she did so.

"Not your temper, though admittedly, that's an eye-opener." Tristan glanced over at her, then returned his gaze to the oilskin tarp that hung between them and the gray sky. "Eleanor Piper. I've thought about you daily, if not all day every day, since we met. I meant it when I said I thought of you naked, for how could I not? But I also thought of you dining with me. Dancing with me. Breaking your fast in the morning over the newspapers with me. I've thought about children, Eleanor. Children."

Eleanor frowned. She was losing the thread. "What about children?"

"Eleanor. Please, this is hard for me. I've had affairs with women before, but I have never, and I mean absolutely never, thought about those women being the mothers of my children."

She shook her head, not wanting to understand. The idea that he'd had affairs with women before made her stomach churn.

"But you? I've already picked out names, like I'm some kind of sodding family man. I've already decided that they'll have your lovely multicolored brown locks, and my devastating blue eyes."

"What?" Eleanor was confused.

Tristan sat up and took her hands. "Eleanor, I love you. I'm sorry I hurt you. I want us to be together so badly that I'm willing to name our firstborn after your father."

Eleanor couldn't bring herself to say anything. Everything he said was perfect, and she couldn't imagine anyone ever wanting her badly enough to say these things.

"If it's a girl…?"

Tristan grinned at her. "Even if it's a girl. Maybe especially if it's a girl. Wouldn't it be hilarious to have a pig-tailed little thing skipping 'round the house and calling after her, 'Bruce, Bruce, darling?'"

"You're trying to make me laugh." Eleanor warned.

"I am. Is it working?" Tristan asked.

"I'm not done being angry."

"Absolutely fine. In the meantime, may I still call you Eleanor? Perhaps El. Ellie. What should I call you? Darling? Sweeting? Devastating Goddess of My Erotic Dreams?"

"That last one sounds a bit long." There were a few silent moments where he looked at her expectantly. She had to get out her anger or she'd never feel good about herself. "You left the house and didn't speak to me after I protested that I didn't want to be kicked off the expedition. If it was such a big misunderstanding on my part, why did you sulk so dreadfully?"

Tristan dropped his head, his shaggy and unkempt golden hair flopping into his face. "That. Yes. Rather poor sportsmanship on my part. It is rather a kick in the arse to be told that a cold, desolate mountain is better than being married to me."

"We were only talking about courtship then."

"Even worse." Tristan sighed and took her hands again.

She stared at where his hands enveloped hers. His thumbs caressed the backs of her hands. He was warm. He was safe. He said he loved her. She had the sudden urge to burst into tears again, but she managed to keep her head about her. She didn't want him to think she was crying about marrying him. She nodded.

His blue eyes roved her face in such an earnest manner, it made her squirm to be so avidly viewed. But she let that thought go and examined him right back. He was beautiful, even here in this gray gully, cold and wet, deadly winds howling above them.

"I've bollocksed this up completely, haven't I?" Tristan gave her a wry smile. "I'm sitting here confessing my adoration for you, utterly convinced you feel the same about me. And now, you feel awkward because clearly you don't." He sat back, staring into the small space they occupied. "Don't I just deserve that."

Eleanor fought the urge to go to him, smothering him in assurances that she didn't feel. But she held herself apart. This was important. She needed to sort out her feelings, and his nearness made her dizzy all on its own. Couple that with his earnest declarations of love, she was positively nonsensical. "Give me a moment to think."

Eleanor dropped her head in her hands. She was in a gully in Scotland with a sprained, possibly broken ankle that was swelling up to resemble a pale hot air balloon with a devastatingly attractive man. Oh, who was also completely in love with her. Top it all off with an astoundingly foul-smelling cheese, dried apples as hard as pebbles, unbreakable hazelnuts, and remarkably good whisky. She let herself fall back against the wall, thinking how strange it was to round her spine like that, since she wasn't wearing a corset.

How very strange it all was.

Tristan stretched out, returning to his side, studying her as he propped up his head with one hand.

Eleanor looked down at him, not knowing how to cope with this man's bizarre conversation. "I am beginning to think you're daft."

"But handsomely daft?"

"Tristan." She tipped herself over to lie on her side, echoing his relaxed position. It felt dangerous and perfectly appropriate all at once.

"Eleanor." His normal joking demeanor, the flirtatious façade, crumbled, and Eleanor was left staring at him. The real him.

"There you are." The urge to touch his face was powerful, but she restrained herself.

"It takes a lot for me to stop making jokes," he said. "But I am absolutely serious about you."

"What do I have to give up in return?"

He shook his head. "Nothing."

"How can I be certain?" Her heart still stung from his previous actions. She'd get over it, but it would take some doing. She wasn't petty, but she was steadfast, and betrayals hurt so very much.

Tristan turned onto his back and looked up at the tarp. "I suppose you can't. But we can put anything we like in our marriage contract. If you want a line in there that says I cannot forbid you from climbing a mountain, I'll sign."

Eleanor felt as if something was shifting into place inside of her. There was something at work here, more than just her mind.

For once, he didn't speak. Didn't joke. He merely stared up at her. Abruptly he took a breath but didn't expel it. He looked down the gully. "Eleanor. May I kiss you?"

Chapter Fourteen

TRISTAN COULD ONLY see her lips at this point. She was talking and flirting with him, and he was doing his best to stay focused, to answer her questions and parry her barbs. But holy hell, it was becoming near impossible to pay attention. His body was snapping from exhaustion to exuberance, and he needed something to distract himself.

She didn't say anything, leading him to believe that he had once again, completely bollocksed up whatever this was between them. But suddenly he realized that this was her thinking face. The expression when she was thinking about why it could be a bad idea and why she might *do it anyway.*

"I think that would be fine," she said finally, her eyes downcast.

"If you don't want to kiss me, don't be afraid to say no." It killed him to say it, but he needed to make sure she wasn't intimidated by him. He desperately wanted to kiss her, but he also didn't want to kiss a woman who didn't want it.

She raised her velvet brown eyes to his. "I would really prefer it if you would."

He swallowed hard. His body was already reacting to her. There were many things he would like to propose in order to hear such proper words from her. He would love to find all the things she preferred. He went to his knees, pulling her up as well. Kissing a woman while lying down was too much temptation for him. At least, it was when the woman was Eleanor.

And he meant to be chaste. A virginal peck on the lips. He was trying very, very hard. But, as usual, things got away from him.

He tilted her chin up. She eyed him through her inky lashes before closing them in preparation. It gave him a moment to study her up close. The subtle spray of freckles across her nose. A virtually unnoticeable pock scar near her hair line. The perfect skin underneath all of it, as if she were made of marble or milk.

He pressed his lips to her soft mouth. And dear God, she melted into him. They matched bodies from knee to chest, and his lust sprang to life, urging him to explore deeper. Her rapid breathing distracted him, another signal to the animal in him. He deepened his kiss, pushing his tongue at the seam of her lips, until she opened her mouth and let him in.

She gripped at his shirt, the heat of her fingers pressing through all of the insulating fabric. He wrapped his arms around her completely, pulling her into him. His body was no longer content with kisses. She was soft, and without a corset, he could feel her body mold to his.

The taste of her was sheer madness. It was nectar, it was honey, it was the explosion of a thousand Mount Olympuses in his mind. Before he could think, he reached down and cupped a handful of that incredibly luscious arse. It felt so ripe and perfect in his hand. She moaned in response, and the sound made him hard enough to pound nails.

He pulled away, releasing her with a burst of superhuman willpower. "I'm sorry," he panted.

Her eyes were dark and wild, her lips wet and rouged from his kiss. "For what?"

"For pushing. Eleanor. I can't merely kiss you. It isn't safe for you, for us, to be doing this here."

"Safe for me?" she asked.

"Safe for your virtue." He dared look at her again, her dark locks disheveled, and the lust plain on her face. It was some unseen magnetism that made him unable to part their bodies even further. She drew him in. But no. No. He had control. He had willpower in spades. Didn't he?

"What if I don't want it anymore?" she asked, her voice grave and quiet.

"Want what?" he asked, because surely, surely she could not mean what he thought she meant.

"I will say this once, so there is no room for your agonizing."

"I don't agonize," he protested, knowing full well that he absolutely did.

"I'm not certain I'm getting off this mountain. I want to know what it would be like to be with you."

She might as well have hit him over the head with a hammer. His mind spun in every direction. "First, we are in fact getting off this mountain alive," he said.

The lust that had been so clear on her face dimmed. Oh, that had been a real offer. It wasn't a joke or a temptation. She'd meant it. Which, of course she did, because she was Eleanor, and Eleanor didn't make empty threats or promises.

"And second," he continued, "you can tell me to stop any time and I will stop." He reached for her, and was pleased that she reached for him in return. She threaded her fingers through his, and even her smooth palm was dissolving his body into drunken desire. This was real. He nuzzled her perfect, shell-like ear.

"Did you know what I thought when I first saw you?" she asked as he trailed kisses down her neck. Her beautiful, soft throat. He could bury himself here, smelling her hair, pulling her earlobe into his mouth. She gasped when he did so, and he filed that reaction away for later.

"What was that?" he asked, pulling her fully into his lap. She was his right now.

"I wonder what he looks like naked," she said.

And he laughed. Because she'd thrown his own words in his face, but also because she said what she wanted. "I'm happy to oblige." One of his hands roamed her back, and the other worked the buttons on the high collar of her shirtwaist.

"I'll do mine if you do yours." Her hands moved to her own buttons. She squirmed in his lap, a motion that did no favors to his control.

Once again, he was totally stunned. He didn't want to spend any amount of brain power on his own buttons, so he sat there like a complete mump and watched her unbutton her top. Slowly, the pale, smooth, expanse of her skin was revealed. She wore an odd sort of under-jacket, unlike any he'd ever seen before. It had straps over her shoulders and barely went past her ribcage. He didn't know what it was, but it was unusual, and he liked it.

"It's old-fashioned," she said. "But it was the best design for our purposes."

He slowly pushed one strap so that it fell off her shoulder. Her skin was hot, despite the cold temperature. It was fascinating to see how that woolen strap hung. She slid off the sleeves of the shirtwaist, her skin suddenly prickling. Another distraction for him.

"Your turn," she commanded.

He didn't want to stop tracing invisible lines on her skin. He wanted to trace each path with his tongue. He wanted to spend days touching her, tasting her, drinking her in. "Do you want to take mine off?"

She nodded, her tongue slipping out to touch the side of her mouth. Relief washed through him as she worked the top button of his shirt. She completely forgot the waistcoat, but he did not care. His hands had been shaking with effort to keep them to himself. Now, he could caress her as she unbuttoned his clothing.

"Oh, damn your buttons!" Eleanor huffed.

"Yours are worse," he murmured in her ear, before kissing the soft spot behind it. He could care less about his own shirt. His mouth wandered down her neck. He nudged the other strap off her shoulder with his nose, then kissed the skin where it had lain.

"You could just lie back and relax."

"I want to see you, though. I want to see all of you." Her eyes were dark and intense, asking more of him than anyone else had ever wanted. It caught something in him, some circuit that engaged for the first time. He did feel worthy of her now, the way she asked for him.

"You will," he promised. But she was perched on him, giving him the perfect angle of her small, high breasts. "But let me make you feel good first."

She was cautious, and he moved slowly for her sake. Her ran his roughened fingertips down to where the fabric cupped her breast. He pulled the fabric down, exposing her and her perfectly taut nipple. He ran his thumb over it, and she squirmed. He leaned forward and took her lips.

He worked one hand into her hair while the other exposed the second breast, thumbing that nipple in the same way. Tristan shifted his body, scooting Eleanor off his lap and onto the ground. Repositioned, he dipped his head to lick the valley between her breasts before moving to one side. He licked her nipple, letting the cool air do its own work. His other hand moved along her leg, pulling up the heavy woolen skirt and its petticoat. She still wore her thick woolen stocking on one leg, having discarded the other when he'd examined her ankle.

Her hand slid into his hair, scratching his scalp ever so lightly with her fingernails. He whimpered. Something about that possessive gesture from her made him want to spend right away. How did she know to do that? His focus returned, and he continued sliding his hand up past her knee, to the soft bare flesh of her thigh. He unclipped the garter holding up her woolen stocking, rolling it down to give himself more space to play.

Her thigh shook as he took a great handful of her leg. He paused his ministrations to her breast. "Is your ankle all right? Do you need me to stop?"

She looked down at him, her mouth open as she panted. "Don't. Stop."

Tristan grinned and moved to the other breast, her fingers still entwined in his hair. He continued his exploration of her thighs until he reached her center. The wet seam was tantalizing. He ran his finger up and down it, intentionally going slowly enough that even an inexperienced virgin might buck at the teasing.

He delved in between her folds and found that perfect nub. She thrust against his hand. God, it was incredible to have her react to him like this. His cock strained in his trousers, rubbing against her hip. Her hand fisted his hair and pulled him up to look her in the eye as she sputtered and arched. Her cry, unfettered by decorum, was a potent aphrodisiac.

Having given her one climax, he caught her lips, kissing her deeply as he used his fingers to coax her into another. "My beautiful Eleanor, I want to see you come again." He nipped at her breast, one then the other, letting the cool air do the work for him. "Let me see."

Again her back arched, wordless noises of pleasure echoing off the walls. She returned to herself, catching his soaking hand. "My turn," she panted. "Clothes. Off."

A thrill ran through him at her commands. She struggled to keep her composure, and she looked every inch debauched. Her gorgeous breasts were displayed to the air, her nipples wet and pointed from his kisses, her skirts pushed up to her waist. His fingers skated across every one of his buttons, and soon he dropped his waistcoat to the ground, shucked the braces from his shoulders and pulled his shirt over his head. "Do you like what you see?"

Her expression was feral. "You're so beautiful, Tristan."

"As are you, my darling." He unbuttoned his trousers and let them fall. He finished undressing, trying very hard to not think about her staring at his painfully throbbing cock, because that would end things sooner than he would like. He lay down beside her.

"It's not what I thought it would look like," she confessed.

He searched her meaning. "My cock? What did you think it would be like?"

She shrugged. "Smaller, I think."

He threw his head back and laughed. He cupped her jaw with one hand, kissing her lightly on the lips. "Would you like to touch it?"

She nodded, biting her lip, as if now she were shy. He didn't think it was a game or a ploy on her part, and it was driving him absolutely out of his mind. She gripped him in her smooth pale fist.

He let out a steadying breath. What else could he think about? Bugs. He could think about bugs. She slid her hand up to the tip, her thumb swiping the moisture leaking from the tip.

"Oh," she sighed, in a way that sounded both pleased and revelatory.

Bugs were not enough.

"Are you well? I'm not hurting you, am I?" Eleanor was very concerned.

He shook his head, unable to speak, for fear of spending. "Eleanor. I'm so very close. And I would very much like to be inside you."

"I would prefer it," she said.

He flipped her on her back, taking another steadying breath. He needed to last. "Is your ankle—"

"My bloody ankle is bloody fine. Give me your cock."

Tristan gritted his teeth. She was a marvel. "Your preferences are going to drive me mad."

He rubbed the tip of his cock on her blessed little nub, and it made her legs widen. Of her own volition, her hand rubbed at one of her nipples. He stared, fascinated by the white skin massaged by her delicate fingers. She seemed like she might be getting close again. What a fucking wonder she was.

"Are you ready?" he asked.

She nodded, lifting her head to see. He circled her entrance with his cock, trying to relax her, make her ready. Was she ready enough? He'd never bedded a virgin. He moved slowly, entering her inch by inch, trying very hard to pay attention to any discomfort on her part. But she felt like slick perfection, warm and boundless. He slid all the way in, and to his surprise, she clutched at his arse, pulling him into her.

Another gesture of possession that almost made him lose control. She was his, perhaps, but more importantly, he was hers. He liked that thought. In the world, he could take care of her, and at home, she would take care of him. He thrust gently, listening to her breath catch with the friction between them. He touched that nub again, and moments later, her quim pulsed on him, milking him, pulling at him.

He yelled as he came, the release from months of seeing her, the release from their dangerous fall, the release from loving someone and finally knowing they loved him in return. "Oh fuck," he whispered, cursing as luxuriated in between her legs. Her hands ran along his arms.

"I feel like an absolute fool, but—"

"—I love you," he interrupted. "I love you more than every-thing I've ever felt in my entire life put together."

She smiled, almost a bit sly. "Have to be first, don't you?"

He pulled out, finding a rag that once wrapped the parcels of food. He cleaned himself and her with it. He gestured to her. "Please. What were you going to say?"

"I love you, Tristan Bridewell."

Balling up the rag and throwing it across the stone gully, he gave her his most arrogant look and said: "I know."

She threw her head back and laughed. He couldn't help him-self, he leaned forward and licked the beautiful column of her neck. She shrieked. "What are you doing?"

He couldn't go again right away; there was some time to wait. "The trespass has been committed. I like to revel in my choices."

"But aren't you tired?" she challenged.

"Do you have something better to do?" he challenged back.

"Let me rest. Then we'll see," she said, righting her clothing.

For the sake of the cold, he donned his clothing, and they lay together in the darkness of the gully. "What are we going to do?" Eleanor asked.

"We're going to get married, obviously. It's going to be very challenging to have rendezvous this entertaining if we aren't."

Her laughter rang like small bells in the darkness.

"Is that a yes?" Tristan asked, a strange nervousness clanging through him.

"It is a yes, but I was asking about getting out of here. Getting to safety." Just as she finished speaking, her stomach growled.

Tristan felt her words like another command. A less sexy one, but a dire one. She couldn't walk, so it was up to him to figure out what to do. How to bring home his bride.

⇛⇚

ELEANOR AWOKE ALONE. Their chamber was humid from her breath and her body heat, but Tristan's absence was notable. After all, if she wasn't touching him, where could he have gone?

At least there was time for her to take inventory of herself. The ankle was still swollen and sore, but slightly less so. Or perhaps that was merely optimistic thinking. The rest of her body felt sore in a different way. She felt raw between her legs in a way that made her smile. Their coupling had been extraordinary. No wonder people got married.

So, where was he? She dressed and, gathering courage to face the cold winds, she threw off the oilskin tarp and peeked out of the gully that had been their makeshift love nest. The fog had subsided, but the sun was still obscured by clouds. Movement caught her attention, and she turned. There was Tristan, striding along the rocky hillside, the climbing rope wrapped across his chest. He looked magnificent, as if he were a hero out of a fable.

Once he got within earshot, he immediately apologized. "I'm

sorry you had to wake up alone. But I had an idea, and I couldn't wait." He heaved the rope off his shoulders and slid down into the gully, kissing her on the lips as if their connection was comfortable and easy.

It thrilled her that it felt that way. She could stand with having a greeting kiss after every return. "What is your idea?"

"It occurred to me that we could tie you onto my back, and I could carry you down." Tristan began tidying up their cave, throwing off the blanket and stowing packets of food and what was left of the whiskey in the hole in the ground.

She frowned. "I'm not terribly light, I'll have you know. I don't think it's wise."

Tristan paused then looked up at her. "I will attempt to say this without offending your sensibilities."

She put her hands on her hips. What insult could he manage at this point?

"I have seen porters carry loads three times their own weight up and down mountains, with a clever use of ropes to balance the burden. Don't you think we could do something similar?"

It was a good idea in theory, but Eleanor didn't know anything about either the physics or the physiques involved. She stared at him, trying to imagine where ropes would even go. "It may take some trial and error."

"Do you have better things to do?" Tristan asked, his face as blandly polite as if he were truly asking her the asinine question.

"Valid point, sir." Still, she frowned. Where would the ropes go? "What is the best way to distribute the weight on the porter?"

Tristan grinned and motioned to his waist. "Around the waist, around the chest, and around the forehead is what I've seen."

Well, she was not putting a climbing rope around his head. This rope was far too thick, and the idea of it slipping down around his neck, choking him, was far too unappealing. She'd concentrate on binding herself to him around his waist and chest. Her face heated at the thought, as her memories of last night flashed through her attempts at focusing on her new problem.

After he finished tidying away all of the makings of their love nest, hiding the evidence that anyone was ever here, he came over and attempted to sit next to her on the rock she perched on. It was the only natural seat available, but it didn't work well for two across.

"That's not right," Tristan muttered as he got up, and he swung his leg around behind Eleanor, sliding onto the rock as if he were mounting a horse, with her in front. "There we are." His breath hit right below her ear, in that space he had discovered last night.

She shivered. "How am I to think now?"

He rubbed her arms, his touch deep and intimate. "I have no doubts in the power of your mind."

She nodded, thinking about the type of seat she would manufacture with the climbing rope. One that could be comfortable enough for her for the miles downhill and then to wherever people might be. And then Tristan's hand molded around her breast. Instantly, she felt ready for him again. Her nipples strained to hard points, and now that she knew what to expect, she felt the wet heat between her legs. "Tristan—"

"Hmm?" He used his thumb to tease her nipple through the fabric. "Keep on thinking. I've got this well in hand."

"I can't think when you do that," she said, aware that her voice had dropped to a whine.

"Oh, no? That's too bad." His hand abandoned her breast and pulled up her dress instead. Unlike yesterday, when he took his time getting to the center of her pleasure, this time he went straight for her apex, circling around the hard bud she'd found so much affection for.

Her body arched back into his as he continued his ministrations. She could feel his hard cock pushing into her from behind. Instinctively, she scooted back into it.

"No, my exquisite genius, this is not involving me. You see, you have things to plan while I have nothing to do. And I get bored easily. This is the best way to keep us both focused."

Eleanor had no thoughts of knots or anything but his delicious forearm that flexed down her front, pinning her to him, while he worked his fingers in her wet quim. She gripped his arm as the wave of pleasure crested through her.

"There you are, good girl," Tristan cooed in her ear, the words sending her almost to a second brink.

All right. Eleanor needed to concentrate. Now that she had found her climax, and Tristan had said this wasn't about him, she could focus on the trouble at hand. Indeed, he was dismounting the rock, coming around in front of her, rubbing the sizeable bulge in the front of his trousers.

"Are you sure you don't need anything?" Eleanor asked, very distracted by the sight of him.

"Keep going with that big brain of yours," Tristan said. "I'm quite busy, I assure you."

But he didn't take care of himself, which Eleanor very much wanted to watch. He pushed her legs apart, flipped her skirts up to her waist, and knelt. "But what—"

He grinned, and bent down, put his face right at her quim and licked.

"Oh, God," she blurted, not meaning to blaspheme. But it was the only thing she could think in that very moment. Suddenly, she could no longer sit up. She leaned back, supported by her elbows, watching his golden head move between her thighs. Then she noticed he was pleasuring himself as he did so, and it was not long until she came again, doing her best to not squeeze his head.

"Nicely done, Eleanor," he said, wiping his mouth on the hem of her skirt. He unbuttoned his trousers, still kneeling in front of her. "Let me admire my handiwork for a moment more, please."

He took his hard, bare cock in hand and slid up and down. She watched, memorizing his motions, wanting so badly to touch him in the ways he touched her. He stared at her wet quim, then he gripped one of her thighs, staring into her eyes as he came, and the warm, ropy seed covered her legs. Tristan sat back on his heels, head down, panting, his hand still strangling his cock.

"Are you well?" she ventured, after moments of him not moving.

When he lifted his head, his blue eyes cut right through her. "Eleanor, I cannot tell you how very ideal it is to be stuck on a mountainside with you, facing death."

She burst out laughing. He did too, and he leaned forward, lacing his sticky fingers behind her waist, his head resting on her hip. She petted his back. "I've never had a better time freezing to death."

"Quite pleasant, is it not?" Tristan's voice was muffled by her skirts.

Suddenly, staring at his back, she knew how she would create the rope structure that would take them both back down to safety. "I know how to do it now."

"I'd say so," Tristan said, rising up.

She batted his arm. "Not that. Carrying me down to town."

"Right. So." Tristan procured the same rag they used last night and cleaned them both.

She could get used to such attentions. It wasn't at all like she'd heard coupling would be—none of the dread, lying in the dark, waiting for a new husband to pass the threshold as if he were fording the Rubicon. This was fun and playful, and she knew she should worry about her ruin, and consequences, but she couldn't. Tristan made her feel safe above all else.

"This is going to be a bit complicated," she said, standing.

"I've no doubt it will be. But let's crack on, shall we?" Tristan pulled the oilskin tarp off the gully, the illusion of their love nest well and truly shattered. The wind found its way in immediately, causing her to slip into her now-dry coat. Both of them dressed fully, hats on and mittens at the ready.

Eleanor sat on the rock once more, unmolested this time, as she concocted an improvised webbing for her to sit on, leaving plenty of tail that would serve to tie around Tristan's waist. After the seat was knotted, she bid Tristan come stand in front of her. She held the heavy rope up, visualizing where and how the rope would connect them. "This will take teamwork."

"I'm excellent at teamwork," Tristan said, standing stock still as she'd asked.

She looked at him, seeing his sly smile. "You know, I think you rather are good at teamwork."

Tristan gave her an encouraging look. "Of course. I don't lie. Everyone thinks I'm joking constantly, but it's only because I tell the truth no one wants to say."

"Like how good looking you are?" Eleanor teased, pulling him around, so he faced away from the rock.

"Exactly. Unless you'd rather argue about it?"

"Arms out," she instructed, stepping up onto the rock. She handed him the long tail she'd left when she'd created her webbing. "Hold this." She wrapped the other end of the rope around, feeding the long, heavy cable along with it. "I'm not arguing with you about anything. You, after all, are my ride."

"Yes, I am," he said with a certainty that made her blush.

She ignored his innuendo and instructed him to wrap the rope, helping to thread the rope, never twisting. By the end, the rope was diagonally wrapped around his chest, creating an X in front, and an X around her in back. "Ready?"

"Climb on," he answered, backing up a little more. So she did, her legs at his hips, her skirts disgracefully tucked to cover as much of her legs as possible. And then they cinched the knot that she instructed him to tie at his chest level.

Her chin was on his shoulder, watching him tie, taking a few turns before, yes, there it was. He cinched, and the ropes creaked as she was pulled into him.

"It's supposed to distribute the weight between your hips and your chest. Is it working?" Eleanor was not the lightest member of their expedition. And she was the type of girl that didn't mind an extra scone at tea time.

He took a step, which made Eleanor feel mildly dizzy. "Yes, I think so. Quite." He deftly tied an overhand stopper at the tail end of the cinch, to keep it from loosening. She was proud of him for that quick bit of thinking.

He climbed out of the gully, a dizzying experience that she shut her eyes against. And then he started down the mountain in a very confident direction.

"Do you know where the trail is?" She had to shout, given the wind.

He nodded. "Where do you think I got the rope from?"

The wind still bit at them, and she was glad for his body heat, though she was wishing for another set of wool stockings. He was sure-footed like a mountain goat, taking great strides when the rocks had dissipated into dirt. She kept her face buried in the soft wool knit of his cap, letting her ears take the brunt of the cold. The rhythm was mesmerizing and sure. Almost like being rocked to sleep. Neither of them spoke. Her ankle still hurt, the wind was still cold on her legs and her back, but she felt strangely at peace.

All of a sudden, he stopped and pointed. Eleanor peered over his shoulder and saw the barn where they'd stayed the night before the climb. She almost wept with relief. They continued the descent, losing sight of the barn, and then finding it again as Tristan fairly ran down the side of the mountain.

They were almost there when the barn door flew open, revealing Lady Rascomb. Her cane was at her side, but it was clear she'd heard something and come to investigate, not expecting to see her son with a woman tied to his back. Eleanor kept her eyes above Tristan's shoulder, watching Lady Rascomb's face as it tumbled from concern to joy and back to concern.

The woman whom Eleanor hoped to call mother-in-law waited until they were close enough to hear before she spoke, as she had excellent manners, and was not raised as a merchant's daughter. Eleanor would have yelled, she just knew it.

"You are safe now. Who is hurt more?" Lady Rascomb looked them both up and down, awkward as they were with

Tristan wearing her like a turtle shell.

"Eleanor is. Likely a bad sprain, but enough that she cannot walk on it." Tristan moved towards a nearby rock. "Can you help with untying us?"

They set to work, finally reaching the point of Eleanor standing on her own foot again. But now, Tristan stretched his back, then picked her up, cradled in his arms. "You are much heavier like this."

"That's not how you say it," Lady Rascomb said, leaving the rope where it slid to the grass.

"I don't mind," Eleanor said, "as long as there is something warm in that barn."

They settled in with the blanket bags piled around them and Lady Rascomb plying them with the Highlanders' oatcakes and cheese.

"They'll be here with a wagon soon," Lady Rascomb said, consulting her watch which dangled from a ribbon at her waist. "Everyone agreed on an eight o'clock rendezvous."

"Then why are you here?" Tristan asked. Eleanor recognized that pointed look he gave his mother, the one that cut beyond assumptions and niceties. The expression he gave to those he loved and wanted to take care of.

"I stayed the night out here. I wasn't going to abandon my child." Lady Rascomb looked at him with utter calm.

"Alone?" Tristan went into a sputter. "An English lady stayed alone in a barn in the Highlands? Have you gone mad?"

Her smile was serene, and Eleanor thought about how she would like to learn how to do that—to be calm in the face of someone else's panic.

"Your father was with me. He left at dawn to walk back and gather the others."

"Still. It's irresponsible." Tristan shook his head.

The Highland clearances in the decades before had done what was once thought unthinkable—it made the Scots hate the English even more. Eleanor would not have wanted to stay anywhere on her own. Lady Rascomb was either very brave or very foolish. Eleanor preferred thinking it was bravery.

In short order, they heard the wheels of a wagon and the clop of horse hooves outside. They rose to meet their rescuers, Lady Rascomb offering one of Lord Rascomb's walking poles to help. Tristan rounded exited the barn first, receiving whoops of praise and hollers. Lady Rascomb pushed Eleanor in front of her, and the others whooped even louder at her appearance.

Prudence was the first to crush her into a hug. The slender woman went so far as to pick her off her feet, something that Eleanor was shocked could happen. As soon as her foot was back on the grass, Justine jumped on her, hugging her short arms around Eleanor's neck.

Behind her was Ophelia, and then they were just a knot of women tangled around Eleanor.

"Oh, my Lord, it was terrifying," Justine said in one ear.

"We did it, Eleanor. We did it," Ophelia whispered in the other.

"Come, come," Lord Rascomb boomed from the driver's perch. "Let's get all packed up, make Eleanor comfortable and get them back to the inn. I bet they would be delighted to have a full breakfast."

The women dispersed, and while Tristan used the blanket bags to make her a fine nest on the floor of the wagon, her ankle propped up to reduce the swelling, the other women gathered the rest of the gear left in the barn. Lord Rascomb himself dealt with the heavy climbing rope, winding it 'round with the amount of respect it deserved, considering how much Eleanor had relied on it to save her.

They were on the way back to the inn, the other women chattering while Eleanor's head lolled with lack of sleep.

"What do you want more?" Justine asked. "A cup of tea, a hot bath, or never seeing Tristan's ugly face again?"

Though the question was meant in jest, it jolted Eleanor. She looked at him, and his face revealed the same naked panic. They were entering the real world again, where they had families and obligations, where one couldn't just cozy up to a man for a kiss. There was so much more to do for Eleanor.

"Cup of tea," Eleanor said, giving Tristan a hopeful smile.

"Oh God, no," Justine said glancing between them. Ophelia gave a shy smile, which relieved Eleanor. Even Prudence glanced away, and she was an American. Justine flung herself backwards onto the rest of the blanket bags. "And I liked you and everything."

Back at the inn, Tristan carried her up to her room but had to leave her there. It felt strange to be parted from him, after. A maid brought a breakfast tray, and another set about getting a bath prepared. They hadn't the latest innovations of running water, and thus it still required girls running downstairs to gather up more boiling water.

Eleanor nibbled on the toast, smeared with the best butter she'd ever eaten. Having eaten her fill of the oatcakes at the barn, she focused on drinking down the tea that was still hot. It warmed her from the inside out, but she still didn't like being without Tristan. And there wasn't much of a way to tell him. A note, perhaps?

When the bath was ready and her tea was done, Eleanor hobbled over to settle in. There were aches in her arms and her back that she hadn't even noticed until the other pain was soothed away. She balanced her head on the back of the tub and closed her eyes. She was safe. She had climbed the mountain. Her eyes flew open. But she'd have to tell her mother that she was ruined.

She smiled.

Chapter Fifteen

T RISTAN PACED. HE hadn't had any time alone with Eleanor, and it grated. What kind of tortuous world would keep them apart? It was obvious they cared for each other, so why was it so miserably difficult to speak to her in private?

He wanted to assure her of his continued affections. She needed to know that he intended to go straight to her father as soon as they were back in London. But what with the few days of recovery at the inn, the letters and papers he was obliged to pen to raise money for their Matterhorn attempt, and then the separate carriages and train cars back to Edinburgh, there was absolutely no chance to see her.

The most he'd dared was a scrap of paper with the word *amor* scribbled on it, which he'd slipped into her hand as he'd handed her up to board the carriage. It was ridiculous. They were affianced, at least, in their own minds, and aside from which, he'd had carnal relations—twice—with a respectable lady. That was enough, wasn't it?

They boarded the train to London bright and early. Once again, separate cars. A stop for a meal in York, where he might steal a glance and a smile. He wanted to beat his head against the very train itself. Why must everything be so difficult?

His father sat opposite him, just as they had on the way up to Edinburgh a few weeks previously. It felt like an age since they'd done so. That day and night on the Ben had changed him profoundly. He knew now that he could keep Eleanor safe. That he deserved her, and that together, her brains and his beauty, they could do anything.

"Anything wrong?" his father asked before he cracked his newspaper open and fell into the daily natterings of the world.

Who cared about the outside world? Not when he had to meet with Mr. Piper. When he had to figure out his own financials, to prove to Mr. Piper he could support her. A merchant like him would want to know where the money came from. "I'm anxious to get back to London."

"Oh? It seemed like you were enjoying yourself in Scotland." There was a twitch at his father's mouth that Tristan finally noticed. It was his father's tell for teasing.

Tristan narrowed his eyes. "Yes. I enjoyed my time in Scotland immensely. But I've pressing business to attend to."

"Any of it having to do with arranging a meeting with Mr. Piper?" His father acted as if he were actually reading the newspaper and not torturing his third-born.

"As a matter of fact, yes, I do plan on that. Along with taking a meeting with the man who pulls the purse-strings of my inheritance."

His father's eyebrows shot up. "And who is that delightful fellow?"

Tristan was too agitated to play anymore. "Papa. Please. I'm crawling out my skin because of this."

"Oh, all right." His father dropped any pretense of reading the paper. "I can tell you that in addition to the portion you already receive, I have set aside a small bit from your mother's dowry to go to you upon your marriage. You may tell Mr. Piper that Miss Piper shan't want for anything."

Tristan sagged against the train's cushioned seat in relief. "Oh, thank goodness. I was worried, after talking with Herringbone."

That piqued his father's interest. "About the title's finances?"

"He made it seem like it was in trouble, that there wasn't

enough and he had to marry an heiress to keep the estate afloat."

His father blinked rapidly. "Unless he's made some unwise investments that I don't know about, I can't think of why that would be true."

"Or maybe that he's using it as an excuse to not marry?" Tristan suspected that it had to do with the penniless Lady Emily. He and his father shared a look that seemed to say that was exactly what was happening.

The rest of the trip was made in relative ease, though Tristan was still anxious to be in London. They arrived late, and while Tristan had hoped to speak to Mr. Piper as he picked up Eleanor, the merchant did not show. A footman collected Eleanor's trunks and then Eleanor herself.

"I'll come to you tomorrow," he whispered to her as she wafted by him. She looked back at him with those great velvety brown eyes, and he knew wild dogs couldn't keep him at bay.

ELEANOR ARRIVED HOME well after dark. Her ankle throbbed in pain. She was still using Lord Rascomb's walking stick. She hobbled up the stairs and asked for a bit of ice for her ankle. At least it was May, where the stores of ice were plentiful. She didn't have the energy for a full bath, and she appreciated the work of her lady's maid. Her traveling costume was not as simple as her outdoor clothes were.

Still, it felt good to be home, wearing a new, clean nightshift that didn't smell vaguely of horses or oatcakes or the smoky peat of fires. She was nibbling on a tray of cold cuts when her mother burst into the room.

"You're hurt?" her mother, who had not bothered to meet her at the train station, practically shrieked.

Eleanor could do without the histrionics. "I sprained my ankle quite severely."

"Let me see it," her mama insisted, lifting the poultice of ice and mustard seeds. She made a noise that Eleanor could only assume was anguish. "It's awful! Those people tried to kill you!"

Eleanor laid back against her pillows. "No one tried to kill me. It was a bit of bad luck. And Mr. Bridewell saved me."

"What's this?" her father wandered in. "I hear your mother screeching, then Sellers tells me you're hurt? What in blazes is happening to this world?"

"Papa, I'm fine. It's a sprained ankle. It's still swollen, but not nearly as badly as it was when it first happened."

"It was worse?" her mother keened.

"See here, I won't let them take my little girl and put her in harm's way for some ridiculous political stunt! That's not empowerment, that's endangerment! I won't allow it! Oh, I'll stop it completely! They think they can use up common folk like us? Think again, I say!"

"Stop," Eleanor said, taking hold of her mother's arm. But her mother didn't stop her ridiculous fussing. "Papa," she begged, taking a hold of his arm, though he was still shouting about noblemen.

But this had been her whole life. She'd been the audience for their antics, while they'd barely registered her presence. Like now, when neither of them could stop themselves from their dramatic performances.

"Enough!" Eleanor shouted. It at least cut through their chatter long enough to quiet them. "Neither of you bothered to meet me at the train, so I can't imagine you are terribly upset."

Hollow sputtering came from both of them. Eleanor held up her hand to quiet them.

"I climbed Ben Nevis. I got all the way to the top—we all did—without trouble. We made great time, all of us fitter than we thought we'd be. Then, on the way down, a snow cornice fooled me, and I stepped right through it, and down I tumbled, taking Mr. Bridewell with me, as he was standing next to me."

"He should have—" her mother insisted, but quieted when

Eleanor held up her hand.

"Snow cornices aren't visible from the top. I didn't see it, neither did he. No one is to blame. In the tumble of the fortunately not-too-steep edge, I hurt myself, and then compounded it by walking on it, even when I knew I was hurt. I made the mistake, not wanting to confess to my injury."

"Did the rest find you?" her father growled.

"No," Eleanor answered, wanting to be absolutely truthful, because it was the clearest way to get what she wanted. "The fog drew in too quickly, and we couldn't see. I couldn't walk by then, but we found a ravine to settle into for the night."

"You spent the night alone with that man?" her mother asked, her eyebrows nearly meeting her hairline.

"I did. And the next morning, he carried me down the mountain and we returned to Fort William, and then to Edinburgh, and then home."

Her father crossed his arms across his chest, nodding to himself. Her mother stared at her father.

"Did he—" her father choked. "Did he—"

"Have his way with me?" Eleanor asked with the same serenity that Lady Rascomb displayed. "Yes, he did."

Her father's face turned purple. Eleanor's mother gasped and ran out the door.

"That was either very stupid or very wise," her father said. The mottled purple color was changing to red, which was a good sign. Still, he ground his teeth. "But for right now, I cannot speak to you. I'm disappointed in you. So very disappointed."

He followed the path Eleanor's mother took, slamming the door behind him. Eleanor sat back against the pillows once again, her appetite gone. Their disapproval hurt. Why was her accomplishment of summiting Ben Nevis not celebrated? Why was that feat washed away by the revelation of her virginity? It didn't seem fair. Eleanor felt far more like a woman who had climbed a mountain rather than a woman who'd engaged in carnal relations outside of wedlock. She went to sleep, secure in the knowledge that Tristan would ask for her hand, her father would be forced to accept, and she would live happily ever after.

But the next day, Tristan didn't call. The physician came and examined her ankle, saying the same things that Tristan had said in the gully. He wrapped it with a clean bandage and instructed her to keep her foot elevated. But by evening, she was anxious. Hobbling downstairs, she went through all the calling cards on the silver platter next to the door. Tristan's was not among them.

"Mrs. Piper said you were ill and not receiving callers," Sellers, their butler, informed her.

"Indeed," Eleanor said, managing the stairs with the aid of Lord Rascomb's walking stick.

The next day came and went, and still she'd had no word from any of the members of the Ladies' Alpine Society, nor from Tristan. Her heart sank. After all that, she was just forgotten?

Again?

TRISTAN WAS ABOUT foaming at the mouth. He'd never been so angry in his life. First, he'd been denied at the Pipers' home residence. Then his letters were returned to him. He couldn't get a note to Eleanor, he wasn't allowed to see her, and her father refused to take a meeting with him. He was ready to punch through a wall.

Finally, he staked out the man's offices down at the docks. Tristan dressed down, not wanting to draw too much attention to himself. Still, the quality of his tailoring, his excellent skin, and his polished boots gave him away. Tristan didn't care. He was on a mission. He waited until he saw the Pipers' carriage arrive and the man himself descend.

He waited a few minutes, thinking that he would be in a better mood if he'd had a chance to settle into his workday before being interrupted. Then he snuck in past the man with the slate who'd thrown him out last time. Tristan dodged around the crates being opened and the others being hauled in, the bustle and movement an ideal way to not be noticed.

But it was on the stairs he found his way blocked by a man with an epically flowing silver beard and an eyepatch. "Who ye be?"

Tristan pulled his hat off, an attempt at showing respect when he'd been found out. This had to be Eleanor's Captain Smythe. "Tristan Bridewell, sir. Here to see Mr. Piper."

"And Dreggles down there sent you up?" The bearded man squinted at him. He likely needed glasses, Tristan thought.

"No sir, I did not go through Mr. Dreggles. He denied my entrance last time."

"Oh? That's unusual. Very few are blacklisted round here. Why would Dreggles send a well-dressed chap like you away?"

Tristan's hands sweated into the brim of his beaver-skin hat. He turned it, hoping to not deform it or leave a mark. "Well, you see, I'm here to ask for the hand of Miss Piper, and I don't think Mr. Piper wants that to happen."

The other man's bushy white eyebrows moved like lazy caterpillars sunning themselves. "That so? For Miss Eleanor? Hm. What be your qualifications?"

"I'm er," Tristan stammered. What were his qualifications to be a husband? The accident of his birth? "I'm good in a crisis."

The old man nodded.

"And I'd climb the tallest mountain for her," Tristan said, as if that were a decent argument for marriage. "Or with her, if she wanted to go."

"Good enough for me. Come on, I'll help you with your suit. I've known ol' Bruce for longer than he knowed himself." The old man clapped a hand on Tristan's shoulder and propelled him up the rickety wooden stairs.

Tristan knocked on the door at the top at the old man's urging.

"Come in," Mr. Piper yelled through the door. "Damn it all,

Smythe, I'm behind as it is. What now?"

Tristan opened the door, entering with the old man at his back. The room was sparse. Mr. Piper was at a desk of moderate size, though considering the piles of papers stacked at all angles, a bigger desk was likely needed. In the other portion of the room sat a worn sofa with a number of clumsy needlepoint pillows flung about. Across from it was a low table with a washing up stand. Tristan surmised that some nights, Mr. Piper slept at the waterfront.

"You," growled Mr. Piper. "Smythe, how dare you let this man cross my threshold? He's been the cause of the utter downfall of my daughter. He almost gets her killed, and when she is vulnerable, he takes advantage of her!"

Well, that was good to know that Eleanor had told her parents. Made his position a bit awkward, yes. There was no denying his actions, and no explaining them either, not to a man like Mr. Piper.

"Mr. Piper, with respect," Tristan said, his hands raised.

The man stood, and with his fervor, a pile of papers toppled to the floor. "If you had an ounce of respect, you wouldn't be here! And Eleanor wouldn't be laid up at home, recuperating from an injury you caused her!"

That barb stung a bit. He didn't cause anything. "A snow cornice is a dangerous formation that—"

"I don't want to hear your ridiculous excuses! Get out!" Mr. Piper roared, throwing an inkpot at him.

Tristan ducked, hearing it clatter to the floor behind him.

"Now, Bruce," the older man said.

"Don't you do it, Smythe. Don't you talk me in circles about this. I know a degenerate ne'er-do-well when I see one!"

"Is he not the son of a viscount? That's good business there, to be associated with the nobility. Surely, it is no balm to ye, when ye were expecting a grant from our queen. But it is a step closer than ye were before."

"They pretend to fine manners, but look where it got my

Eleanor! I could kill you for this, Bridewell!"

Smythe gestured at Tristan to stay put. "The boy is a blighter, that's true. But he tells me he loves Eleanor. And that's not a thing you could ever buy for her."

Piper stood still, his hands still balled in fists. "S'that true?"

Tristan nodded his head, then feeling stupid for not speaking, he assured him that way as well. "Absolutely. Yes. More than anything. More than my own life."

"Eleanor says you saved her in the mountains. That if it hadn't been for you, she would have perished there from the winds and the cold. Is that true?"

Tristan hadn't thought about it, didn't want to contemplate Eleanor being at risk alone, as he'd already resolved to be by her side. "I suppose it is."

Piper stared at him, then sat down and wrote a letter. When either Smythe or Tristan attempted to speak or ask a question, Piper silenced them. Finally, he melted a bit of wax, sealed it with a ring and handed it off. It felt all a bit medieval to Tristan, but all he'd hoped for was an audience and he'd gotten that, so he felt he ought to keep his mouth shut.

"Deliver that to my wife at my house. It says you may see Eleanor. Says I've approved your marriage. Says you're a damn lucky prat that I don't kick in your teeth and dump you in the ocean."

Tristan took the letter and, glancing at Smythe, who gave him the nod to leave, he bowed. "Thank you Mr. Piper. This is—"

Mr. Piper growled at Tristan's groveling for his efforts, but that was more than enough. Tristan flew down the stairs and ran to his own hack. He delivered the letter and sat in the front entrance of the Pipers' grand in-town house. He tapped his toes on the cold marble foyer floor. Finally, he was summoned to the upstairs drawing room, nearer to Eleanor, nearer to wedded bliss, nearer to purpose.

ELEANOR HAD BEEN clear about the marriage contract. She'd insisted on being a part of negotiations, despite the lawyer constantly protesting her presence. In the contract, it stipulated that Tristan could not forbid her activities with the Ladies' Alpine Society. It also had a clause paying Mr. and Mrs. Piper damages should Eleanor become injured during a husband-approved expedition.

"Shouldn't damages be paid to me?" Eleanor asked, but the lawyer fussed at her about a woman's place until she had no choice but to ignore him and move on.

They would settle into a Bridewell townhome in the fashionable Belgravia, the upkeep of which would be paid for by Eleanor's dowry. The details didn't matter to Eleanor. What mattered was that Tristan would be with her when she climbed the Matterhorn. That together, they could accomplish the impossible.

"YOU ARE DISMISSED for the evening!" Eleanor called to her lady's maid as she left. Tristan could hear her through the adjoining door of their marital suite. Everything felt new. The furniture was new, the gas lighting throughout the house was new. The indoor plumbing was new. He was the luckiest man in London, and he knew it well.

"Oh!" Eleanor started as she spotted him leering through the adjoining door. "I didn't even hear you."

"I'm certainly not going to languish all alone over here on my wedding night."

"Nor would I have you do so, but . . ." Eleanor trailed off as she dug through the trunks she'd expressly asked her lady's maid to leave alone. "I have some preparations to make."

"I love preparations," Tristan said, coming into her room and taking a seat.

Across the room, Eleanor pulled out small lengths of rope. "You know that I like to solve problems with knots."

Tristan's heart skipped a beat. "I would very much like to be the problem," Tristan said, his throat already dry and his cock already at attention. He would be lying if he had not already had some very explicit fantasies of his bride in the weeks leading up to the wedding, some of which had involved her expertise with rope.

Eleanor smiled, her brown eyes focused on him and only him. His wife. His wife! As of this morning, the bishop proclaimed them man and wife, and if that was good enough for Mr. Piper, then Tristan would tell the whole world to sod off. Eleanor was his.

"I'm glad to hear it, because I thought of you as I designed these knots." Eleanor went to the foot of the bed and started tying. Tristan didn't care. Nothing worked in his brain and frankly, he was all the better for it.

"Shall I take off my boots?"

Eleanor glanced up as she finished tying the next one. "Please."

Tristan's wee little mind, which, compared to Eleanor's vast intelligence, creativity, and imagination was the size of a gnat's, went into a flat buzzing sound. He stood in his stockinged feet and drifted over to the bed.

"May I help you with your stays?" he asked, hoping the answer was an enthusiastic yes.

Instead of that coquettish assent, she looked at him with almost pity. "Oh, no, my love. You won't be touching me tonight."

Panic seared through him. "I won't?"

She bit her lip and shook her head. "I'll be touching you. Because you're mine. Take off your shirt and lie down."

Still, he trusted her, so he did as he was bid, watching her busy with finishing the knots on the far side of the bed. "Give me your hand."

Her voice was thick with lust, and Tristan had no choice but to comply. He gave her his hand, and she slid a strip of silk around his wrist, cinching it tight. This is not what he expected on his wedding night, nor what he expected from his blushing bride. Did he have complaints? Absolutely not.

Tristan quickly pushed his hair away from his face as she rounded the bed, her eyes on the expanse of his bared chest. He wasn't a particularly hairy individual, and of that, most was pale and golden, with the exception of that concentrated line that drifted from his navel down into his trousers. An area that seemed to fascinate Eleanor.

She bent down and kissed him deeply, her tongue sweeping into his mouth. He lost his mind at that moment, giving himself up to his wife, as she had once given herself up to him. The reciprocity was heady. Neither of them was alone. As she broke off the kiss, he realized she'd slipped his other wrist into a silken knot and cinched it tight.

"Clever girl," he said, hoping his admiration was obvious. It was obvious in other places. Like his trousers.

She smiled, kissing down his bare chest. "No interference. I get you all to myself." She unbuttoned his trousers and slid them down to his knees. He helped kick them off as she slid the silk restraints around his ankles. He felt vulnerable, yes, lying naked on a bed with an erection waving about in the wind.

But Eleanor's hands dragging up his legs made his eyes roll back in his head. "I want to take my time tonight, but I knew that if I let you free, we would focus on my desire, and not on my curiosity."

"Your curiosity?" Tristan managed.

She slid one hand up his cock, which made him tense his arse. He couldn't help it. He thrust into her warm, smooth palm. "I've had this inside me, yet I feel like I hadn't gotten a proper look." She conducted her experiment again, and again, he thrust up into her. "Does that feel good?"

He let out a strangled assent. Words were beyond him now. Gently, as if she were a lady leaning down to smell a rose, she licked his length.

"You did this for me, and I quite liked it." She drew him all the way into her mouth, and he nearly blacked out.

It was an inexpert cock-sucking, but since he couldn't think of a bad one, he was pleased beyond all measure. He did his best to keep from all-out spending, as she sucked so hard he thought he might die. And right when his cock was hard and aching and ready to erupt, she sat back.

Her lips shone with wetness. From her saliva, from his cock, it was a heady sight. He hoped she would do him the honor of truly riding him, but instead, she leaned against the footboard. He strained to look at her, and she watched him as she slowly pulled up her skirts, revealing her naked core. She dipped a finger in it and started to tease herself.

He bucked and whined, wanting to be there, to smell her, to touch her, to taste her. Instead, her slow grin turned to a pant as she aroused herself.

"Eleanor, please," he pleaded through gritted teeth.

He watched her as she came, falling apart in front of him. God, he wanted to feel that. He wanted to feel her orgasm pulsing against his cock. "Hm?"

"Sit on my cock," he said.

She leaned forward, giving his waving cock a quick lick that sent him perilously close to the edge. "Only if you say please."

"I said please. Please. Eleanor. Please. My love. My life. My bride. Sit. On. My. Cock."

She laughed, but straddled him, her skirts bunched up all around her. She settled and arranged herself around him until finally, finally, she pressed his cock to her entrance. "For you? Anything." And she sank, mercifully, slowly onto him.

She rode him as promised, him straining to keep from reaching his limits, waiting for her to find her second ascent.

Thankfully he didn't need to wait so long. She fell apart, and an instant later, he did as well, yelling nonsense as he climaxed harder than he'd ever done in his life.

They lay panting, the sweat from Tristan's chest cooling him. She rolled off him, gathering towels she'd set aside. What a clever wife he had. She cleaned herself, cleaned him and freed him.

They lay naked under the covers, clinging to one another.

"The one question I still have from our sojourn in Scotland is a bit odd." Eleanor shifted, as if he might be uncomfortable with her. He didn't like that one bit, so he snuggled her closer, kissing her bare shoulder.

"What is it?"

"Who was it that stashed the whisky and the food and the blanket on the Ben? And why had they not come back for it? How long had it been sitting there, waiting for them?"

Tristan then knew how selfish he was, as it had never occurred to him to wonder. If the cheese had been inedible, and it had been stowed in a cool, dark mountainside, how long had it been there? Decades? "I don't know."

"I want to think they were lovers who eventually got to be together, and they left that cache for us. Another set of lovers who were in need."

He kissed her temple. "We did need it, though we weren't lovers at the time."

"We became lovers," she said. "And it was thanks to the ghosts of lovers past."

"Ghosts, now?" Tristan said. "I don't think ghosts left dried apricots."

"Not ghosts then, but they became them. Because they were ghosts for us. We don't know them, we just know that someone, somewhere, needed a place to stay. And we benefited. I'd like to send them a thank you card, but I don't know how to do it."

"I'd send a selection of fine cheeses, theirs was horrifically inedible." Tristan added, pleased when she laughed. "How about we be grateful? Every day. Because we don't know what happened to that other couple. I can only hope they were as lucky as us."

Eleanor kissed his cheek. "We are lucky."

"I love you, Mrs. Bridewell. I can't wait to whip you into shape for the Matterhorn."

She batted at his arm. "I love you too, Mr. Bridewell. I'll be testing your knots at every opportunity."

He sucked her earlobe into his mouth and gave it a playful bite. "Any time, Mrs. Bridewell. Any time."

The End.

About the Author

Edie Cay writes steamy feminist historical romance. Her debut, A LADY'S REVENGE won the Golden Leaf Best First Book (2020), as well as the Indie Next Generation Book Award (2020). The second in her series, THE BOXER AND THE BLACKSMITH won the Hearts Through History Legends Award, A Man for All Reason in 2019 as an unpublished manuscript, and then went on to win the Best Indie Book Award (2021). The third book, A LADY'S FINDER was a finalist for a Lambda Award, the most prestigious LGBTQ+ literary award in the world. A VIS-COUNT'S VENGEANCE garnered the Best Indie Book Award for Regency Romance as well in 2023.

Previously, she published short stories, poems, and non-fiction in small presses. She co-wrote and starred in several short films and documentaries from MadLaw Media, including "Big 5 Dive" about scuba diving in the Great Lakes, and "How to Be Sexy," a fictional short about confidence and self-worth.

She obtained dual BAs in Creative Writing and in Music from Cal State East Bay, and her MFA in Creative Writing from University of Alaska Anchorage. She has been a professional musician, bookstore employee, and a healthcare worker.

She has participated in several anthologies, including Un-locked, The Grand Mistletoe Assembly, and the upcoming Beneath the Midwinter Moon.

Her next series will be about Victorian women alpinists, out in August 2024 from Dragonblade Publishing.

She is a founding member of the historical fiction collective The Paper Lantern Writers, and helps edit and publish their anthologies. She gives presentations at conferences around the world on the history of women's boxing and other aspects of

Regency culture and writing.

In addition to fiction, Edie writes and reviews for the Historical Novel Society. You can keep up with her on her website, www.ediecay.com, or follow her on Instagram or Facebook @authorEdieCay.